ALSO BY ELSIE SILVER

Chestnut Springs

Flawless

Heartless

Powerless

Reckless

Hopeless

Gold Rush Ranch

Off to the Races

A Photo Finish

The Front Runner

A False Start

Rose Hill

Wild Love

THE FRONT RUNNER

ELSIE SILVER

Bloom books

Published by Bloom Books, an imprint of Sourcebooks
P.O. Box 4410, Naperville, Illinois 60567–4410
(630) 961-3900
sourcebooks.com

Cataloging-in-Publication data is on file with the Library of Congress.

Originally self-published in 2021 by Elsie Silver.

Printed and bound in Canada.
MBP 10 9 8 7 6 5 4 3 2 1

For all the women who've been told
they should smile more.
Fuck that noise. Frown all you want.

Reader Note

This book contains adult material including references to animal death typical with farm life as well as domestic abuse and sexual harassment. It is my hope that I've handled these topics with the care they deserve.

I'd also like to extend a special thank you to Anna P. for performing a very thorough sensitivity read to ensure that Mira and her family have been represented with proper care and accuracy.

CHAPTER 1
Stefan

SIX MONTHS AGO

"DALCA, YOU PIECE OF…"

Here we go. The woman who works for and is engaged to my biggest competitor is going to fly off the handle. Again. Billie Black is especially talented at this kind of behavior. She reminds me of my little sister. Entitled and impulsive. The difference is my sister likes me.

This woman does not.

It's a bold spot to make a scene. I'll give her that. We're in the middle of a public roadway at the prestigious Bell Point Park. Our horses are ready for their race. In fact, hers is standing right behind her with the petite fair-haired jockey they seem to use exclusively now.

I slide my hands into the pockets of my suit pants and quirk one eyebrow at her in challenge. I would be lying if I were to say I don't take some small pleasure in riling people up. File that away under the behavior of a child who didn't get enough attention growing up. Any attention is good attention, and this type of attention is especially amusing to me.

But the raven-haired veterinarian steps in front of the other two women, hitting me with a look that would make a lesser man's balls shrivel.

"Stefan, walk with me." She crooks a finger and heads in the opposite direction without even looking back, like she just knows I'll follow.

I'm not sure what's going on. It feels like I'm in trouble; it looks like I'm in for some sort of scolding. I smooth my hands over the lapels of my suit jacket and clear my throat by way of saying goodbye to the two women glaring at me and spin on my heel. Billie makes an immature gagging noise as I walk away, but I tip my chin up and keep walking after the woman who has piqued my interest since the first time I laid eyes on her.

Dr. Mira Thorne. My favorite equine veterinarian in the area for more than one reason. The woman is beautiful. But more than that, she's smart. Cunning. Thinks quickly on her feet. She's impressive in so many ways.

She's a *challenge*.

And I love a challenge.

I've seen her save more than one horse down at the track with her quick thinking. She may be younger than the other track veterinarians, but it strikes me that she could probably run circles around the rest of them.

Her impressive brain doesn't stop me from admiring the way her hips sway as she marches away from me, straight toward the barns. She takes a hard left near a tractor and moves to the other side where no one will see or hear us. My stomach flips.

What the hell is going on?

Dr. Thorne is an alluring woman, and I'm still human enough to admit that. There's an arrogant edge to her cool exterior, hawkish intelligence in her eyes. A spark that, with the right fuel, just might combust.

She spins on me, her dark eyes pinched as she homes straight in on mine. I like that she doesn't shy away from eye contact, and I meet it, even if there's a minor part of me that's concerned about what she's going to say next. Something feels off.

"How can I help you, Dr. Thorne?" I force my voice to sound smooth and confident, even though I'm brimming with questions.

"It's more about how you can help yourself."

I tilt my head at her, studying her face, admiring the straight line of her nose, the angle of her brows, the puffiness of her lips, and the stubborn set to her jaw.

"I'm going to give you a bit of advice, Stefan." I like the way she calls me by my first name—the way it sounds in her mouth. "The horse-racing business is a tight-knit industry in this area. This community is small, and Ruby Creek is even smaller. Making enemies of Billie and the Harding family is not in your best interest. You compete on the track, not off."

I almost want to roll my eyes. "Thank you for your input,

Dr. Thorne. But unfortunately for Billie and the Harding family, I like to compete everywhere."

She nods at me slowly, turning my words over in her head as her arms come up to cross under her full breasts. They're magnificent. I've noticed over the past couple of years that she tries to hide them with layers. Sometimes, when it's damp and cold, she wears this big= brown Carhartt coat, but today she's wearing a fitted, quilted vest over her long-sleeved T-shirt that does her nothing but favors. It nips in around her waist, and I swear she almost can't get the zipper all the way up.

But I don't stare. I'm not a total Neanderthal.

"Then you'll need to find another veterinarian to use."

I scoff. "You can't be serious. All because I made a perfectly fair offer to buy one of their horses?"

Her chocolate eyes are all fire now. "First of all, that was a very subtle attempt at blackmail, and we both know it. But bravo on walking that line so skillfully. This time it's different, Stefan. You've gone too far. I don't work for men who employ predators."

I rear back, ice racing down my spine and stiffening my entire body. "What did you just say to me?"

Mira drops her chin and offers me an unimpressed look. "You heard me. You're a smart man, so don't play stupid about Patrick Cassel. You've taken this vendetta too far by weaponizing your employee."

Every ounce of humor drains from my body as I stare back down at this woman, who is accusing me of something I would *never* do. Patrick Cassel is the jockey I've hired to ride my horses. Do I like the guy? Not particularly. But he wins, and I like to win.

"I would *never* do that. Not in a million ye—"

She cuts me off. "He intentionally took Violet down on that track. Purposely injured another comp—"

My spine stiffens as I fist my hands in my pockets and interrupt her right back. "That is still under review."

"Shouldn't be. I overheard him confirm it when he cornered her, terrified her, and told her he wouldn't do it again so long as she slept with him."

My throat feels tight as I blink stupidly at the veterinarian, trying to wrap my head around what she's just told me. Trying to keep the rage surging up inside me at bay. I can't let how distraught this makes me show.

"Is she okay?" is the first thing I think of, and I blurt it straight out. The thought of him doing something like what Mira just described makes me feel borderline murderous.

She blinks a few times, assessing me. "Yes. She's small but mighty."

My breath rushes out in a whoosh. Mira has no reason to lie to me about this. She's been nothing short of professional, even though her friends and employers have labeled me as the Big Bad Wolf.

But apparently, she's not done knocking me on my heels for today. "I also have my suspicions about what he's doing to the horses he works with."

"What is that supposed to mean?"

"I saw him inject one with something before a race last weekend."

"One of mine?"

"No. But it doesn't matter whose it was. He was acting off, looking around like he didn't want anyone to see. It just didn't seem right. Between you and me, you need to be careful. Both of these things could come back on you and your business."

"I…had no idea." *And Patrick Cassel is a dead man walking.*

She shakes her head, and her chest heaves under the weight of a tired sigh. "The worst part is I actually believe you. I don't think you're the devil everyone makes you out to be, Stefan. Here's your chance to prove it. Find a new jockey, and I'll continue working for you."

I almost laugh. She looks so serious, so deadly serious. "Isn't *that* blackmail, Dr. Thorne?"

The smile she hits me with now is pretty much a snarl. She reaches out and pats me on the chest, right over the front pocket of my suit jacket. It's almost condescending.

"No, Mr. Dalca. It's a *perfectly fair offer.*"

I bark out a laugh as she spins on her heel and walks away. She just spat my words right back at me with a pretty smile. She knows she's got me by the balls, and she's absolutely delighted about it. On top of that, she's walking away with the last word.

I hate not getting the last word.

"Let me take you on a date, and we'll call it a deal. I'll fire Patrick," I call out—only half-joking.

It's her turn to laugh now. It filters back toward me, melodic and amused.

"No chance, Stefan. You'd fall in love with me, and then I definitely couldn't be your vet."

And with one sly wink over her shoulder, she's gone. Back around the tractor, melting into the race-day crowds at Bell Point Park, thinking I'll fall for her whole smart-mouthed, confident persona.

Challenge accepted.

★★★

FIVE MONTHS AGO...

Second place. Again.

The whir of the track immediately following a major derby rages behind me as I stand at the fence line watching the horses cool down after a hard-fought race. I'm disappointed. I hate losing, and I'm not above admitting I especially hate losing to Gold Rush Ranch and all their happy, sunshiny positivity and family-like vibe. I swear I can hear them cheering above the buzz.

I know it's petty—I know I'm jealous. But I really thought this was my year. I thought I had a horse who could beat the spunky little black stallion. My horse, Cascade Calamity, is well bred. He's an athlete—a competitor—but the Gold Rush horse is a force to be reckoned with.

They had two races in hand heading into the final leg of the Northern Crown, so while I knew I couldn't take the crown, I definitely thought I could prevent them from taking it again. Back-to-back crown wins with that horse will make Billie and her boyfriend so much more smug and obnoxious than they already are.

ELSIE SILVER

"He ran well." Nadia slips her hand into mine and gives it a tight squeeze.

I give her a curt nod, still looking out at the track. "He did."

"Maybe next year." She says it sweetly, but with a total lack of understanding.

Nothing is certain in this sport. Some racehorses have long, healthy careers, but the vast majority of them don't. They get sore, they get sour, and I'm not about to push my horses beyond what they're capable of doing. I'm not going to ruin an animal just to win a race, and it's my feeling this boy is about ready to retire. He's sound, he's happy, and he's had a very winning career. I can stand him at stud somewhere, and he can spend his days eating grass and making babies.

I respect him enough to let him walk away from the sport while he's still healthy. Could I run him into the ground for another season and make some cash? Probably. But I refuse to do that to an animal who has run his heart out for me and my business.

He deserves better.

And despite what Billie Black—who clearly hates me— likes to run around telling everyone, I am not a dick. Well, at least not to my horses.

"You know what you need to do."

I peer down into Nadia's mahogany eyes. She's grimacing at me because she knows how much I'm already dreading what I have to do next.

My shoulders heave under the weight of a heavy sigh, and I give her a terse "Yup."

A quick squeeze on her slender shoulder and I'm gone, pushing my way through the bustling crowd toward the winner's circle. I hate watching the race from the owner's lounge, surrounded by the sorts of people I can't stand, the types I turned away from when I left Europe. Money. Excess. Lack of sense. Obsessed with their image.

I hate it all.

So I watch down at track level, among all the regular Joes. It feels more real down here. More separated from how I grew up. And I'll do almost anything to distance myself from that.

I make my way through a sea of oversized hats and fancy dresses. Derby day is charming to be sure. The excitement is palpable. It's hard not to get swept up in the thrill. But right now, as I approach the winner's circle, all I feel is dread.

I need to walk in there and congratulate my competitors. The Gold Rush Ranch team. Billie Black. The Harding brothers. The little blond jockey who always looks at me like she feels sorry for me. That expression might be worse than the total distaste the fiery trainer aims my way.

With the circle in sight, my steps falter. Dr. Mira Thorne is also there with them, a sultry smile on her lips and a twinkle in her big dark eyes. My stomach flips at the sight of her, like it always does. I must be a glutton for punishment because getting turned down by her has become one of my favorite pastimes.

The crowd presses in around the circle—reporters, cameras, fellow owners, and jockeys. Everyone comes out of the woodwork to ask questions and offer their congratulations.

It's the classy thing to do, and I'm not about to play into their hand with what they think about me. I'm aware they hate me—more than the average athlete hates their closest competition. But I don't need to give them more reasons to.

Kill them with kindness.

Walking up with a forced smile on my face, I try not to stare at Mira. I have a good idea of how this is going to go, but it still needs to be done. I stop right in front of Billie, who hates me more than any of them. She's the ringleader in the campaign against me—that much is clear. And I suppose there's a part of me that can't blame her.

All is not fair in love and war where she's concerned. And that chip on her shoulder has proven impossible to smooth out.

"Miss Black." I thrust my hand out in her direction. "Congratulations on another crown win. Absolutely incredible."

And I actually mean it. Back-to-back wins are practically unheard of. An exceptional feat, to be sure.

But her shapely brow arches with pure disdain. "You think I'd shake your hand?"

I should have known she would make a scene.

I tut at her, replacing a fake smile with a smug smirk. "I thought you might value good sportsmanship."

She steps in closer toward my hand, looking around herself with a wide phony smile before whisper-shouting, "*You* are going to talk to *me* about sportsmanship?"

"I'm happy to let bygones be bygones."

She stares back at me, slightly slack-jawed. *If looks could kill.*

10

"I don't make deals with the devil, Dalca. Some people might look the other way where you're concerned, but I'm not one of them."

"Billie." Vaughn, her fiancé, comes up behind her, snaking an arm around her waist. He leans in close to her ear with a small smile, and I swear he says, "If you don't have anything nice to say, say nothing at all."

Her gaze flits up to his, and she gives him a small nod before turning away from me. He doesn't though. He stands there and glares at me.

If looks could kill.

"Don't suppose you're up for a handshake either?" I shouldn't say it, but they're all so childish. It's difficult not to stoop to their level.

He shakes his head and turns away from me with a disappointed sigh. I make a point not to look around myself. I'm not above feeling some level of embarrassment. And being entirely ignored by some of the biggest names in the business stings. Something I refuse to show.

Shoving my shoulders back, I turn to Violet, who is positively beaming on the back of the black horse. "Remarkable win, Mrs. Harding."

She looks down at me with a slight smile before placing her small hand in mine. She never has been as hard on me. Instead, she looks at me with pity—which is definitely worse.

"Thank you very much, Mr. Dalca. Your stallion ran well too."

From behind Violet, I can see her husband storming

through the crowd, looking like he might take my head off. The man is massive and terrifying, and I'm probably out of my league where he's concerned.

"Stefan." Mira sidles up beside me, wrapping her hand around my elbow. "It's time for you to go."

I tilt my head in her direction with a quirk of my cheek. "But why, Dr. Thorne? I'm having so much fun."

Her lips purse together like she's trying to hide a smile. "Because Cole Harding will legit murder you for waltzing in here and making trouble."

She tugs me away from the center of the circle, other people already pushing in to take our spots.

I bristle a bit as she leads me toward the surrounding fence. "I'm not making trouble. I'm offering my congratulations like any good competitor would."

She stops with a sigh and hits me with her signature stern stare. "*I* know that. But them?" She hikes a thumb over her shoulder toward her closest friends. "They don't see it that way. The best thing you can do is leave. Send a card in the mail if you need to congratulate them. Please just don't make a scene. Let them enjoy this."

I shoot her a disbelieving look. Billie Black might be her best friend, but we both recognize I'm not the scene maker in this scenario.

"I know." She runs a hand through her hair. "I *know.* Please?"

"Please what?" That word sounds so damn good on her lips.

"Please, just go." Her eyes are wide and pleading. Absolutely distracting.

12

I tap at my lips and stare up at the sky dramatically like I'm considering what she's told me. "What's in it for me?"

"Stefan." Her tone is so scolding.

I pin her with my gaze. "Let me take you on a date, and I'll leave like you want me to."

She shakes her head, and this time she can't contain the smile that touches her mouth. "You're insane, you know that?"

Can't blame a guy for trying.

I wink at her before I turn away and call back over my shoulder. "Yeah, but that's what you love about me."

She groans, and I chuckle under my breath as I leave.

Yep. Just insane enough to keep trying.

CHAPTER 2

Mira

MY BREATH COMES OUT IN PUFFS, WHITE AGAINST THE NIGHT sky, as I trudge down the steep stairs from my apartment. I had been warm. I had been dead to the world, blissfully floating through a deep, dreamless sort of sleep.

Until the alarm went off.

It only took one glance at the webcam set up beside my bed to tell me there was about to be another new arrival at Gold Rush Ranch.

The last one for the season—thank god.

This has happened every night this week. It's the end of February. Foaling season—at least for racehorses, who need to be born early in the year. And it seems as if every single mare at Gold Rush Ranch has gotten together over a bale of hay and discussed syncing up their births just to spite me.

I imagine them like women, sitting around sipping a green smoothie, planning out how cute it would be to have their babies at the same time. How they could all play together, go to school together. *Ha ha. Imagine if they dated one day! How precious.*

We wanted the foals this year to be born as early as possible to give them every advantage on the track. But back-to-back-to-back? This is just torture.

The night is quiet and wet. Rain mists down continuously, causing a chilly dampness that leaches the heat from your bones and creeps into all the layers you've tried to guard yourself with. Spring in Ruby Creek is a different beast from what you'd see in the city. The elevation change ensures that, and Canadian winters aren't known for how mild they are. We butt up against the Cascade Mountains, which means it's frigid even when there isn't snow. Cold in the winter and scorching hot in the summer.

My leather gloves wrap around the steel barn door and heave, the wheels screeching as I slide it open. A quiet nicker greets me as I head down to the last stall. It's lit with warm infrared lights and glows a sort of orange color in the otherwise dark foaling barn.

We have seven mares on the farm who were due this year, six of whom have already foaled out. Four this week alone. In the middle of the night, no less.

Sadly, the mare from last night didn't make it. Everything seemed fine. Baby was up and nursing—until she collapsed. It doesn't happen often, but it does happen. And it sucks every goddamn time.

I've wanted to be a veterinarian since I can remember. I'm well aware it's not all sunshine and rainbows, but it doesn't stop the bridge of my nose from stinging when I think about it.

Now we've got this beautiful red colt, with flashy white legs and a wide blaze over his face, who doesn't have a mom. What's worse is he's our first—and only—foal sired by the farm's celebrity stallion and two-time Denman Derby winner, DD.

He's the special foal we've *all* been waiting for.

For the past twenty-four hours, we've been taking turns bottle-feeding him. Every single person on the ranch has put out feelers looking for a mare who may have lost a foal because what this little orphan needs is a mare who will adopt him. A nurse mare. Without one, his chances of survival aren't great. He *really* needs that colostrum.

I peek into his stall, trying not to tear up at the sight of his tiny sleeping form, before moving on to the next stall. *One thing at a time, Mira. You can't save them all.*

"Hey, Mama," I coo at the dark bay mare, who is already down on the ground, sweat slicked across her neck. "How we doing, huh?"

I run my fingers through her thick forelock as she gives me a slight head bob, her eyelids closing under the gentle pressure of my hand. This isn't Flora's first rodeo. From what I understand, she's produced several nice foals for the farm and is the great-granddaughter of the first-ever racehorse at Gold Rush Ranch, Lucky Penny.

The interconnectedness of it all is almost saccharine in

its sweetness. The two grandsons of the couple who founded this place are running it with their partners and making international headlines. Still breeding racehorses off that very first bloodline.

I'm not an overly sentimental woman, but even I must admit it's pretty adorable.

I crouch down behind Flora, lifting her thick black tail while rubbing at her haunch to watch for contractions, checking my watch to time them. The second one comes, but not so fast that I need to stay here and crowd her.

That's the philosophy I try to carry forward with the animals I treat. How would I want a medical professional to react in this situation? I haven't had a baby before, but I imagine having a doctor hover and stare at me would be stressful.

So I extend the same courtesy to Flora and head into the staff lounge attached to the barn. Might as well make some coffee. *Again.*

I flick the lights on, put a pod in the coffee maker, and then slump down in the cushy armchair, feeling the weight of my exhaustion. It's like the marrow in my bones has turned to lead. My entire body feels heavy. But I've always wanted this career, and I've worked too hard and too long to complain now that I'm finally here. *People have survived worse, Mira.*

Dragging my phone out of my pocket, I fire a text off to Billie as promised, and I wait for the hot water to flow through the pod and create a hot caffeinated drink for me. Billie is the head trainer here at the ranch as well as the owner's fiancé, but she's also become one of my closest friends over the last couple of years. We initially bonded over a close call with her stallion, DD. And then she was like a fly I couldn't shake off, hugging me and inviting me to girls' nights. Talking to me like we'd known each other for years. She's one of those people who just has a way of making you want to be around them. Her energy is as addictive as her language is colorful.

Mira: Ginger is foaling. I'm at the barn.

She's been sleeping with her ringer on, waiting for this final foal. Billie is usually cool under pressure, but she's nervous after last night. With a fresh reminder of how wrong it can all go, I can't blame her for feeling that way.

It only takes a few moments for her to respond, even though it's just after 2 a.m.

Billie: You really need to hire someone to help you.

Don't I know it. The problem is, I'm kind of a loner. As an only child, I take pleasure in my solitude. There are very few people in the world I can spend extended periods of time around without eventually feeling agitated by them.

Mira: Fucking tell me about it.

It's the only response I can muster as I shove my phone back into my pocket, grab the cup of steaming coffee, and wander back into the barn. I hear Ginger's labored breathing and soft grunts now, all normal. I peek in and time another contraction, which are slowly getting closer together. She won't be long now. Provided everything goes the way it's supposed to, it rarely takes long for a foal to be born.

As I sip my coffee, I move back over to the small orphan colt's stall and watch his tiny rib cage rise and fall where he's snuggled up in the straw. I'm worried sick about him. I grew up on a farm. I'm a scientist, so I like to think of myself as rational. But as much as I've trained myself to look at much of what happens to animals in this line of work as the natural circle of life, now and then, you get one that just kicks you in the gut for no good reason. Something so unfair that it clenches your heart in a fist and won't let it go. And this nameless colt is that for me.

I feel powerless to help him, and I *really* hate that. It almost makes me want to wake him and feed him again, even though I can see from the chart on his stall that Hank was here only a few hours ago and gave him a bottle then. He needs to rest, and I recognize that I just want to wake him to comfort myself. To convince myself that he really will wake again and stand on those wobbly, gangly legs. This shouldn't be how DD's first foal hits the ground.

It should be a moment of celebration, not sadness.

When my phone rings in my pocket, I don't even bother checking the number before I hit answer and say, "Go to sleep, psycho. I'll call if I need your help."

But it's not Billie's voice I hear. "Dr. Thorne? It's Stefan Dalca."

Stefan Dalca is pretty much everyone's least favorite person. He's solidified himself as enemy number one to most people at this farm for the arrogant shit he's pulled or for the arrogant shits he's employed. And to be honest, the only reason I haven't entirely written the guy off is because I kind of like him. He's a good client at the clinic. He takes meticulous care of his horses, he pays his bills early, and he keeps his appointments—in a lot of ways he's a good guy.

"Listen, if you're calling in the middle of the night to ask me on a date, the answer is still no."

Stefan is also relentless—and I kind of get a kick out of it. He asked me out six months ago as a joke. And now it is *the* running joke. He smirks and offers a date in lieu of paying a bill. He winks and offers a date in exchange for throwing a race. A woman with better sense would tell him to back off, but I've always been drawn to the man—against my better judgment—so he usually gets a headshake and an eye roll followed by an "in your dreams" with a small tip of my lips.

"I called the clinic, but—"

"That's because it's closed. You can't be calling me at all hours of the night, Stefan. I don't even know how you got my personal number. I'm not on call. We open at nine—"

He cuts me off with a crack in his voice. "It's an emergency. I need you at my farm as soon as possible."

I pull straight up to the big barn doors at Cascade Acres. My footfalls echo in the otherwise quiet barn as I run down the alleyway to where lights are on at the back.

"Stefan?" I call out breathlessly. "I'm here."

"Over here," he barks back from only a few stalls ahead, just as I see his wide-eyed barn manager, Leo, step out into the aisle.

The man presses his lips together and shakes his head at me as I turn down into the oversized foaling stall. Stefan is hands-on with his horses, and it's irritating that Leo, who is supposed to know something about this business, is standing here like a bump on a log while I've spent the drive over talking his employer through what to do to salvage a dangerous situation.

Stefan is down on the stall floor, kneeling beside a motionless foal, his hands braced on his knees and his head bowed.

His voice comes out quiet and lightly accented when he finally speaks. "I've been trying to resuscitate her the way you told me to. I think she's dead."

I step in and check the chestnut mare, who is standing above the foal's body, quickly. She looks tired but isn't bleeding excessively. Thankfully, nothing looks emergent with her—it's the foal that has me worried. "Mom looks okay for now."

"I burst the bag just like you told me to." His voice is thick, and blood covers his naturally tan arms and white T-shirt.

Red bag deliveries are dangerous, messy, and rarely end well. The placenta separates and the foal is born prematurely.

I take a deep breath and then kneel beside Stefan. "You did great. You did everything right."

He looks at me now, his green eyes almost mossy in the low light. There's no smirk on his face tonight. He looks genuinely gutted.

I drop his gaze, pull out my stethoscope, and listen for a heartbeat. Finding none, I place my hand gingerly over one of his. "I'm sorry, Stefan."

He nods, unable to meet my eyes. I hate this part of being a vet. The dealing with people part. The dealing with feelings part. Animals live their life in the moment. They are eternal optimists—they don't know any better. But people are complicated and traversing their emotions isn't my strong suit. I'm not a talk-about-your-feelings type of gal.

With my other hand, I awkwardly pat his back. I'm aware my bedside manner leaves something to be desired, but I'm good with the animals, and in my book, that's what counts. It's moments like this where my tongue ties in a knot, and my otherwise quite exceptional IQ short-circuits.

"Did I miss something?" he asks, his voice so thick it makes me blink away unwanted moisture in my eyes.

I sit back on my heels and heave out a sigh. "You didn't miss a thing. This is just…nature. It's sad and gritty sometimes. But what you did saved your mare's life. In the wild or without supervision, they'd both be gone."

He nods but still doesn't look at me, so I opt to sit beside him in silence, holding vigil over the lost foal. What more is there to say, really?

The world is a cruel place sometimes.

CHAPTER 3

Stefan

DEATH SUCKS. THIS IS SOMETHING I ALREADY KNEW, BUT watching something so young and innocent die is different. It's just *wrong*. It makes me feel almost nauseous. All the prepping, all the money, all the knowledge. None of it matters when the universe shits on you.

I stand and pat the sweet broodmare, whose eyes are fluttering shut with exhaustion. "You did good, pretty girl," I say as I slide a hand down her face. "You did good."

And then I walk woodenly to the bathroom to wash some of the blood off myself. I'm a goddamn mess. I look like Carrie on prom night, and as much as I hate to admit it, I feel like I could cry.

I haven't cried in years. I've become far too closed-off for that. And I'm sure as hell not going to do it in front of Dr. Thorne. It would probably just give her something to run back to all her annoying friends with. Something to mock me about.

I'm not stupid. I know they think I'm terrible. I'm not oblivious to the fact that there are almost certainly jokes made at my expense around Gold Rush Ranch. Did I resort to questionable tactics to buy their championship-winning stallion out from underneath them? Yes. Did I hire a jockey who may have set out to harm their horse and rider? Yes. Did he also turn out to be a sleazy predator? Yes. But I had no knowledge that he was going to do that. And I *never* would have instructed him to do so. I might not describe myself as a "good man," but I'm not morally corrupt enough to actually hurt someone. Plus, I'm not finished with him. He'll get what's coming to him if it's the last thing I do. There's a special place reserved in hell for men who hurt women, and I plan to ensure he gets there. At any rate, the last thing I need to do is give them ammunition to take me down when all I want is to succeed in this business.

Making my way to the top has been my singular focus for years now. I've done what it takes to get ahead. To establish myself. I promised my mother on her deathbed I would take her dashed dreams and make them a reality. So here I am, trying my best and not all that concerned about making friends along the way.

I watch the dark-pink water swirl down the drain until it runs clear before drying myself off and heading back to the stall. Dr. Thorne is in there tending to Farrah, the mare who just lost her foal. She's hooked up to fluids and who knows what else. Mira has wrapped the filly in a blanket and moved her out of the stall.

"Is she going to be okay?" I ask as I lean on the doorjamb.

Mira's fathomlesss dark eyes shoot up to mine. She looks serious. She looks *tired.* Blue smudges beneath her eyes mar her beautiful face. Mira Thorne is alluring, and I'm not immune to it. Black hair and similarly dark, almond-shaped eyes. A slight smirk always on her lips, like she thinks she's smarter than everyone around her.

And she just might be right. Though I'm sure I could give her a run for her money if I wanted to, but I don't. Out in Ruby Creek, the pickings for veterinarians are slim, and Dr. Mira Thorne is damn good at her job.

"Yeah. I'm just going to get her hydrated, get some antibiotics through the system, just in case. We'll have to keep a close eye on her for the next while."

I just nod, feeling the sadness of the lost filly like a weighted blanket across my chest. I feel responsible. Like I could have done more. Should have hired better people. Should have called Mira sooner. Should have had my own on-site veterinarian. Should have done *something.*

Like she can see my turmoil, Mira looks at me, her expression perfectly sincere. No trace of that smirk she's usually giving me. "Hey, you did everything you could. More than most people would. This isn't on you."

In moments like this, I feel distinctly out of my element. I wasn't raised on a farm, and I don't have a background in this industry. I just waltzed in with a checkbook and a keen mind and set myself to learning, as well as hiring and buying the best. Maybe she's just being nice. Maybe I could have done more.

I watch Mira work quietly and gently beside the mare,

mumbling things to her I can't quite make out. She has a way with the animals that I admire. I could use a little of her gentleness sometimes. I recognize that the way I've gone about doing things has rubbed some people the wrong way. But I don't concern myself with their opinions. Instead, I think of my mother, who, after years of protecting me, got taken out by the asshole she married. The one who got off on knocking her around. I think of her, hooked up to tubes and wires after that plane crash, telling me she never should have left Ruby Creek.

A place I'd never heard of.

Telling me she should have stuck around and trained racehorses.

A part of her life I'd never known about.

Then she dropped a life-altering bomb on me.

And then she died.

He died, too, but he took my mom with him. In his stupid small private plane, the kind that rich people have a bad habit of dying on. One final *fuck you* to the son he never liked. She never could quite leave him, so the plane crash took them both. So bitter and so sweet all at once. And I missed out on so many years with her while she shipped me off to private schools to keep me safe and away from him, my supposed dad.

She was battered and bruised and so damn injured. With her hand in my hand, she took her last breath, and I promised to bring her back to Ruby Creek. A small town on the other side of the world. And then with all the vast amounts of cash that asshole left behind, I set out to make her dying dreams come true.

Life isn't fair, and neither am I. Especially not when I have a promise to fulfill.

I storm through the barn and grab a shovel on my way out the door. It's dark and cold, and it's raining again, but I don't care. I'm a mess already.

Shovel in hand, I head down toward the small lake on my property. The one that separates my house from this barn.

The one where I spread my mother's ashes. And beneath the big weeping willow to the east of the water, I dig a hole.

This place is about to become a cemetery for everyone I can't manage to keep safe.

"Stefan, sit down."

I barely hear her silky voice over the rush of the rain falling. I shake my head and keep throwing dirt back into the hole. When I retrieved the foal's body, Mira looked at me sadly. I don't want her pity. I don't want her to look at me like that. I just want to bury the foal and then carry on with my day like this shitty fucking night never even happened.

I freeze when I feel her hand come to rest on my back again, her slender fingers lying across the expanse between my shoulders, heating the skin beneath through my soaked shirt.

Her touch is warm. But her voice is not. "Sit. Down."

"I can't. I need to finish filling this hole."

Her other hand shoots out and wraps around the wooden handle of the shovel. "No. It's my turn."

I stand up straight now and peer down at her. "This isn't what I pay you for."

She rolls her eyes at me but yanks on the shovel. "Don't I know it. But I'm going to do it. So back off."

"You look tired," I say, looking her up and down, her stern face peeking out from beneath the hood of her raincoat.

Her gaze scans me, and that signature smirk touches the edges of her lips. "I guess I'm in good company." I get distracted by her mouth for just long enough that she yanks the shovel right out of my hands. I expect some sassy comment, but she just turns around and starts shoveling scoops of heavy, wet soil into the big hole.

My feet root to the ground as I watch her work, misty rain falling around us as the sun comes up over the Cascades, casting a blue glow across the valley. It's eerie and beautiful all at once, and suddenly I feel just as tired as I accused Mira of looking.

I sink to the ground right where I am, not caring about how wet or muddy I might get. I'm past that point. It feels like I'm having an out-of-body experience—that's how tired and stunned I am.

"Why are you helping me?" I blurt out to the woman in front of me, who I could have sworn is completely indifferent to me but is going out of her way to help me right now. At the very least, her friends hate me. Helping me would probably be a crime in their books.

She doesn't look up. The shovel clinks and rasps against the small pebbles in the pile of silty dirt. It smells fresh and earthy between the soil and the lake and the rain.

"Because you needed help," she eventually responds.

"What are all your friends going to say about you doing this?"

She stops now, jams the shovel into the ground, and puts one booted foot on top of its edge as she looks down at me. Her eyes are intelligent, and her cheeks are pink, and her chest rises and falls with the exertion of digging. "Not sure. I don't usually ask their permission to do what I think is right."

I scoff and stare at the upturned tip of her nose, the way a droplet of water drips off it. Leave it to the woman who saves lives for a living to be all morally superior when I'm so clearly morally gray. I wonder what she really thinks of me.

"You know what they say about assuming, Dalca. And you definitely shouldn't make assumptions about me." Mira glares at me so hard that I drop my eyes. I'm not in the mood to face off with anyone right now. So I sit, lost in thought, getting soaked to the bone while my veterinarian finishes covering the grave. I don't even bother interrupting her to take the shovel back. She doesn't strike me as the type of woman who needs my help.

Plus, I'm probably no gentleman as far as she's concerned.

When she's done, she drops the shovel on the ground and comes to stand over me. Her warm breath puffs out in front of her as she speaks. "I'll be back later today to check on Farrah. You should get some sleep."

"Are those the doctor's orders?" My tone is condescending. It's kind of my default mode—I sometimes talk that way without even meaning to. I sound like a spoiled rich

ELSIE SILVER

kid with mommy issues even though I'm thirty-four years old. *Adorable.*

She puts her hands on her hips and quirks one shapely brow in my direction, scolding me silently. "Never believed you were quite the dick people make you out to be. But when you talk like that, I can see it."

I clench my jaw, working my teeth against each other, internally berating myself. When I finally look up to offer her an apology, she's walking back toward her Gold Rush Ranch truck, hips swaying with a gait that defies how exhausted she must be right now.

I should have thanked her. She helped me. In the dark. In the rain. And I acted like a sullen little prick.

Her friends call me *Dalca the Dick*, but right now is the first time I've actually felt like one.

CHAPTER 4

Mira

BILLIE AND I FALL SIDE BY SIDE ONTO THE COUCH IN THE stable lounge. We let our eyes flutter shut while more coffee brews.

I'm so tired that I feel like I'm drunk. The kind of tired that pushes you past exhaustion right into giddiness. I need to sleep, but I can't. We've got a beautiful new filly on the farm that Billie delivered last night after Stefan called me away on the emergency.

Flora had a healthy, uneventful delivery and gave birth to a perfect doppelgänger filly. Dark bay with long eyelashes.

Seeing a happy, healthy foal was the lift my heart needed after leaving Dalca's farm this morning. Losing a foal is never easy, but seeing how hard he was taking it made it even worse. I'm well aware I'm not a comforting person. I'm not a hold-your-hair-back-while-you-barf kind of friend. I didn't get the nursing gene. But I do know how to make myself useful, and sometimes that's an okay way to comfort a person too.

"Thanks for taking over with Flora," I mutter quietly.

"Hey, no worries. It was kind of fun. It also never fails to kill any inkling I might feel about wanting to have a baby."

I snort.

"Seriously, Mira. Something that big coming out of something that small is terrifying."

"Vaginas are very elastic. You'd bounce back."

Billie groans. "Ugh. Why is everything so literal with you? You're like Amelia Bedelia."

"I loved those books," I chuckle.

"Speaking of idiot savants, how was Dalca the Dick? He sure kept you there long enough."

"His foal died," I say bluntly. Sometimes Billie needs to be sobered up a bit.

"Well, shit. Now I feel like the dick."

I peek over at her and see her amber eyes shrink-wrapped in a layer of wetness. That loss hits a little too close for her with DD's orphan baby lying in a stall by himself not a hundred yards away. "You should. Red bag delivery. It was a tough night."

She grunts and blinks rapidly. "Did the mare make it?"

"Yes…" I say, trailing off suggestively.

Billie turns her head and hits me with wide eyes. "Why did you say it like that?"

"Are you being intentionally dense because of the person we're talking about, or are you just so tired that you're not firing on all cylinders?"

Billie is whip-smart. To pretend the first place her mind went wasn't our orphan colt would be ridiculous. Just ten minutes down the road is a mare with no foal whose milk is in full swing.

The math is pretty simple.

She blinks and nibbles at her lip. "Would you believe me if I told you I'm just super tired?"

I huff out a laugh and shake my head as I get up to walk toward the coffee machine. "Better fix your attitude, Billie. Dalca the Dick just became your best shot at saving that colt."

I pull up to Cascade Acres with two coffees in tow. I basically *am* coffee now. My blood is straight-up caffeinated, and I need it to make it through the rest of this day. Not only am I physically tired, but I'm emotionally exhausted. Vaughn, one of the owners of the ranch, told me to close the on-site clinic and get some sleep. It still means I'm on call for emergencies, but at least I'm not dozing in the new state-of-the-art facility while I pretend to work. I don't even think I could safely treat a horse right now if I wanted to.

That's the side of this gig that people seem to forget about. Some days, you feel sad right down to your toes. It's hard to shake.

But at least there's coffee.

Sweet, sweet bribe coffee. Because somehow, I'm the one who must waltz out here and convince Stefan Dalca to let us borrow his mare for the orphaned foal. Probably because

I'm the only one who is on reasonably good footing with the man. I tried to convince Hank, the sweet older barn manager, to do it. But he just laughed good-naturedly at me and said he's too old for the drama we "kids" are into.

A comment I resent. I avoid drama at all costs. Good thing Hank is so damn loveable, or I'd have pressed harder. Violet offered to go, but the scowl Cole gave me—like he might skin me if I sent her over here—had me turning her down. That motherfucker is scary when he wants to be. And Billie and Vaughn? That wasn't even on the table. They both *hate* Stefan, which is why this situation is going to require some finesse.

So I gave in and opted to take one for the team.

I walk in through the big sliding barn door and peer around. Usually, Gold Rush Ranch bustles with staff at this time of day, but this farm is pretty quiet. It's a much smaller operation. I still kind of assumed there'd be people working.

"Stefan?" I call out into the echoey alleyway.

I stop and wait for a response but hear nothing, so I keep walking toward the tractor with a trailer full of soiled wood shavings attached at the end of the barn. As I pass by the dark-stained wood Dutch doors on the stall fronts, I see the odd shovelful of waste flying out of one of the last stalls into the trailer—clearly someone is mucking stalls out down here. I'll get them to point me in the right direction.

Except when I peer down into the box stall, I don't see the staff member I was expecting to find. I see Stefan Dalca, wearing fitted black jeans, a black T-shirt, and a dark scowl on his face. AirPods are in his ears, and he obviously has no clue I'm here. So I watch him for a minute.

Dark-blond hair and golden skin give him a glow. Long limbs, corded with muscle, move with a confidence most men try to fake. But on him it looks natural. There's something alluring about his slightly dangerous vibe and the mysterious accent.

Everyone else sees Stefan all polished in an expensive suit at the track and thinks that's his go-to look, but they miss the version of him doing the dirty work at his farm. Stefan tossing hay bales off a truck in a fitted T-shirt and jeans is a memory I have stocked away for rainy days. The way his arms rippled and sweat slid over his temples. Away from the public eye, this man is a farm boy, with glowing skin from days spent working in the sun.

"Are you having a stroke, Dr. Thorne?"

My head snaps up, surprised by the sound of his voice. His smug veneer has slid back in place perfectly. This is the version of Stefan I'm accustomed to. Quick-witted and sarcastic. Frankly, it's easier to take than Sad Stefan. That was really doing a number on me.

I smile though. Because I absolutely got caught creeping. Something has inexplicably drawn me to the way this man looks. "No. But I think I might have fallen asleep."

He leans against the pitchfork in his hand, matching the way I'm leaning against the stall door, head tilting like he's assessing me. Stefan Dalca is a bright man; you can tell by the way his green eyes spark when he talks. *Nothing short with this one,* as my nana would say.

"What can I help you with?" He looks like some sort of farmer porn leaning on that pitchfork.

"Where is all your staff?" I gesture down the barn alleyway with one coffee cup.

"I sent them home. Needed to be alone."

"So. You're…mucking all these stalls by yourself?"

"Well done, Watson."

"Dick," I murmur, chuckling as I hand him the extra coffee.

"For me?" He reaches out for it slowly, eyeing me with suspicion.

"Yup."

"Is it poisoned?" His green eyes go bright as they dance with dry humor.

And I find myself laughing and joking back, like a total traitor. Like when he asks me out and I brush him off with a stupid giggle. "Nope. Just black. Like your soul."

His eyes drop as a wry twist takes over his mouth. I expected him to laugh at that, but it almost looks as if my words carried some weight. A heavy silence fills the stall, and I work to come up with something that might salvage this conversation. I can't afford to blow this. I really need his help. That foal really needs his help.

"You, uh, want some help?" I gesture down at the pitchfork.

His brows pinch together. "Why would you do that?"

"Because I'm a good person," I say brightly.

"Because you feel bad for me after last night?"

"Nope." I pop the *p*, trying to sound extra convincing.

His head tilts in an almost feline way, like he's got me totally figured out. "Because you want something from me?"

I sigh, frustrated with his ability to see right through my ruse. "Listen. Do you want the help or not?"

"Pitchforks are hanging by the feed room down the alley-way." His chin juts out in that direction. "You can take the other side." And then he gets back to sifting through the wood shavings and flipping the dirty ones skillfully into the trailer.

Saying nothing further, I grab the pitchfork and get to work. I grew up on a farm. My parents are blueberry farmers, but we still had some livestock. Chickens and goats, that kind of thing. So scooping shit isn't exactly new to me. I go inward and get lost in the repetitive nature of the job. The scrape, the shake, the toss. It's almost therapeutic. And I'm so tired that I'm pretty sure my brain departs altogether, letting my body and muscle memory take over entirely.

Stefan and I work silently and efficiently. I'd be lying if I said I'm not surprised by his work ethic. He always looks so polished and prissy, like a total square, when I see him. Expensive suit, perfectly coiffed hair, absolutely in control *always*. So these last twenty-four hours have been a surprise. My forehead wrinkles under the pressure of trying to reconcile the two different versions of this man. He's a walking, talking contradiction, and I can't help letting my mind wander to the golden manual-labor version of him.

This version is what I like in a man, and it's tripping me out. Thinking of Stefan Dalca as anything other than our competitor and a dick in general feels traitorous. If my friends could read my mind, they'd read me the riot act.

Especially when he hops up onto the tractor, turns the

key, and lets his tongue slide out over his bottom lip as the machine roars to life beneath him. He drives it casually, inching forward down the alleyway so that the trailer lines up with where we're working next. His corded forearm ripples where it's slung casually over the wide steering wheel.

And I blame everything that I'm noticing about Stefan Dalca on the delirious level of exhaustion I'm experiencing today. With all my faculties about me, there'd be no way I would check him out.

His gaze moves over to me, and I drop my head quickly, raking through perfectly clean shavings like I missed something. Hoping upon hope that he didn't notice me staring at him. *Again.*

We finish the barn, fill the hay nets, and lead all his horses back in from their time outside. We don't talk, we just do. He must be almost as tired as I am, and I figure I'm gaining some good karma points for helping him today.

I think? Probably not any good karma points with Billie. But whatever. She doesn't need to know what it took to soften the man up. She'll just be happy when she gets what she wants.

The metallic clang of the last stalls being latched echoes through the barn, and he finally turns to regard me. A light layer of dust from the shavings coats his dark-gold hair.

My fingers itch to brush it off for him.

"Now are you going to tell me what it is you want?"

I brush the shavings off my fleece coat instead, mulling over the best way to respond to him. It strikes me that playing dumb with Stefan won't be a winning strategy. So I smirk at him. "Yes."

He chuckles and stares up at the ceiling, shaking his head. "You must want it pretty bad to have spent the last few hours doing physical labor with me."

I wave him off. "I can handle physical labor. I need your help though."

He leans back against the stall and quirks an eyebrow, urging me on.

I take a deep breath and open my eyes wide. It sounds bad, but I've learned a few tricks throughout the years for bringing men around to my way of thinking. A well-placed doe-eyed look has brought many a gruff old horse breeder around to splurging on a lifesaving procedure. Does that make me a bad person? I'm not sure, but I'm willing to toe that line to save lives. As far as I'm concerned, it's just me doing my job to the best of my abilities.

Stefan snorts, hitting me with a smirk of his own. "Don't use that look on me, Mira. Just spit it out."

For crying out loud. This guy really is the worst. "Fine. I have a foal that needs a nurse mare. Without one, he won't survive."

He just stares, green eyes pinning me in place.

"And you have one…"

"Whom does the foal belong to?" His voice is calm, measured. He shows no signs of surprise.

Might as well just spit it out. "Gold Rush Ranch."

His lips roll together in thought, and I run my sweaty palms down over my jeans. He'd been a good enough guy to turf Patrick Cassell the very day I told him about what the jockey did to Violet. He marched straight back to the barn and fired the weasel on the spot. Pulled him from the race they were heading into and ate the entry fee with no questions asked.

Hopefully, he'll be good enough to do this too.

"Okay." His reply is simple. So simple that it almost confuses me.

"Really? Just…okay?"

His responding grin is wolfish. Boyishly charming. And the dark smudges beneath his eyes do nothing to detract from how handsome he is.

"Yes." He pauses. "Well, I have a couple of conditions."

Yup. There it is. Wiley bastard.

I roll my eyes. I can't help myself. And I flick my hand, motioning for him to spit it out.

"One, I want to keep them here on my farm."

Good god. That's going to be a hard sell. "It makes more sense to have them at Gold Rush with the clinic on-site."

Stefan waves me off. "It's a five-minute drive. You'll be fine."

My teeth grind at his dismissal, but I tamp my agitation down and focus on how badly that foal needs a mom. "Fine," I grit out.

"And two." The man looks downright gleeful. "You let me take you on a date."

Motherfucker.

He scratches his chin thoughtfully. "Actually, three dates."

Mother. Fucker.

"You can't be serious," I whisper-shout at him, watching

40

his eyes flashing with something I don't recognize. I think he secretly gets off on agitating people, self-serving prick that he is. "You're really going to make that running joke part of this deal?"

His lips tip up. "That's rich coming from the woman who brought me a coffee, spent hours helping me, and tried to hit me with her best damsel-in-distress face to get what she wants."

I shake my head at him with wide eyes and fists propped on my hips. "I can't believe how thoroughly you outmaneuvered me. You're willing to use a dying foal to corner me into this? Man, I feel like I just got schooled."

"You did." He smiles smugly, looking altogether too pleased with himself. He knows I won't be able to say no. Not only because I want to save that foal, but because I won't let my friend down.

"Why three dates?"

"Because it's more than one."

My foot taps. "Why not two?"

"Because it's fewer than three?" He says it like a question.

"Okay, then why not five?"

"Are you asking for more, Dr. Thorne?" The smile he hits me with now is downright devastating.

"So basically you've taken your running request and added two punishment dates?" My voice is incredulous.

"They won't be a punishment for me." He grins, and I almost want to slap it off his smug face. I wish I didn't want to save this horse so desperately, or I would. I also wish I didn't admire his tenacity. I definitely wish my stomach wasn't fluttering over why Stefan Dalca wants to take me on a date so badly.

I am a smart girl who is about to do something very stupid.

"Fine. But they will not take place in Ruby Creek, they will be platonic, and you can't tell *anyone*." I turn and head toward the door before he can respond, looking forward to escaping to the safety of my truck.

"Whatever you say," he replies smoothly. "I just can't fall in love with you, right?"

I chuckle as I twist the doorknob to leave. "Oh, Stefan. I think you already are."

I smile into the crisp afternoon air at the sound of his laughter behind me. I may be stuck with the guy, but I don't have to make it easy for him.

Can't let him win every round.

CHAPTER 5

Mira

"No. No fucking way. No, Mira. No."

Violet looks between Billie and me with wide blue eyes, like she's trying to figure out how she can smooth this over. I've just told them about Stefan Dalca's stipulation but conveniently left out the date part for obvious reasons. There are some things the people you love just don't need to know. I will make that sacrifice in secret.

And I don't want to watch Billie full-on erupt either.

"I told him it was fine."

Billie is *riled*, amber eyes narrowed and her head shaking vehemently. "No chance am I sending DD's first baby into the lion's den. Over my dead fucking body."

"Well, it'll be your dead body or the foal's."

"Jesus, Mira. That's dark," Violet pipes up, running her hands through her hair.

Billie glares at me. She doesn't like what I've just said, but she can't deny the truth of it either.

"Man," Billie sighs raggedly. "He's such a dick. I hate this." Her hatred for the man isn't news to anyone. His tactics rub almost everyone the wrong way, but he almost ruined her and Vaughn—something completely unforgivable in her book.

"He isn't so bad." Violet is obviously more forgiving.

"Listen. It is what it is. Are we saving the foal or not? Because the way I see it, he's kinda got us by the balls. It's five minutes down the road. I can check on the foal daily and report back. In the fall, we'll wean him and forget this ever happened. Then we can all go back to openly hating Stefan Dalca."

Billie sighs.

Violet nods.

I think that's as close as I'm going to get to agreement from these two, so I slap my knees in closing and push up to stand. "Who's going to help me load up the trailer?"

Both women stare back at me with frustration and resignation in their eyes. But then they stand and follow me out to help anyway. It doesn't take us long to lift the foal and get him positioned in the trailer. He's still so wobbly and weak, it's definitely not ideal having to transport him. But it's close enough that I figure the reward outweighs the risk.

"I'm coming with you." There's a hard set to Billie's jaw but also a slight wobble. She's trying to be strong, but this is killing her inside. She feels so deeply—loves so thoroughly. She's got this boisterous exterior, but she's incredibly sensitive.

I grab her shoulder and stare back into her face. "Not today, B. Let me do this for you. Let me do my job and get them settled." What I don't say to her is that there's a chance the mare doesn't accept the foal. I don't want her there if that happens. "We can go together tomorrow and check on them. Let's keep it as quiet and private for them as possible today."

She nods once, tersely. We're talking about skittish animals, and she knows that sometimes what we want isn't really what's best for them. And she's willing to sacrifice her own comfort for that—it's part of what makes her such an exceptional horsewoman.

Violet scoots in beside her, fitting herself into Billie's side like a puzzle piece. The two of them are so cute together, it almost makes me gag. Soon to be sisters-in-law since they're each with one of the two brothers who own Gold Rush Ranch.

We're all friends, but I still always feel a bit like the third wheel. And that's not on them, it's on me. I've never been big on loads of friends or the whole girl-tribe thing. But these two just sort of claimed me and haven't let me go, and I'm not complaining. Billie and Violet are easily the best friends I've ever had. It just still feels weird to have these people that I'm accountable to after being a loner for so long.

I hop in the truck and buckle up, rolling down the window as I slowly pull out of the circular driveway in front of the main building.

"Wish me luck!" I call out to them with a wave.

Lord knows I'm going to need it.

★★★

"Who are you?"

The girl at the door is eyeing me like I'm yesterday's

roadkill. Even she knows I shouldn't be here. She has head-phones around her neck and is wearing an oversize T-shirt with tight shorts barely peeking past the hemline. I can see gum in her mouth every time she opens her jaw wide to chomp back down on it. The pink scrunchie that holds her blond hair in a high ponytail makes her look like a walking, talking attitude problem, complete with a bow on top.

The house itself is beautiful, like it's made for the land that surrounds it. All river rock and natural wood beams. A rounded front door with a wrought-iron-framed window at the top. It's big, but not gaudy. It's classy—just like Stefan.

"I'm Mira. The vet." I hike a thumb over my shoulder back toward the farm, where I left the unnamed foal in the trailer because Stefan is nowhere to be found and I need some help. "I'm looking for Stefan."

She looks me up and down, still chewing her gum like a cow would chew its cud. I can't tell how old she is, but she strikes me as young. Too young to be with Stefan.

I hope.

God. I hope he's not slimy enough to con me into three dates when he has a girlfriend.

"Stefan!" I startle when she turns and yells up the curved staircase behind her.

Within moments he's jogging down the stairs, torn jeans hugging his legs in an almost distracting way.

"Nadia, would it kill you to take a few steps and look for me?"

Nadia rolls her eyes and storms off. Stefan offers me a tight smile as he reaches down to slide his feet into a pair of

46

worn work boots. This angle gives me the perfect view of the muscles in his back as they ripple beneath the plain white T-shirt. I figure if I'm going to be forced to go on fake dates with the man, I might as well enjoy the view.

I'm only human.

A human who is currently way overworked and way undersexed.

"Sorry about Nadia. Taking in my little sister is not the cakewalk I thought it would be."

I sigh in relief. *Sister.* Hallelujah.

He reaches into the closet and pulls out a shearling-lined brown jacket. There's something decadent about the way Stefan moves, confident and borderline hypnotic. My eyes trail down his body, watching the veins in his hands as his long, deft fingers button the jacket.

"Eyes up here, Dr. Thorne," he coos with a knowing smile.

I like this more playful version of Stefan Dalca. Not the uptight, almost too-smooth version of him everyone sees down at the track.

I decide to roll with it. "Why?"

"Because you might fall in love with *me* if you stare for too long." Even the light lilting of his accent is more pronounced here on the privacy of his farm. Like he's not trying as hard to project a certain image. He's comfortable and teasing.

It's weird. And what's worse is I live for this type of banter.

I scoff. "Pfft. Don't worry. You're not my type."

He holds one arm out, gesturing me down the front steps

of his house up on the hill. The property is not as expansive as Gold Rush Ranch, but it just might be more picturesque. It overlooks a valley with a small lake at the base. The barn is just up the opposite slope, and there's a huge weeping willow tree right beside the gravel road that joins the two buildings. Everything nestled into the valley gives it an effortless cozy feeling that I like.

Our footsteps fall in time on the gravel road as we walk down to the stables.

"And why am I not your type?"

I sneak a peek over at him, hands slung casually in the pockets of his jeans. The way he carries himself—perfect posture and head held high—gives him an almost regal air. If anyone thinks he's practically royalty, it's Stefan Dalca. So why he's hung up on me saying he's not my type is beyond me.

"Blond hair." I laugh, watching my breath blow out in a white cloud before me, unwilling to admit that it's not *that* blond, really. In certain light you see the shimmery gold, and I bet as a child it was much lighter. But now it's this dirty color. Either way, it's not my usual dark vibe.

He shrugs. "We can dye it."

I can't help the big stupid grin spreading across my face. I feel like I'm living in the twilight zone. *What the hell am I doing? Are we being friendly? Are we flirting?*

"Okay. Also…you're arrogant."

He gives me a sly look out of the corner of his eye, one side of his sinful mouth tipping up into a cocky smirk. "You'll get used to it."

I shake my head. "You're just proving my point." He doesn't respond, but I see his body stiffen slightly as we walk past the fresh grave we dug last night. His eyes fixate forward on the barn. "Okay. What about the Mafia ties? Everyone says you have mafia ties."

Small-town gossip is vicious, and I'm not sure how or where this rumor started, but people around here spread it like wildfire. Probably the accent, the murky past, and the boatloads of unexplained cash.

As the daughter of an Indian farmer and his white hippie wife, I'm not oblivious to how judgmental rural towns can be. Having to always work harder to fit in or succeed isn't new to me.

He stops at my question, turning toward me slowly. The energy in the air shifts from laid-back to something more ominous. "And what do you think about that?"

Our eyes clash as I assess him. I swear I can see the humor drain out of them right before me. "I think you're all bark and no bite."

He huffs out a quiet laugh and starts walking again with a subtle shake of his head. "You are something else, Dr. Thorne."

I take a few long strides to catch up with him. "I'm going to take that as a compliment."

"You should," he replies with complete sincerity as we approach the Gold Rush Ranch trailer parked in the lot before us. Before I have time to ruminate on that last comment, he continues, "Okay. What do we do now, Doc?"

I blow a loose piece of hair away from my face. "I'm

going to need your help walking him into the barn. He's very weak. Let's just get him into a stall on his own first. I'm going to need some of the mare's manure, and I've got some Vicks VapoRub."

His nose wrinkles. "For what?"

"The manure we need to rub on the foal. The Vicks is to block her sense of smell. Hopefully that will be enough. Is she a mellow mare? A mild tranquilizer is also an option."

"She's always been very calm. Why would you tranquilize her?"

I peer back at him as I pull open the trailer door. "She could react poorly. She could reject the foal. This isn't guaranteed."

Stefan presses his shoulders back stiffly, his lips pressing into a grim line. "I didn't realize that was a risk."

I step up into the trailer, muttering to myself, "Sometimes I wonder how you got into this business at all."

I feel him step up behind me, but he says nothing.

"Hey, little buddy." I run my hands over the foal, happy to see he's still standing. "Out we go. Stefan, just support his body in case he stumbles."

Between the two of us, we get the small colt out of the trailer and into a warm stall. Stefan stands in the doorway staring at him with a sad look on his face while I swipe some of the rub into the mare's nostrils a few doors down. Then with one gloved hand, I pick up a few pieces of manure from her stall before heading over to rub it along the foal's back. Right where she might sniff while he nurses. *Hopefully*.

To Stefan's credit, he doesn't even flinch. And when

everything is as set as it's going to get, I turn back to the tall man waiting behind me. The grim expression on his face and red-rimmed eyes are a perfect reflection of my own face.

"Ready?"

He gives me a steady nod. "Yup. Let's do it." There's a hard set to his angular jaw now. Our time for joking has passed. He almost looks nervous.

"Okay. Let's get him up."

I'm not big on praying. But I send up a small prayer now. I'll take all the help I can get to make this work.

CHAPTER 6

Stefan

MY HEART HAMMERS AGAINST MY RIBS AS WE WALK THE TINY colt down the concrete alleyway, small soft hooves clopping quietly through the barn. I feel like a shmuck. Here I am, joking around and flirting with Mira, feeling all proud of myself for squeezing three dates out of the woman while a horse's life is on the line.

And this might not even work.

I'm usually comfortable with morally gray business decisions, but this time I just feel like a dick. Mira saves lives for a living, and I leveraged that passion for my own gain. Asking for the dates was a shot in the dark, just like it was the first time I did it and every time since. But her turning me down has me fixated. I want to know Mira Thorne in ways she can't even imagine.

Truthfully, I should probably feel worse. But watching her work, so steady and focused, just makes me more attracted to her. I've studied my ass off since starting this venture to learn as much as possible about the business. My closest friend, Griffin—who I bought this place from—is my go-to source for horse information. But orphaned foals haven't come up in our chats yet.

Mira slides the stall door open and takes a deep breath. Her eyes meet mine over the back of the foal, and she gives me a decisive nod before we step into the stall.

I'm nervous. It's so unlike me. But, god, I really want this to work. I don't even care who owns the foal. The truth is, I'd have done this even if she said no to the dates. Plus, I don't dislike Billie Black or the Harding family enough to wish this upon them. Watching my foal die this morning was heart-wrenching. I've come to love these animals, and watching them suffer is torture in a league of its own.

"Hey, Mama. Meet baby. He's a real sweet boy." Mira's voice is deep and smooth. She doesn't use a high-pitched baby voice. It's almost like she could hypnotize the horses into acceptance with a tone like that. Or me. I'm a sucker for her sultry voice.

She flicks her head back at me, effectively dismissing me as she holds the small red foal and lets the mare walk toward it. Stepping back into the doorway, I watch raptly. I'm not a superstitious man, but I'm not taking any chances tonight.

I shove my hands into my pockets and cross my fingers. I think I'd cross my toes if I could.

The mare's dark globes for eyes assess the colt, and her ears flick around in confusion as she tries to sniff him. To the colt's credit, he may be weak, but his sense of smell is just fine. I watch his head snap toward her udder, ears pointing exactly in that direction, and spindly legs follow. His back moves right beneath her flared nostrils. They're glistening with the rub that Mira smeared there, but she must catch some small scent of the manure because she gives him a small nuzzle on his bony haunch with her top lip.

I don't miss the small gasp that slips past Mira's lips. She holds her hands up off the foal like he burned her and steps back slowly. Carefully. Like she doesn't want to break whatever momentary connection the two horses seem to have formed.

My fingers hurt from how hard I'm squeezing them across each other. I don't move, even as Mira's body comes to pause only a few inches away from mine.

Within moments, the colt shoves his head beneath the mare's belly and nuzzles at the overfull udder. Trying to figure out something he hasn't quite learned how to do yet.

I glance down at Mira's tense body—raised shoulders and hands fisted in front of her breasts—feeling her heat seep into the front of my body. The only part of her moving is her chest, with the rise and fall of her deep breaths.

The stall is almost entirely silent. Until a noisy suckling noise fills the space. Followed by a ragged sigh from the woman standing in front of me. In wonder, I watch the content mare go back to the hay net before her. Mira's thick black ponytail flops forward as she drops her face into her hands.

The relief pouring off her bleeds into me, and I pull one hand out of my pocket and place it on the nape of her slender neck, giving her a reassuring squeeze. "You did it."

She just nods. She doesn't shake me off; she stands there, soft skin beneath my palm, watching the mare and foal accept each other like life meant them to be together no matter how tragic the circumstances.

"Fuck. What a relief." Her voice is hoarse, but I can't see her face to confirm how emotional she might be. I absently brush my thumb across the base of her skull, and after a beat she clears her throat and steps away. "Let's leave them for a bit." Mira turns to exit the stall but doesn't meet my eyes.

Usually, she covers her vulnerability with a smirk—but not today.

I shouldn't have touched her like that. I'm like a cat playing with his food. But all I really want is for her to see that I'm not a bad guy. I don't always play by the rules, but I'm not a *bad* guy. I grew up with one, and I refuse to become him.

I move away, letting her pass. Wishing my hands were still on her. I don't know why the woman intoxicates me the way she does. Her eyes, her lips, her cool exterior, the sensual hum of her voice—it's all driven me to distraction since the first time I met her down at the track. Her no-nonsense way of handling me while being perpetually gentle and sweet with the horses was a contradiction that fascinated me then and still does now.

She's an equation I'd love to solve.

Or maybe the broken little boy in me just wants her to treat me the way she does a horse. *With love.* I shake my head at myself as I turn to follow her. The thought of her softening up for me is the ultimate carrot she could dangle. I want nothing more than to watch her melt.

I don't love Dr. Mira Thorne. I barely even know her. I'm just fascinated though—inexplicably drawn to her. And I'm too damn accustomed to getting what I want to let it go.

"What now?" I ask as she marches toward the lounge area, complete with cushy brown-leather couches, a pool table, and a fully stocked bar.

She straight-up ignores me for a few beats before flopping down onto a couch with a loud sigh. "Now we wait a bit and see what happens."

I follow suit and drop onto the couch across from her, propping my feet up on the table and resting my hands across my ribs. "You look tired."

She hits me with an unimpressed look. "Charming, Stefan."

"Why don't you sleep for a bit, and I'll keep an eye out."

"No." Her head drops back, and her eyes close.

If she's half as exhausted as I am, she must feel like utter garbage. But I don't argue. Mira doesn't give off the vibe that says she wants to be coddled. So, if she wants to be dead on her feet, good for her. I'll support it.

"What's the accent?" she asks without opening her eyes.

"Romanian." I keep my eyes wide open. Truthfully, I can't peel them off her.

"You're Romanian?"

"I was raised there."

"You just look so...I don't know. Not Romanian?"

Yeah. I'm not sure how it took me so long to figure that out either. I'm about to ask her about her family's background, but after only a few moments, her fingers fall open and her pillowy lips part.

She's out like a light.

She looks younger and…softer somehow while she's asleep. More innocent. The sight of it stirs some instinctual part of me, and all I want to do is take care of her. Make sure she's comfortable. That she rests for a while.

I walk over to the large wicker basket at the end of the couch, pull out an Aztec-style wool blanket, and drape it over her gently. She stirs slightly, but only to nuzzle her cheek into the couch.

She looks so damn tired.

I figure I can sleep tomorrow while she'll probably have to work. With one final glance over her sleeping form, I walk back out into the barn alleyway to the stall with the mare and foal. I flip the latch and creep in. My chest warms seeing mom standing and dozing with sprawled-out baby sleeping happily beside her. They're a perfect match. Red and red. You would never guess they aren't related.

I step into the stall, closing the door behind me, and slide down onto the ground near the foal's head. With my back against the wall, I let my gaze travel over his spindly body, warm under the glow of the red lamp hanging above. He looks weak but peaceful.

I'm momentarily transported back in time to the horse I had as a child. The same color as this foal, but not with flashy white legs and face. An entirely different type of horse. But he was *mine*. He was my reprieve from the hell that was living in my childhood home.

I lean forward and let my hand trail over the sleeping colt's leg to his knee, where the white stocking blends into the coppery brown of the rest of his coat. My body moves of its own accord, coming to kneel beside the small horse. My palm rests over his rib cage, feeling it rise and fall in a steady rhythm. He may not be out of the woods yet, but his breathing is strong. I think he's a strong little horse.

A fighter.

When I move up to his head, cupping the round plate of his cheekbone, he nurses in his sleep. A sweet suckling noise that makes me smile. This guy knows what's up. He's not down for the count yet. And I'm going to make sure he succeeds.

I lean back against the wall, resting my elbows over my knees, vowing internally to make sure this is the healthiest foal anyone has ever seen.

★★★

"Wakey, wakey."

My foot wobbles from a kick, and my eyes flutter. The first thing I feel is stiffness as I try to get my bearings. Stiffness in my joints…and in my pants.

Mira's voice filters into my consciousness. Something that is definitely not helping the morning wood situation. "Up we get, Sleeping Beauty. I made you coffee."

And there she is, standing in the stall's entryway, looking a tad disheveled. How I imagine she'd look after a night spent in my bed. Soft and lacking the snarky smirk that's always plastered on her face.

I scrub at my stubble, trying to wake myself up. A small chestnut face moves into my periphery. The foal is looking at me like I'm absolutely fascinating. Farrah is just ignoring me—the weird guy who slept on the floor of her stall.

Mira steps closer, leaning down slightly to hand me the mug of steaming coffee in her hand.

I peer down into the mug. "Cream this time?"

Her eyes flit away shyly. "You didn't seem big on the black coffee, so I tried something else. How do you take it?"

I just don't want you to think my soul is black. It had been a joke when she said it, but I'd let it bug me anyway. I'm inexplicably concerned with what this woman thinks of me.

"This is fine," I reply gruffly, taking the coffee from her, willing my raging boner to disappear. *Hello, morning wood.*

"Okay, get up. I need to check these two over."

I take one thoughtful sip of the coffee before I calmly say, "I can't get up right now."

Mira scoffs. "Of course, you can."

I grin back at her, and after a beat, her confused eyes trail down to my lap and then go wide as she puts all the pieces together. "Oh." She clears her throat. "I'm, uh, just going to get a few things from my truck then." And then she darts out of the barn.

I can't help but chuckle as I bang the back of my head on the wall a few times. That's not the reaction I was expecting from her at all. She acts like a siren, but the mere mention of a boner, and she can't get away fast enough.

After a couple of minutes, I stand and lean back against the wall of the stall. I sip the hot coffee and scan over the mare and foal again. The foal comes closer, clearly curious about the person who spent the night sleeping with him. His soft nose rubbing against my jeans, nostrils flaring wide as he tries to take in my scent. Bulging black globes with chestnut lashes fanning down as he wiggles his lips against my shoulder curiously.

Damn. He's *really* cute. I reach my free hand out and rub the fuzz of his goofy little forelock between my thumb and forefinger before letting my palm slide down over the wide white blaze on his face. His eyes flutter shut, like he's enjoying the feel, and I can't help but smile at how sweet and trusting he is. How unmarred by the world—by life.

"He's pretty sweet, isn't he?" Mira's voice interrupts the dark turn in my head. She's standing in the doorway with a stethoscope around her neck and her ponytail slicked back harshly against her scalp.

"Does he have a name yet?"

She sips her coffee and shakes her head. "No. I think Billie didn't want to get attached, so she was pretending to have a hard time coming up with something.. You know, in case he doesn't make it."

It's the perfect opportunity to take a jab at the other woman, but I can't bring myself to do it. "What's his breeding?" I ask, curious about the colt's lineage.

Mira continues to sip her coffee and stare at me. Her eyes flit momentarily to my crotch, and I swear her cheeks pink a bit, but I don't get long to think about that before she says, "He's the black stallion's first foal."

I blink at her. "The one I tried to buy?"

"Yup."

"Jesus. Did you have to tranquilize Billie to get him over here?"

"Don't be a dick. She's been sick over this foal. She hates you, but she wants him to survive more."

Feeling properly chastised, I hide behind my cup of coffee for a moment before changing the subject. "He needs a name. It's important he has a name."

"Why?" Her voice is quizzical as she steps in and holds the stethoscope over the nameless colt's ribs.

"Because he's going to make it. A name ties him to this world. It gives him an identity. Means we recognize his existence."

I see the searching look she gives me. It's quick, but it's there. Full of curiosity.

Every time I ran away as I child, I'd end up with the local villagers who lived nearby. I'd hide out in their homes and listen to their stories, their teachings, their connectedness. That immense sense of community—it all stuck with me. Rather than growing up to be a man who was afraid to fall into my parents' footsteps, I decided it was my goal to prove that I wouldn't. I'd have a wife, I'd have a family, I'd have it all, and I would treat them like gold.

She rolls her lips together but doesn't look up from where she's staring down at the foal. Her mouth moves silently as she counts his heartbeats.

"Then name him. He needs all the help he can get," she says as she steps away. "I'll be back later to check on him again. I need to go open the clinic. Can you make sure he's nursing throughout the day? I'm going to do a blood draw when I come back. I'm probably going to bring Billie—she needs to see that everything is good. So can you either keep your mouth shut or make yourself scarce?"

I nod, trying to hide my amusement over her thinking she can dictate my behavior or whereabouts on my property. My gaze follows her decisive movements as she packs up her kit and heads out. I shouldn't check her out the way I am, admiring the roundness of her ass in the pair of dark-wash Levi's she's wearing. But goddamn, she fills them out so well.

Her hand taps the frame of the stall door as she leans back in, tongue darting out over her bottom lip. "And, uh, thanks for the blanket last night."

"Next time I'm joining you." I wink, and she just rolls her eyes.

I should try harder to keep things professional and not let my curiosity about Dr. Mira Thorne take over my brain. I shouldn't think with the wrong head.

But the more time I spend with her, the more of a challenge that feels like. I like a challenge…but keeping my hands off Mira isn't one I'm sure I want to take on. The woman is not my biggest fan, this much I know.

But then I've got three dates to make her *want* my hands on her body.

CHAPTER 7

Mira

NICE STEFAN IS TRIPPING ME THE FUCK OUT. I'VE SPENT almost every appointment today trying to figure out what to do with my opinion of him.

I stare out the big floor-to-ceiling windows of the clinic as I wait for the X-rays I took to develop. Taking in the rolling hills around Gold Rush Ranch, I mull over the past thirty-six hours. I had Stefan neatly classified into a file where I put people I feel mostly indifferent about. He'd done some shitty things, but I'd also been witness to him being a decent human being. He was morally neutral. One experience sort of canceling out the other.

Past tense.

Now?

I don't know. Watching him these last couple of days threw a wrench into all my preconceived notions. Was he a cocky prick? Yes. But was he also charming and sensitive? Yes.

Should I be mad at him for forcing my hand on the

dates? Ugh. Probably. But I'm not. And I don't really want to analyze why that is. I especially don't want to think about the possibility that he's using me to get at my friends.

I thought I'd be worried about leaving the foal there with him, but I'm not at all. He slept beside it, for crying out loud. I watched the way he ran his deft fingers over the colt's face—the expression of wonder on his own had been like a punch to the chest.

No, I'm not worried about the foal at all. I feel it in my bones that Stefan is going to name him and love him the way he deserves. It had been the look in his eyes, the gentleness in his touch. He was nothing if not determined.

For one mindless moment, I wondered how it would feel to have Stefan run his hands over me that way. It was *such* a bad idea. It would backfire spectacularly, especially with my friends. But it almost made me want it more. Under different circumstances, he'd be a fun onetime thing.

The door swings open, shaking me from my reverie.

"How's the baby?" Hank grins at me as his broad frame fills the front door, his cheeks and ears red with the bite of the cool air outside, and I marvel at how the barn manager still looks like he has a tan in the middle of winter. I guess years spent in the sun get you a perma-tan. People pay good money to look like that.

I smile at the older man who swooped in to help Vaughn run the farm when an alleged cheating scandal broke. The man who's been a mainstay in Billie's life since her teen years and a close friend of Dermot Harding, the founder of Gold Rush Ranch.

"He's good. The mare took him right away. It was amazing."

He stomps his boots on the mat at the door before approaching the front desk. "Well, you know how it goes. Sometimes it takes mere minutes, sometimes hours, and other times not at all. You should give yourself a pat on the back."

I reach over my back dramatically, patting my shoulder with a big grin on my face. I have to confess, I'm feeling proud of myself for working this out. I don't even care about the three dates I agreed to go on with Stefan. I can totally handle them. Maybe I'll get a good meal out of the deal. My stomach growls just thinking about it, and I resolve right here and now to make sure Stefan takes me for a super fancy meal.

He's gonna pay for this trick, and I'm gonna enjoy the hell out of some delicious food.

"You did good." Hank beams at me, his eyes crinkling at the sides as he leans over the counter. He's so sweet. A surrogate father to pretty much everyone at the farm now. It's probably close to time for him to retire, but I have a feeling Billie will have to drag him kicking and screaming off this property. It's never going to happen.

"Thanks. How's Trixie?" He tries to bite back a smile at the mention of the new woman in his life. They met at Cole and Violet's wedding and hit it off almost instantly. She lives in Vancouver, just ninety minutes down the road, and they take turns visiting each other when their schedules allow it.

It's freaking adorable.

"She's wonderful. So different from anyone I've ever met or thought I'd be with. She keeps me on my toes."

I can't help but laugh because the woman is a character. "I'm so happy for you. On your toes is a good thing!"

"Is it ever." He clicks his tongue and shakes his head. "Never settle, Mira. Sometimes what you want isn't what you need."

"You giving me dating advice, Hank?" My lips tip up at the thought.

"Yup. You spend too much time working for a woman your age."

I flinch. This is a sore spot for me. I've known I wanted to be a veterinarian since I was tiny. It was my single-minded focus through school and into university, straight through vet school. Did I miss out on social experiences to get where I am? Yeah, but it was worth it.

Unless you ask my extended family on my dad's side. They always have something to say about me needing to start a family. They mean well, and I know it's a cultural thing, but it gets old fast. And while my parents would never say that to me, they don't correct them either. It's like none of them completely appreciate how hard I worked to become a doctor of something, that I graduated at the top of my class, that I worked my ass off to do it. At twenty-seven years old, I'm more educated and more accomplished than anyone else in my family career-wise, and yet none of them seem to want to celebrate my achievement.

Basically, my love life revolves around the purple rubber boyfriend that lives in my nightstand and all the thirst traps

I browse on TikTok. I don't have *time* for a relationship, even if I wanted one. So my silicone friend is perfect. He doesn't need anything from me, and he doesn't get in my way. I don't owe him anything except to charge him up now and then. And that's about the level of commitment I can handle right now.

"Hey, I didn't mean that in a bad way." Hank's brow crinkles in concern.

"Oh, nah." I wave him off. "It's all good. Just distracted today. Did you need something? I'm planning to close up shop soon."

I'm aware I come off a bit cool sometimes. I'd like to say I don't mean to…but I think I do. I don't like people meddling in my business. I'm not a spew-my-personal-issues type of girl. I've been told I'm intensely private.

I say I'm just independent with clearly defined boundaries.

Hank straightens, and I smile at him kindly, trying to show that all is well without having to verbalize it. I'm not big on explaining myself when I don't think it's necessary. That's one thing I like about animals. They judge you by your actions.

"Billie is meeting me here. I'm going to drive her to Stefan's. Consider me her…bodyguard? Or Dalca's, considering my job is probably to hold her back from killing him. I'm also her getaway car if she does."

I huff out a laugh as I shut down the monitor at the front desk. "Billie should hold it together. His willingness to help is what's going to save her foal."

One corner of Hank's mouth quirks up as his eyes scan my face, a little too curiously. "I wouldn't put it that way to her if I were you."

I wink at him. "Wouldn't dream of it."

The door swings open right at that moment. "Wouldn't dream of what?" Billie asks, stomping her boots on the mat and shaking out the thick chestnut braid from under her hood.

"Oh, geez. It's pouring," I say, trying to change the direction of the conversation.

"Yeah. Just started." She looks up with a smile. "We good to go see the baby?"

"Are you?" Hank asks with the quirk of an eyebrow.

Billie grunts and rears back, like she's offended by the question. "Why wouldn't I be?"

I cut in. "I think what Hank is trying to say without actually saying it is, 'Are you prepared to behave civilly?'"

Her amber eyes narrow at me. "Yes."

Hank and I both laugh.

"What? I am. I will be just as civil as Dalca the Dick." A knowing twist takes over her lips. "And don't worry, Violet just read me the riot act. She even said he's not as bad as I think he is."

She shudders, shoulders shaking dramatically. Hank's eyes flit over to mine, like he's a freaking mind reader, and I glance away, grabbing my keys, feeling grateful that neither of them actually is.

When I jump into my vehicle, I take my phone out and open a blank text conversation with Stefan. He only ever calls me, and texting feels more personal somehow. There's a casual familiarity that comes with texting that I'm not sure is a match for a client and me, but I need to make sure he won't pull some sort of childish shit once we get there.

> **Mira:** Hi. We're on our way. Can you throw me a bone and just stay away for a bit?

He texts me back almost instantly.

> **Stefan:** Maybe if you beg.

Ha. That'll be the day.

> **Mira:** You'd like that, wouldn't you?
> **Stefan:** Absolutely.

Perv.

> **Mira:** Go fuck yourself.
> **Stefan:** You shouldn't talk that way. It's unbecoming.

He's not wrong. I've been spending too much time around Billie. But would it really be so hard for him to be compliant this once?

> **Mira:** Okay. Please go fuck yourself.
> **Stefan:** I think I will. ;)

I shake my head, half-amused and half-agitated. He can't just give me a straight answer. It's so typical of him. Between him and Billie, I'm going to have to pray for some superhuman levels of patience these next several months.

We travel to Cascade Acres separately. There isn't a lot of spare room in my truck with all the equipment I have to haul around. And Hank isn't wrong. Having a way to get out of there isn't his worst plan. *God, I hope Stefan stays away.* He and Billie are like water and oil. Or gasoline and a spark.

When we pull up, I direct them where to go and unpack what I'll need for tonight's checkup. I'm working overtime right now, but the Hardings gave me a generous compensation package, including lodging. Sure, the apartment is a far cry from fancy, but it beats living with my parents to afford my student loan payments. They've done so much for me that I don't mind spending a few extra hours here and there, going above and beyond.

When I round the corner into the immaculate barn alleyway, I'm transported to the morning Stefan and I spent mucking out stalls together in quiet companionship and shared sadness over the lost foal. The truth of it is, I hadn't planned on doing that. I could have just asked him the favor straight out, but he looked so downtrodden. And I'm a sucker for a wounded animal.

"Mira. You saved him." Billie's eyes sparkle as she claps her hands together when I enter the stall. "He already looks so much better!"

Hank's palm lands on her shoulder, his green eyes glittering with the same grateful emotion as hers.

"Okay, well, let's not take this overboard," I say, prepping my tubes for the blood draw.

"No, I'm serious. Thank you. I know it means you have to spend time here with that asshole, but...well, I'm not sure how I'll ever repay you."

Oof. If she had any idea what it really cost me, I'm not sure I'd be so securely in her good books.

She hugs the foal's neck, planting a kiss on his little head before turning to the bright chestnut mare with the flaxen mane. "Thank you," she says, voice cracking as her hand trails over the mare's delicate face. "You're the best mama in the world."

"She's a special mare, for sure," I murmur as I shoo them out of my way.

Billie and Hank look at her with so much love my heart squeezes. If everyone could stop making me feel so emotional these last couple days, that would be great.

"Skedaddle, you two. You've seen he's fine. There haven't been any confrontations. Let's call this a win. I'm going to take blood and wait to collect a fresh fecal sample."

Billie wraps her arms around me. She's a hugger, and she has been since that first day I met her when DD had his bout with colic. I am not a hugger—public displays of affection are not my thing—but I let her do it. These are the sacrifices you make for your friends.

"Thank you. I'm so lucky to have you as my friend." She squeezes me tight enough that it dislodges all my traitorous thoughts. They swirl in my head, increasing my internal shame over my growing tolerance for Stefan Dalca.

On one hand, I don't owe anyone any explanations about my feelings or choices. On the other hand, even just knowing I agreed to three fake dates with him is making me feel guilty and traitorous.

"I need to get these done and out of the way as quickly as possible." I pat Billie on the back woodenly, hoping that will signal to her the hug is over.

She pulls away, laughing. "Love you, my Ice Queen."

I can't help but roll my eyes at her nicknames. Pornstar Patty for Violet, Bossman for Vaughn, Big Bro for Cole… Dalca the Dick for Stefan.

"Love you too, B. Catch ya later, Hank!" I wave casually before turning back to the horses.

I'm relieved when they finally leave—that's enough attention for one day. The compliments, the hugs, the intense levels of thankfulness…they're all nice, but I find them overwhelming and never know quite how to react appropriately.

So, while I wait for the foal to give me the sample I need, I pull out my phone to browse social media. I find one of those dumb personality-type quizzes and start typing in my answers. Essentially zoning out while I lean up against the frame of the stall door.

"What are you doing?"

A voice startles the hell out of me, and I jump, feeling my back press into a hard chest while two gentle hands slide beneath my elbows to keep me upright. *Stefan.* I'm too shocked to even move out of the embrace.

One of my hands flattens over my sternum, where I can feel my heart thumping. "You scared the shit out of me," I pant. It's after dinner, and the barn has been quiet and empty. "What the hell kind of stalking skills are you practicing?" I spin, feeling the chill of the air against every spot that has been warm pressed up against him. It almost makes me want to spin back around and sink into his embrace. *Almost.* "I didn't even hear you at all!"

His mossy eyes scan my face, the slight bump in his nose just adding to the intensity of his face. Most people would get a break in their nose fixed, but on Stefan it just adds to his look. His mystery. I hope he never fixes it.

He takes advantage of my shock and swipes my phone out of my hand. "Then you're definitely not Black Widow. She would know someone was approaching." He smirks, and it's both annoying and adorable all at once. "*Which Marvel superhero character are you?*" he reads the name of the quiz out loud, and I will my cheeks not to pink. I can take dumb quizzes if I want. "Sounds very scientific."

I roll my shoulders back. "You do it. I bet you'll get Thanos."

His nose wrinkles, and he throws a hand over his chest dramatically like he's offended. "The big purple bad guy?"

I offer him my sweetest smile and quirk my head to the side as if to say, *If the shoe fits.*

He just grunts and goes through the quiz.

"You have to answer honestly," I remind him.

He doesn't look up at me, but I don't miss the way his jaw pops at the comment. "I am always honest. I don't abide lying."

Well, that joke fell flat.

I step beside him to peer over at my phone right as he

submits the survey. The wheel spins as "calculating" flashes across the screen. Like there's some legitimate process to matching this up.

Tom Hiddleston wearing horns pops up on the screen, and I burst out laughing. "Loki!"

He grins now, eyes twinkling with mirth, and hands me my phone back. "I'm going to have to get a hat like that."

"Oh, yeah. That would be hot." His head quirks almost instantly, and I try to cover the slip of my tongue. "The god of mischief," I say, nodding. "That's pretty accurate. Maybe their science isn't so bad after all."

He peers down at me, looking altogether too confident. It does funny things to my insides. Laughing with this man in a dim barn when I'm not supposed to enjoy his company at all is bad. *And did I just accidentally call him hot?* I should know better. I should *do* better.

But I've always been one to want things I shouldn't.

"Speaking of mischief," he says, eyes scanning my face in a way that heats me to my core. "You owe me three dates."

I smile back at him, meeting his stare confidently. "Yeah. I've been thinking about that. I think I'm due for a *really fancy* meal. I mean, I want to give that black Amex of yours a real workout."

"Charming." His mouth twists wryly.

I wink. "Cute coming from the guy who conned me into going on dates with him just to prove a point."

We smile at each other in the dark barn, a battle of wills raging between us.

"And what point am I trying to prove?"

"Oh, come on, Stefan. We both know this is just an obnoxious power play. That you're trying to prove you have the upper hand. That you have me up against a wall."

His smirk morphs now into something more feral as he leans in. He moves across me, his head coming to my ear while his opposite hand cups my elbow, holding me close. His proximity, the feel of his breath against the shell of my ear, it all makes the soft hairs on my arms stand on end. I desperately hope he can't feel it.

"Trust me, Dr. Thorne, if I had you up against a wall, *you'd* be the meal."

My breathing stutters, and I jerk my arm away from him. I have no clue what to say to that. I have even less of an idea of how to react to his level of confidence. I'm too out of practice. Hell, I'm too inexperienced. So I just hit him with my best unimpressed, glacial stare.

His responding chuckle is dark and sensuous. It feels like hot wax on bare skin. I want to hate it, but my tongue darts out over my bottom lip.

He turns to leave, and only now do I notice he's wearing gym clothes that hug his body in the most delectable way. I'm too confused to even stop myself from staring at his perfectly round ass as he strolls away looking completely unaffected.

And I'm too speechless to even respond to the parting remark he tosses over his shoulder. "Pick you up at six on Friday."

God. I'm in so much trouble.

CHAPTER 8

Stefan

Mira: You can't pick me up. Someone might see. I'll meet you at your place at six.

I READ THE TEXT A FEW TIMES. IT STINGS MORE THAN IT should, and it feels distinctly improper to not be picking her up—no matter how fake the date is. Call me old-fashioned, but I enjoy ringing the doorbell. Not being able to hold the car door open for her when she gets in has the gentleman in me twitching. I've been enough of a brute where Mira is concerned that I feel like I owe her that chivalry.

I've spent the entire week avoiding her because what I whispered in her ear a few days ago was crossing a line I shouldn't have crossed. And I didn't like the way she shut down afterward.

The worst part is, I can't actually say what it is I want

from her. Am I attracted to her? Yes. But I don't think it can ever be more than that—even if there's a part of me that wants it. I really need her as a veterinarian. My horses do too. Risking that seems like a colossally stupid idea.

So platonic dates it is.

Friends.

I could try to be her friend so that the dates aren't just awkward disasters.

Or I could let her off the hook for the dates altogether.

But I shake that thought out of my head. I'd rather prove to her I'm not the bad guy she thinks I am.

And why does what she thinks of me matter?

That's the real question, isn't it?

Because I'm pretty sure I've made things awkward by reverting to the private school douchebag I grew into as a teenager. In fact, it seems an awful lot like she's avoiding me. I know she's been here to check on Farrah and the foal, but she comes at random times, and I haven't received a single message from her since that day when she told me to stay away while she had Billie here.

She hasn't even said anything about me naming the foal *Loki*. I put a tag on his stall, so Mira's seen it, but she hasn't said anything. I imagined a snarky text from her about it, but nothing came. The name makes me smile, and the more time I spend with him, the more I think it fits.

As he gets healthier, he keeps getting spunkier. When I go down in the evenings to hang out and brush him, he likes to play with my shoelaces. His toothless gums snap at them and pull the strings curiously. And then when he gets them apart and I move my foot, making them drag across the ground like a snake, he spooks. He jumps back all wide-eyed with flared nostrils like they might attack him.

It's nice having some company.

In the morning when I come to check on him before I go for my workout, his shrill baby whinny rings out through the barn. One morning, I figured I could leave the stall unlatched while I came back with extra grain for Farrah, but he pushed it right open and went on an adventure through the barn. The little prick had fun evading me, making me chase him around like a total amateur until I got a rope wrapped around his neck and led him back to his stall with a big grin on my face. I'm still glad no one was here to see that episode.

And I'm especially glad that dying horses don't pull stunts like that.

The lively rat is growing on me every day. It's nice having someone who needs me. And the moment that thought flits through my head, my phone screen lights up with Ruby Creek High Calling, and my stomach plummets.

Nadia moved here a year ago from Romania after being kicked out of her aunt and uncle's house. She's struggling—I can tell—but no one has ever equipped me to be the parent and guardian of a nineteen-year-old with a massive chip on her shoulder. Nannies and headmasters raised me, and I ran in a pack of poorly behaved rich boys—unfortunately, Nadia's upbringing isn't so different. She failed her senior year here, so she's back for a second try. And terrorizing all the teachers and administrators in the process. No one in this small town is equipped for her.

"Yup," I answer the phone brusquely.

"Mr. Dalca, this is Principal Cooper. Can you come down to the school for a conversation with Nadia and me?"

I sigh out in frustration. "Is she okay?"

"Yes." The man's voice is clipped.

"Okay. I'll be right there."

What's it going to be this time?

My mouth goes dry when I swing open the door. Mira is standing on the front landing wearing a gray cable-knit sweater dress with cream thigh-high socks beneath a pair of tall black-suede boots. A thick black-wool coat with over-sized buttons and matching cream-plaid print falls open at her sides, like a present that has already been partially unwrapped. She looks cozy and sensual all at once, with her black hair smoothed out straight, a heavy mane spilling down over her shoulders.

She looks *edible*.

"What are you wearing?" Her face scrunches up as she looks me over from top to bottom.

"What do you mean?" I peer down at my clothes, checking for a stain or something.

She looks slightly flustered as she waves a hand over me. "Just the turtleneck. And the glasses."

I open one arm to usher her into the house. "What about them?"

She ignores the gesture and licks her lips, shaking her head as if to clear it. "Nothing." She laughs sharply. "You look like you were shooting a professor-themed porno or something."

I wink at her. "Maybe I was."

Mira rolls her eyes and dramatically tips her head back with a groan. I don't miss the way her cheeks pink at my joke. And as much as I should regret the comment, I don't. She's the most fascinating dichotomy. Confident and cool while being shy and awkward all at once. She keeps me on my toes. I just never quite know how she's going to react.

"Let's go get this over with." She hikes a thumb over her shoulder.

I ignore the punch her words deliver. "So, minor change of plans."

Her slightly upturned almond-shaped eyes narrow at me, and I swear if looks could kill, I'd crumple to the floor on the spot. "No. No change of plans."

"I don't think I can, in good conscience, leave my sister home alone tonight."

Her puffy lips roll together. "Why?"

"She had a bad day and could use some company. I promise I still gave my Amex a workout on your behalf. I have excellent wine and beautiful food, and if you come in, I will provide you with a perfectly platonic home-cooked meal."

Her eyes dart behind me into the house, like she's trying to gauge if I'm lying. A growl rumbles in my chest. "For crying out loud, Mira. Let me feed you and then you can turn around and go home. In fact, you are welcome to leave anytime you want. I'm not going to murder anyone in here."

She steps into the foyer begrudgingly and mutters, "No, you'll just be filming porn."

I laugh, closing the heavy door behind us before reaching out to take her coat and hang it for her. I try not to focus on the hum of the zipper as she bends down to remove her boots.

"Leave the boots."

Her eyes dart up to mine. "Inside the house?"

I just shrug. Trying to play it casual. "Yeah. You look nice." What I don't say is that those boots and socks are giving me all sorts of ideas that I shouldn't be having about her. What I don't say is that I'd like to see her in *just* the boots.

"This way." I saunter further into the house, leading her to the open-concept kitchen.

"Your place is so cozy. For its size, I expected it to be different."

"Thanks. I think?"

She chuckles as we enter the kitchen, my favorite room in the house. It's surrounded by floor-to-ceiling windows that slide open onto the patio overlooking the small lake out front. The living room and dining room all blend into the big open space with vaulted ceilings. Warm cream tones play off dark-stained wood and exposed stones.

Mira walks to the oversize island in the center of the kitchen and props herself up on one of the stools before looking over at me expectantly while I try not to stare at the expanse of creamy skin between the hemline of her dress and high socks. That small tease of bare skin feels particularly stimulating in the comfort of my home.

"Well? You promised me wine. I could really use some wine."

"Pfft, you and I both." I round the island and slide over two bottles of red wine. "Pinot noir or cabernet?"

She reaches out, dainty fingers wrapping around each bottle as she pulls them toward herself. Her lips roll together as she eyes the bottles. "Let's start with the pinot."

I chuckle. "Start with, huh?"

She smiles back at me. "Would be a shame to let these go to waste."

I shake my head as I reach for the bottle with the purple label. The tips of my fingers graze hers, sending a tingling sensation up through my joints, right into my wrist, morphing into an ache in the crook of my elbow. I drop my eyes and turn away quickly, trying to put the feeling of her nearness out of my mind as I uncork the wine.

I hate the way she throws me off balance.

When I turn back around to decant the bottle of wine, Mira is sneaking a furtive glance over at the leather couch, where Nadia, her wavy blond hair freshly washed and falling loose to her shoulders, is curled up reading a book with her sound-canceling headphones on. Under the glow of the floor lamp, with her doll-like face scrubbed free of makeup, she looks younger than she often does.

I don't love easily, but when I do, it's fiercely. Which is probably why my mother's betrayal stung as badly as it did. There may be fifteen years between Nadia and me, I may not know her that well, but she's all the family I've got left, and I love her with every bit of my soul. I've wanted to protect her for years, and now that she's finally back with me, I probably won't ever stop. I may not have been able to protect my mother, but I will protect Nadia if it's the last thing I do. Leaving her behind killed me, and I'm happy to have her here no matter the added challenge. I would burn the town to the ground for her, and today I almost did.

"Is she okay?" Mira asks.

I pour us each a large bell of deep-red liquid and slide her glass toward her. "No. But she will be. She's tough." I swirl the wine and inhale the cranberry scent, letting my eyes bounce between the two women before me. "People see that strength and try to tear her down. I think some people—men in particular—thrive off that. She's young now and has me to make them regret that type of behavior. But in a few years, she won't need my help at all." I smirk into the glass as I take a drink, letting the flavor of cherries and menthol pour across my tongue. "She reminds me a bit of you."

Mira takes a sip, snuggling further down into the upholstered stool, and looks back over at my little sister with renewed interest. "May I ask what happened?"

My molars grind against each other unbidden. "I received a call from Principal Cooper asking me to come down to the school. There were issues all last year, and this year is nothing new. She's nineteen now, but the transition to living in Canada hasn't been an easy one. Not to mention what our family has been through the last few years." Mira's eyes widen in interest, but she doesn't make a move to ask anything further. Something I appreciate. "She failed a few classes last year. She's retaking them, and it seems to me that she's got a target on her back."

I stare down into the wineglass, swirling it, trying to keep my agitation from creeping out and taking over. "Apparently, the principal saw her and felt her skirt was too short. So, in a hallway full of her peers, he made the girl who has already been singled out as the one who failed last year kneel on the floor to prove the skirt didn't meet their dress code by one inch." My lips press together almost painfully as I shake my head at the memory.

"Excuse me?" Mira leans forward, her eyes flaring with rage that is reflected in my own. "Did you flatten him?"

I chuckle darkly. *I wish.* "I'll admit I went nuclear. I don't know how I'll send her back. Or if it's even my place to. She's smart—too smart—but she's also proud, and this was a real blow to her pride." The memory of her tearstained face still has the power to set me off.

"No shit." Her words come out with a bite. "Stefan, you can't send her back to that school. There are other options, and she won't be missing out on the experience of being at school at this point in her life. Whatever you do, don't let her see that patriarchal assholes behaving poorly don't face consequences."

Her words land like lead in my gut.

But the fierce spark in her eye makes my heart race.

CHAPTER 9

Mira

STEFAN OOZES CONFIDENCE IN THE KITCHEN, SOMETHING I didn't expect to find so attractive. I watch him chop and stir and move around the industrial-style space with such ease that I almost wonder if he was a chef in a past life. The wine is delicious, just like he promised. It tastes expensive, but I also drink wine straight out of the bottle on girls' nights, so it's possible I'm not the best gauge for fancy.

He seems quieter, less jovial, since that conversation about his sister and the sexist pig of a principal. He's lost himself in cooking, and after my second glass of wine, I give up on trying not to check him out. Never mind porn—he looks more like my unfulfilled professor fantasies. The black rims of his glasses contrast perfectly against the bronze glow of his hair. The turtleneck makes him look uptight and proper, but I know better, and it just adds to his allure.

I shouldn't be looking, but I'm defiant. It's a character

flaw. When someone tells me not to do something, it makes me want to do it more. I'm Eve picking the apple just to see what happens. Want me to settle down and have babies? I think I'll throw myself into my education and my job. Want me to hate Stefan Dalca? I think I'll start fantasizing about him instead.

It's not healthy. And I still have two dates to go.

He's standing at the stove right now, stirring something that smells unbelievable. His body sways gently with the motion of the whisk, and his ass fills out the dark jeans he's wearing in a way that has me gawking while quietly sipping my wine.

"Gross," Nadia huffs as she slides onto the stool beside me.

"What?" I say, pretending something interesting above the cabinets has caught my eye rather than her brother's ass.

But she's not buying it. She quirks a brow and gives me an unimpressed look. Yup, *nothing short with this one.*

"Men suck," she says, and I see Stefan stiffen out of the corner of my eye. "Be careful."

I lean forward and stare at my glass, watching the red liquid slosh against the sides as I swivel it on the white-marble countertop. "Some do. They aren't all bad. Principal Cooper sounds like a real piece of shit though."

She snorts. "On that we can agree." A small smile touches her pink lips. "Total pig."

"Have you considered finishing what you need to finish online? That's easily done now. I did that in university with a couple of classes."

"Really?" Her voice sounds hopeful as she fiddles with her fingers, elbows propped on the edge of the counter.

"Definitely. Grab your laptop. Let's look it up while he finishes cooking."

She bounds out of the kitchen almost instantly with a hopeful smile on her face, blond waves bouncing as she goes. When Stefan turns around, his eyes find mine, but I can't tell what he's thinking. Can't tell if I've overstepped. He leans back on the opposite countertop, palms against the edge of the marble, and stares at me like he's never seen me before this moment.

"What?" I ask, struggling to catch my breath.

His green eyes twinkle as they scour my face, tracing every feature like it's the first time. And then he shakes his head and turns back to the stove. "Dinner will be ready in fifteen minutes."

When Nadia returns, we search the web for what her options are while I polish off a third glass of wine. On one hand, I feel like I'm completely ignoring Stefan. On the other, I'm not sure I care. I'm having fun helping Nadia.

This date isn't so bad after all.

Once Stefan finishes cooking, Nadia and I set the table while chatting about her strengths and favorite subjects at school. Math and sciences are a breeze. It's the language arts and language-based classes that are killing her. She's fluent in French and Romanian, so English is her third language. I can barely speak two languages. According to my family, my Punjabi is an "embarrassment," so in my book, struggling with her third one is understandable.

The duck dish Stefan made is heaven. Crispy skin, served over a bed of creamy polenta with a fresh bitter-greens salad topped with blue cheese and walnuts.

"Oh my god," I moan. I'm feeling loose from the wine, and in the back of my mind, I identify the sound as almost sexual, but I don't care. It is truly succulent. "The only thing missing is a blueberry reduction for the duck."

"Yeah?" Stefan asks with a quirk of his head as he sips a glass of wine from the second bottle.

"Yeah. My parents own a blueberry farm. I'll hook you up when they come into season."

"Can I come pick blueberries?" Nadia asks excitedly.

I snort. The charm of picking berries has pretty much completely worn off for me. People actually pay my parents to come pick their own berries, something that never fails to make me chuckle. But I refuse to quash her enthusiasm. "Of course."

Dinner carries on much the same, but I still catch Stefan staring at me over the candle lit in the middle of the table. The flame highlights the blend of colors in his irises—the greens, the golds. His eyes are beautiful, and throughout the meal, I remind myself not to get lost in them. In *him*.

"That was incredible." I lean back and toss my napkin on the table beside my very empty plate. "Thank you." I smile at him, and it's genuine.

I've had a thoroughly enjoyable night. Relaxing even. I've felt my carefully placed walls crumble, and right now I don't feel like beating myself up about it. There's something distinctly intimate about tonight. Something sweet that I don't want to overanalyze.

But it doesn't mean I don't need to leave before I do something I'll regret.

"Nadia, do you have your driver's license?" I ask, staring at the glass of sparkling water before her.

She scoffs, sounding distinctly teenager-like in that moment. "Of course I do."

She hasn't touched the wine tonight. At nineteen, she's of legal age here, but she hasn't asked, and Stefan hasn't offered. "Would you be willing to drive me home and then pick me up tomorrow morning?"

She shrugs. "Sure."

Stefan stares at me from over the flame. His pointer finger circling the top of his glass while he gazes at me. It's almost hypnotic.

He doesn't offer to drive me, but that's for the best. His eyes are a bit glassy, his smiles a little easier. We have both thoroughly enjoyed the two bottles of wine.

I break the spell when I say, "I'll help clean up."

"You absolutely will not. You're the guest," he replies smoothly, leaning back in his chair.

He oozes class and control. Looking like a dreamboat professor out for a glass of wine at some fancy lounge after a long day of fending off the advances of his overeager students. I can't help but giggle at the path my thoughts have taken after single-handedly drinking what equates to a full bottle of wine.

"Well, in that case, Stefan…" He quirks his head, one

dimple popping up on his cheek as it hitches, hanging on my words in a way that not many people do. "Thank you for the truly outstanding meal. I had a delightful night."

"Yeah. I actually like this one," Nadia says absently, now browsing through her phone.

I burst out laughing, slapping a hand across my mouth to cover my guffaw.

"Nadia, go put your laptop away and get what you need to drive Dr. Thorne home."

She salutes from her forehead without even looking up at him as she replies with "Sir, yes, sir," and then slowly moves toward the stairs, eyes not leaving her phone.

I stand as Stefan ushers me toward the front door. His palm briefly presses into the small of my back as he guides me into the hallway, and I feel the imprint of his warm hand through my sweater like a brand. There's a catch in my breath and in my step at the feel—the familiarity of the touch. It sears me. I feel like if someone looked, they'd be able to make out the swirls of his fingerprints against my milky skin.

Words fail me as he holds the long plaid coat out for me to slide my arms into. The wine has my mind going places it absolutely should not, and the press of his firm body behind mine leaves me feeling heady. He's not even touching me, but I swear I can feel the weight of him against my shoulder blades, guiding them together and pressing on my lungs. His mere presence sticks to me like static cling.

"Thank you for coming tonight," he whispers, his accented voice endlessly deep, turning me to face him and smoothing down the lapels of my coat. Like we do this all the time.

He takes a hold of my wrist and presses a swift, feather-light kiss to the center of my palm. Something that feels intensely personal.

My tongue darts out to wet my bottom lip as I gaze up at his proud posture and the troublemaking glint in his eye. "Thank you for having me."

I smile, but it's watery and uncertain. The man has me completely off balance. My pulse beats in my stomach. Nice Stefan threw me for a loop, but Doting Stefan, who cooks and cleans and loves his little sister, is straight crushing my ovaries.

Any man could do those things and you'd find him attractive, my mind assures me right before he leans in and presses a kiss to the sensitive spot just below my ear.

Then my mind goes blank. Goose bumps crawl in slow motion, covering my entire body. The feel of him towering over me, the rasp of his stubble against my cheek cause all coherent thoughts to flee my mind along with the air from my chest.

Nadia's steps thump down the stairs, breaking the spell. I step back quickly, trying to even out my breathing and be strong enough to still look him in the eye.

"One sec," I whisper, my voice cracking in the most obvious way. "I'll be right back."

I dart into the kitchen and then return to wait while Nadia ties up her laces. I can feel Stefan's gaze on me as though he's trailing a finger everywhere he looks. My body hums as I recall the rough scrape of his stubble and the hot press of his hand.

I need to get the fuck out of here.

With a casual wave over my shoulder, I escape onto the front porch and start walking to my truck, sucking in deep breaths of cool air as I go. A few moments later, Nadia catches up and slides into the driver's seat.

Pale eyebrows knit together suspiciously. "All good?" she asks.

I pull out the carton of eggs I hid in my coat and smile at her with all my teeth. *The perfect distraction.* "Yup. Did I mention I'm well acquainted with where Principal Cooper lives?"

"Good morning, Dr. Thorne."

Stefan's voice used to make me roll my eyes. But now it just feels like someone is sliding silk around my neck. Probably to make a noose, which is what thinking about Stefan this way is going to get me.

A death sentence. At least where my friends are concerned.

"Hi, Stefan," I say stiffly as I check the mare and foal over carefully. Nadia just picked me up and drove me back to my truck at Cascade Acres, so it seemed like the perfect time to do my daily check on the horses.

"How is Loki today?"

I snort. I got a kick out of the nameplate when I saw it. My fingers itched to fire him off a text message about how he named a horse after himself. But for the sake of keeping our professional boundaries clear, I resisted.

"Full of piss and vinegar." I smile as I turn, but the grin quickly slides off my face as I take in the sight of him and the hunter-green bespoke suit he's wearing. The man wears an expensive suit like he was born in it. Like whoever came up with suits as a thing was looking at Stefan when the idea struck them.

It's borderline criminal.

The crisp white shirt underneath has a few buttons open, and a perfect V of tan skin at the top of his chest shows, just below where his Adam's apple bobs. It's not borderline, it *is* criminal. And me looking at him like this, dragging my tongue around on the barn floor, is even worse.

I don't even know if I can blame the wine anymore this morning.

"Where are you off to looking so dapper?"

"The police station and then the city." His voice dances with amusement as his eyes home in on mine.

I school my features. This is one of those situations where I'm better off listening than talking. "Oh?" I reply, turning to pat Farrah.

"Mm-hmm. It seems they have some questions for me. Someone egged Principal Cooper's car last night. Of course, we were all at my house having dinner. So I just need to clarify that for them. May I put you down as a witness?"

I should argue; I don't really want anyone knowing I was at Stefan Dalca's house for dinner. But I don't want to come off guilty either. "Of course." My lips tilt up in a grimace at the white lie.

He just stares back at me, and it unnerves me to my

core. I seriously hope I'm not blushing, but I can't risk saying anything, so I blink and offer him an even bigger smile. *Enthusiasm, Mira.* "Hope everything goes okay."

"Everything is going wonderfully," he replies, his voice softening as his gaze burns across my face.

He doesn't sound mad. *Fuck. This is awkward. He couldn't possibly know.*

"Well, good luck." I sound lame, even to my own ears. "I'll be back tomorrow to check on them."

I beam brightly, grab my case, mouth, "Excuse me" as I squeeze past him, and try to force myself to walk with a confident swagger down the barn alleyway toward the parking lot rather than sprinting away like I want to.

"Hey, Mira?" he calls out right as I reach for the door handle.

"Yeah?" I toss back into the echoey barn, continuing my forward motion.

"You owe me a carton of eggs."

Well, shit.

CHAPTER 10

Stefan

LOKI ISN'T ACTING QUITE RIGHT. WHILE HE HAS TRULY BEEN living up to his name as the god of mischief, he seems lethargic tonight. Dopey. He was fine before dinner when I checked him, but now at 10 p.m. he isn't quite right.

I've been avoiding Mira this week, and I'm quite certain she's been doing the same. The tension between us is thick enough to cut with a knife, and I don't think either one of us has figured out what to do with that just yet. I should let her out of the remaining two dates. A better man would. But I'm greedy. I want to prove to her I'm not the evil dick they've made me out to be.

I just didn't predict craving her the way that I am.

I want her back in my house, laughing and smiling. All soft and warm. I want her in my bed—even though that would ruin a few friendships on her end. And that isn't fair.

But tonight, I need to contact her for purely professional

reasons. My thumb swipes across the screen of my phone as I pull up her contact information and tap the phone icon. I watch Loki's little eyes grow heavy on his drooping head. He looks so small and vulnerable, and I can't stop myself from going into the stall to crouch beside him and rub his shoulder while the phone rings in my ear.

"Hello?"

It's loud wherever she is. It sounds like she's out having fun—after all, it is a Friday night.

"Mira, it's Stefan."

"Hi?" She's clearly confused about why I'd be calling her at 10 p.m. on a Friday.

"There's something wrong with Loki."

She doesn't even miss a beat. "I'll be right there."

Her heart is so damn pure. Far more pure than someone like me deserves.

Within twenty minutes, she arrives, bursting through the door looking like some sort of country goddess.

"I'm here!" Inky-black hair billows out over her brown-suede bomber jacket as she struts down the hallway. Her long legs are poured into a skintight pair of jeans, and the ornate cowboy boots on her feet click swiftly against the concrete. I'm still not accustomed to seeing her in anything other than her cargo pants and oversized Carhartt jacket.

She drops her kit and looks up at me, cheeks rosy and eyes narrowed. "Tell me what's wrong." She doesn't waste any time digging into the box that carries all her general medical stuff, only grabbing a small flashlight and her stethoscope.

Her level of seriousness alarms me. This is what poor

Loki gets for having me take care of him. I'm a goddamn angel of death. I can't keep anyone safe.

"He was fine when I checked on him before dinner." She comes close, listening to his heartbeat and nodding, urging me on. "I came down to check on him before bed, and he seemed lethargic. I mean, look at him. He's been a bit of a terrorist lately. He's not himself."

"Diarrhea?" She looks around the stall and stands up straight, eyes landing on what looks like very liquified poop. *How did I not notice that?* She pinches the skin on his neck and when she lets go, it stays pinched together, not returning flat as it should with a properly hydrated horse. Next, she opens his droopy lips and presses her thumb against his gums, testing how quickly they pink back up under pressure. Her movements are efficient, not panicked, but prompt.

"Okay. He's dehydrated. Orphan foals are prone to infection if they miss out on colostrum—which he did for a few days. Just stick with him while I grab some stuff from my truck."

She darts out of the stall, and I'm left patting the small chestnut horse and murmuring to him. "You're gonna be fine, little dude. I'm sticking with you. And did you know Mira is the best vet I've ever known?" His eyes flutter, and his head bobs. "It's true. She's very impressive." My voice cracks.

I hear her steps behind me and feel her dainty hand land at the top of my back. Her fingers pulse against my spine in a light squeeze before she pulls an IV pole into the stall and gets to work, setting up a drip.

"Fuck," she mutters to herself as she struggles to find a

suitable spot for the catheter. Her thumbs work, pressing down the line of his neck, trying to make a vein bulge. The only sign that she likes what she sees is a quiet grunt and then the precise movement of her hand sliding the needle into the spot she selected. "Good boy, Loki. Tough man. You're a fighter, aren't ya?"

Within a few moments, Mira has the gauge taped to Loki's neck and the line attached. Hopefully, whatever is in that clear bag hanging above us is what he needs. I don't think I can bear the thought of anything happening to him.

"What now?" I ask quietly from where I kneel beside her.

Mira's lips press into a thin line as she looks down at me and sighs so heavily her shoulders rise and then fall. "Now we wait."

★★★

"Coffee?" Mira is back, peeking down into the stall from between the bars. "It might be a long night."

"I thought you left?" I ask sullenly, feeling kind of low and introspective. I guess that's why I haven't moved off the stall floor. Again. I don't want to leave Loki. Just in case. So here I am, leaning against the wall once again.

"Nah. Figured I'd camp out with you for a bit." She kicks the stall door open and steps in with a steaming cup of coffee in each hand. "I think I might have gotten it right this time." She grins mischievously as she comes to stand before me.

The scent wafts off the hot liquid as she folds herself down about a foot away from me. "Is there booze in this?"

"Yeah." She smiles as she blows on her mug. "I found some Bailey's in the fridge. You look like you could use some."

I peer back at her, following the strong angle of her pronounced cheekbones down her perfectly straight nose.

"No Bailey's for you?"

"I'm technically on call. They generally frown on practicing veterinary medicine while under the influence. I take turns being on call overnight with a few other vets so the area is covered for emergencies."

"I didn't know that," I say thoughtfully.

"Of course not. You just call me directly when you need something." Her laughter is light and airy as she leans in to sip her coffee.

"Black coffee for you?"

"Like my soul." Her lips tilt up in a wry twist, but her eyes stay focused on the horses before us. Farrah hangs her head over Loki protectively. I marvel at the way she's taken him over, the way she cares for him when he's not even hers. Or maybe he is hers now.

While Mira stares at them, it gives me the freedom to stare at *her*. To let my gaze roam appreciatively. She looks beautiful tonight—fun—far too done up to be sitting on the dirty floor of an oversized foaling stall with the likes of me. "What's with the getup?"

She quirks a brow. "You asking if I was on a date?"

"You mean we're not exclusive?" I feign offense, even though internally the thought of her out with another guy makes me see red.

"Are you dating someone?"

99

I scoff. "No. Not for a while now."

"So you just…go without?" She sounds so curious.

"I didn't say that either, did I?" Mira shimmies her shoulders taller and looks away. "Things have always been pretty casual in that department for me since I moved here. Women aren't exactly lining up to date me in Ruby Creek, and having my sister in the house makes it awkward."

"But in the city?" She's still avoiding looking at me, picking at a piece of wood shaving on the rubber mat beside her.

"What happens in the city stays in the city. This farm is my refuge. I wouldn't bring just anyone here. Anyway, stop changing the subject. All dressed up tonight?"

"Girls' night at the country bar. Sober for me. Super fun." Sarcasm seeps from her tone.

"With who?"

She gives me a dry glance now. Like I'm asking a stupid question. "Billie and Violet."

I just grunt. What am I supposed to say? They hate me and have me pegged as a lot worse than I am.

"You know, I think under different circumstances you'd all get along."

I scoff at that. "And why is that, Dr. Thorne?"

"Because when it comes down to it, we're all just good people who love their horses."

"I'm not so sure I'm a good person."

"Hmm." She tips her head like she's mulling that over.

"Hmm what?"

"I disagree with your assessment."

"Oh yeah? You told them that yet?"

"No," she says quietly before hiding behind the big mug again. That stings worse than it should. It's one thing for her to tell me I'm a good person here in the quiet barn where no one else can hear her and another for her to say it to her friends. She might not think I'm so bad anymore, but she's not rushing out to tell anyone about it.

"How's Nadia?" Mira asks, effectively changing the subject.

The liquid drips into Loki's line as he leans close to Farrah, seeking her warmth. I consider lying to Mira but opt for the truth. "Not so good."

She nods silently, and I continue. "She's led a privileged but traumatizing life. I've done what I can to keep her safe. But I don't think it was enough."

"Why not?"

That's not the question I was expecting. "Because she's still sad and lost and desperate for love."

"Why?"

God. I forgot how brutally blunt she can be sometimes.

"Because we grew up watching our dad viciously beat our mother."

Her head bounces back against the wall, and she exhales. "Fuck."

"Yeah. He liked to leave the bruises where no one could see. That way he could still package her up in a fancy dress and tote her around to all his classy events. Everyone was spared the horror, except Nadia and me." My lips roll together, itching to spill it all, hidden down low in this warm stall encompassed by the quiet munching sounds of the surrounding horses with this woman who has slowly become something like a friend. "With the age difference between us, she got stuck at home while they shipped me off to boarding school in Switzerland. She was a baby when I left. But we got summers together, I guess." Now I know why I got the boot and she didn't. But I don't feel like going there right now. "As soon as I graduated from that cesspool, I went straight to university in London. I didn't want to go home. I was worried I'd kill him if I had to live with him again. So I stayed. I did my degree and then moved on to the London School of Business for my MBA."

"Did you kill him in the end?"

Not exactly. "No."

"I would have killed him." She nods her head succinctly, like she's very satisfied with her conclusion. Mira Thorne is kinda dark, and I like it.

"A plane crash did that for me instead. Unfortunately, his plane crash took my mother with him."

"Jesus. That's depressing. How long ago was that?"

"Four years ago."

Mira nods. "Right before you came to Ruby Creek." She doesn't miss a damn beat.

"Yeah. My mom grew up here. It seemed like a good way to be close to her at the time."

"At the time?" If she's shocked by that revelation, she doesn't show it. She just looks at me. Her dark eyes are soft as they slide over me like she can read my mind.

"Yeah. Sometimes it feels like I have no idea what I'm doing." I can't hold her gaze for long. I rest my head on the wall and stare up at the warm lights above us.

"I think we all feel like that sometimes."

I swallow audibly. She's probably right.

"And when did Nadia move here?"

"As soon as she could legally—about a year ago. She was stuck living with *his* sister until she turned eighteen. Then I got her on a plane straight here. It's been an adjustment for her. I wasn't there enough through her most important years. I should have gone back. There's a lot of baggage to unpack." My free hand presses down into the rubber mat of the stall floor to ground myself. The top joints of my fingers ache with the pressure as I grasp at the flat surface. It almost hurts. But I probably deserve that.

"You feel guilty." It's not a question, the way she says it. She knows. It's hard to get anything past Mira.

"Yeah." A ragged sigh escapes me, and I run my free hand through my hair. "And I don't even know where to begin on making it up to her."

I start when her hand covers mine, like a warm blanket over a cold soul. Her fingers slide between mine, prying them up off the floor. Tangling together.

With one squeeze, she carries on, like we hold hands all the time. "What's going on with school?" She sips her coffee, but I can't tear my eyes away from her hand on mine. She has elegant hands, long fingers, but they don't feel soft and manicured. Her nails are clean and natural, trimmed neatly, and I can feel the light callus on her palm against the top of my hand. Mira works with her hands, and I can feel the proof.

I can feel everything.

"Umm." I cough in an attempt to clear my throat,

where my heart is currently lodged. "I told her I'd support whatever she wanted to do. I mean, she's a nineteen-year-old woman. She went back for a couple days, but it sounds like there were a lot of cruel jokes flying around." My teeth grind just thinking about it. "On one hand, going to school with a bunch of kids is probably really humbling. On the other hand, I'm not sure what she'll do all day if she does the online school thing for her last few courses. I'm worried she'll be lonely. Or, worse, bored." I groan. "God. A bored Nadia would be dangerous for everyone in a hundred-mile radius."

Mira laughs, deep and raspy. It's sensual. Her hand feels hot over mine. I swear I can feel her heart beating through her palm. Forcing mine to beat in time with hers.

"She'll be fine," she says with another gentle squeeze of my hand. "We womenfolk are smarter and stronger than you all give us credit for."

She means it in a joking way, but the tension between us as our eyes lock onto each other is anything but lighthearted. I've always been drawn to Mira, but this is torture. I feel like she's reached right between my ribs and wrapped her delicate fingers around my lungs. Like if she wanted to, she could squeeze too hard and cut my breath off entirely.

The moment drags on and feels like it lasts forever, but with a sharp inhale, she stands and brushes off her pants. She doesn't explain herself, just goes about checking Loki again before unhooking him and urging him to nurse with a few gentle pushes toward Farrah's hind end. I must admit he's starting to look more perky. Within moments, he's latched on and feeding. At the sight, Mira's shoulders drop on a heavy sigh, a small smile touching her lips.

This is a good sign. My heart hammers when she turns that pleased expression down on me. And suddenly, I wonder what it would be like for her to gaze at me like that between her thighs. I wonder how low her voice would go then—how my name would sound on her lips while she comes on mine.

"Better?" I ask, veering back into reality. Because getting between Mira's thighs is a bad idea. I'd probably never want to leave.

"A little. Too early to say," she replies as she slides down the wall.

But this time, she sits close enough that our shoulders graze against each other.

And after a few beats, she reaches for my hand again.

CHAPTER 11

Stefan

I NEED TO TAKE A BREAK. MY EYES ARE ABOUT TO CROSS FROM how long I've spent staring at a spreadsheet. I press my fists into the sockets of my skull and press gently until I see white.

On Friday night, I stayed in Farrah and Loki's stall, so afraid to disturb the tentative truce that Mira and I seemed to have come to. I sat there so long, feeling the press of her fingers between mine and the heat of her body so close, that we fell asleep. Her head tipped to the side and rested against my shoulder, and what was I supposed to do then?

I didn't want to disturb her, and I didn't want it to end either. I tried to stay awake as long as possible, but sleep overtook me at some point, and I woke up to the feel of cold air against my side and the sound of Mira shuffling around the stall.

She didn't say anything to me. She looked groggy, and it felt like she was avoiding looking at me.

I wanted her to come back and grab my hand again.

To snuggle up against me once more.

But I knew that was too much to ask.

And she clearly thought that would take it too far because she packed up and left with a quiet "See you later. I'll be back in the morning."

I didn't even bother going back to my house. I stumbled into the barn lounge and sprawled out on the leather couch there. And that's exactly where I've spent the last two nights so I can watch Loki.

The good news is the colt seems to be steadily improving. The bad news is I'm barely functional. If it wasn't for the one-on-one time with Mira, I think I'd feel an awful lot like I'm doing Billie Black a favor.

That's a thought I sweep away. I'm doing this to save the foal who's living in my barn. The one who deserves every fighting chance available, no matter who owns him.

With a deep sigh, I head to the front door, where I grab my favorite shearling coat and slip my feet into a pair of boots, hoping some fresh spring air will rejuvenate me.

I walk down the winding road from the house, past the lake where my mother's ashes are sprinkled, feeling conflicted about her, as is my new normal. It's a trip missing someone so deeply but also being so unforgivably angry with them. I'm still not sure how to make heads or tails of that, even after four years.

When the barn comes into view from around the far side of the huge weeping willow, I see Mira's black truck with the gold logo and canopy cover parked out front. In a paddock just next to the barn, Nadia leans against the fence looking down at the ground where Mira is crouching over a horse that is flat out on his side.

The hell are they doing? My heart races. Lately, every time Mira is here, it's because something isn't going right. I pick up my pace, cutting across the grass to reach the paddock as quickly as possible.

"That's *it*?" Nadia's disbelieving voice is what I hear first. "Just like: incision, yank it out, and then snip?"

"Yup." I can hear the smile in Mira's voice. "That's it."

"Huh." Nadia's blond curls bob with her head.

"So the next time those pencil pricks have something shitty to say to you, you can tell them in detail how you'll castrate them."

What the…?

I get to the fence beside Nadia to see Mira disposing of what looks like… Oh. *Oh god.* That's hard to look at.

I'm not especially squeamish, but I'm not keen on watching a fellow male get castrated. I know it's a horse, but still. It just hits slightly too close to home.

"Stefan, did you realize how simple this procedure is?" Nadia asks, sounding a little too excited by the prospect. "I really almost feel like I could do it myself!"

Mira hits me with a knowing grin as she stands and tosses her gloves into the same bucket as the poor horse's family jewels. This woman is terrifying. "I'll get you to help me next time, Nadia."

"Jesus Christ." I drag a hand through my hair and shake my head. "What are you two hellions up to here?"

"Turning a stallion into a gelding. And teaching Nadia how to handle all the immature teenage boys who think the best way into her pants is terrorizing her." Mira slaps her hands together with a satisfied smirk on her face. "I wish I could be there to see their faces."

"What happened now?" I turn to my sister, instantly concerned about what's going on in her personal life. I'm not involved enough. I don't know how to be. And every time I try, I get the distinct impression she doesn't want me to be.

She waves me off, looking happier than she has in a long time. "Don't worry about it. I won't need to deal with them anymore after tomorrow."

"Why is that?"

"Because tomorrow I'm cleaning my locker out and getting my distance learning packages. The next day I'm starting a new job."

Jesus, what poor sucker hired Nadia?

But I opt to be outwardly supportive. Maybe some responsibility would be good for her. A purpose is good for coping with trauma, and I want my sister to succeed in life. Even if the girl is like a hurricane that leaves chaos in her wake. I want her *happy.* "That's great. What's the job?"

Nadia's full lips stretch out over her face, and she looks genuinely excited. "I'm Mira's new assistant at the clinic!"

I blink, trying to wrap my head around that. And then I look at Mira, who softens her features and shrugs before grabbing her stuff from the ground near her feet. "I've been meaning to hire someone" is all she says. As though Nadia is a perfectly qualified and natural choice.

She doesn't act like she's going out of her way to help my sister. To help *me*. She doesn't prance around acting like she's doing us a favor or extending some great kindness.

But she is.

And after everything I shared with her on Friday night, this feels like more. It feels like someone caring about us— something that hasn't happened in a very long time.

★★★

"I brought your eggs," Mira calls into the barn the next morning.

She's been coming back to check on Loki every evening and first thing in the morning before the clinic opens. Twice a day she's been here, running herself into the ground because I'm a greedy prick who wanted to keep the upper hand in an imaginary war with her employers.

"Mira, I was joking about that."

I'm sitting on the concrete floor just outside the stall waiting for her, feeling like a full-blown shmuck for using a woman who would make a special effort to help my little sister.

"Trust me. You want these eggs. They're from my parents' farm. I collected them myself."

Now I feel even worse, if that's possible. But I still take them from her outstretched hand.

"I also brought you a coffee." She holds the paper cup out to me with an amused tilt to her shapely lips.

I'm going to hell.

"Mira. Honestly. You don't need to do this."

"I know. But I like watching your face when I try to guess what type of coffee you like. It's worth the few bucks that cost me."

She pushes it toward me again, urging me to take it from her hand. When I finally do, she moves past me into the stall to check on Loki.

"Good morning, sweet baby boy," she coos. "And you, pretty mama, how are you?" I hear a quiet kissing noise and know she just pressed her lips to the mare's soft nose. I've seen her do it before. And it made my chest pinch then too.

I conned a lifesaving, sister-helping, horse-kissing angel into going on dates with me just because I could. I feel like dirt, and there's a part of me wondering why it's taken me this long to get to this point.

When she finally emerges from the stall, she locks it behind her, drops her workbox on the floor, and comes to the other side of me. I watch her boots as she slides down the wall to sitting. This time, she's only a few inches away from me. I can't figure out why she's sitting with me when she could leave and carry on with her day.

"Seems like sitting on the barn floor is kind of our thing," I say.

She laughs, a soft chuckle. A noise I want to take and suck into my mouth. I want to swallow her whole. Devour her. I don't deserve her, but goddammit, I'm not sure I've ever wanted another woman more.

"How's the coffee?"

She quirks an eyebrow at me as I take my first sip.

"What the—what on earth is this?"

Her head tips back, and she laughs, a full laugh that warms me from the inside. One hand falls across her chest, and the press of her forearm against her breasts makes them strain against the plain gray T-shirt she's wearing beneath her open coat. "Yup. Worth every penny."

It tastes like some sort of caramel cupcake blended into a coffee. It's atrocious. But she bought it for me, and that makes me want to drink it.

"I'm going to drink this, but I'll put you out of your misery. I take my coffee black."

"Was that so hard? Why didn't you just tell me?" She shakes her head, looking amused.

Because I'm a greedy bastard who liked feeling taken care of.

"Because the coffee doesn't matter when I'm in your company." I meant it to come out teasing, but it doesn't— because I mean it.

I take another sip as silence settles over us like a heavy blanket. I can hear the hum of the heater and the soft munching from Farrah's stall. The smell of fresh wood shavings blends with the sweet smell wafting up out of my coffee mug.

"I want to end our deal. You don't need to do the last two dates. I'm happy to help Loki, no matter what. I should never have put you in that position."

Mira scoffs and waves me off. "It's fine." And then with a chuckle and slight shake of her head, she admits, "I had fun on our first fake date."

The word *fake* burns. Maybe it's accurate, but whatever I'm feeling for Mira feels…well, not fake. I nod, effectively plunging us back into silence.

"Thank you for hiring Nadia."

Her head tilts. "I like her. She's got spunk. And I really could use the help. Sounds like she excels in math and sciences, which is exactly what I need. She can do schoolwork and still get some socialization around the clinic. The girls are going to love her."

"Right." I snort. "Billie is going to love having my family around."

"Billie is a good person. She won't hold a single thing against your sister. Plus, she's probably the last person in the world who would judge a person by their family."

I grumble. "Yeah, maybe." Knowing Billie's background, I suppose it's possible.

"It's going to be great. You'll see."

I just nod. My throat feels thick.

"Where did you go to vet school?" I blurt out eventually, trying to fill the space with something. Unsure why she hasn't left yet.

"In Calgary." She smiles wistfully. "I loved it. Every second. The late nights studying. The classes. The stress. I thrived there."

I smile too. I can totally see it. There's an academic side to Mira. She's a bit nerdy. But in the best possible way. There's something about a woman who wields her brain like a weapon and her tongue like a whip that makes me want to worship at her feet.

Never mind physical chemistry, I need intellectual chemistry to hold my attention. Getting lost between the sheets with just any warm body has lost its appeal the older I've gotten.

And I have no doubt that if I stripped Mira down, there would be a battle of wills. She would keep me on my toes, and I'd keep her on hers. And then I'd have her on her knees.

I shake my head, trying to clear my filthy mind.

"Did you always want to be a vet?"

She sighs now. "Yeah. I did. I was constantly tending to the animals on my parents' farm or finding injured animals. Birds." She snorts. "Rats."

"Rats?"

"Hey, man. Even rats need love." She winks at me. I'm pretty sure she just called me a rat in a very roundabout way.

"You've got a big heart. Your family must be very proud of you." It comes out teasingly, but I mean it seriously.

"Yeah. I think they'd be happier if I found a good man and pumped out some babies though."

"Really? But you're still so young."

"It's just a complicated dynamic. I'm the most educated person in my family. My dad is the child of Indian immigrants who have only ever worked the family farm. My mom is this free-spirit hippie who came to pick blueberries one day, found a man instead, and just never left. I love them dearly, but we have vastly different goals in life. I think the fact I'm permanently single stresses them all out."

"Are you?"

"Stressed?"

"No. Permanently single?" I try to keep my voice from going husky. I hadn't even considered the prospect that Mira might not be single, and suddenly I'm feeling a little jealous for absolutely no good reason.

"No."

My teeth clench, and my heart riots against my ribs.

"I'm in a long-term relationship with Mr. Purple."

My brow crinkles. "That's a weird last name."

"He's battery powered and made of silicone. I think it would be weird if I brought him home to meet my parents."

I bark out a laugh. I can't help it. Her delivery is so dry and not at all ashamed. Plus, I was momentarily jealous of a dildo. *Adorable.*

"You could try. But I would like to be present to see it, please."

She doesn't laugh at the joke. "Yeah." Her eyes take on a nervous glint as her lips roll together. "I was wondering if I could ask you for a favor."

Ah, there it is. The reason she's been hanging around all awkwardly. I sip the sweet coffee and realize I'm developing a taste for it. Or perhaps I'm just enjoying her attention.

"Shoot." I'm dead curious what this favor is.

What she doesn't comprehend is I'll do almost anything she tells me to at this point.

Her fingers twist in her lap. "Any chance you'd be willing to use one of those dates we have left to attend a family reunion with me?"

I feel a grin spread across my lips. "You want me to meet your family?"

"Ugh." She looks up at the roof, searching for patience. "No. But I don't want to spend another year being treated like an old spinster who has nothing but an education to crawl into bed with at night."

"Are you telling me you'd rather take me to your family reunion than your dildo?"

She laughs and shakes her head. "Consider yourself the front runner in that race."

"When is it?"

"Two weeks. Not this Saturday, but next." She nibbles at her lips nervously. As if I'd be able to tell her no.

"It would be my pleasure." I drop a hand onto her thigh and give it a squeeze.

She pats my hand gently before standing. "Thank you."

This is when Mira runs. When things get too comfortable, too intimate, she bolts.

"I'll be better company than a dildo. I promise."

She shakes her head again and swipes her kit off the ground. "Doubtful" is her reply as she walks away.

I can't help but appreciate the way her cargo pants hug the round globes of her ass. *The things I'd do to that ass.*

"Bet I can make you come harder too."

She laughs, a girlish laugh. Not her usual throaty husk. "I'd like to see you try."

Challenge accepted.

CHAPTER 12

Mira

I'M WATCHING HANK TROT BRITE LITE IN A STRAIGHT LINE away from me, but I'm thinking about Stefan.

I'm supposed to be watching the pretty gray mare to see where I think the hitch in her step is coming from, and instead I'm replaying the feel of his hand when he wrapped it around my thigh. It's driving me to distraction.

He's driving me to distraction.

Exactly what I've always promised myself I wouldn't let a man do. Let alone a man like Stefan. It's complicated. His entire persona is sketched in blurry lines, and I'm worried I'm getting lost in that fuzz. When I took Billie to see Loki today, I found myself constantly looking around, hoping to catch even a glimpse of him.

I have a savior complex. You don't become a veterinarian or medical professional without that facet to your personality. And everything he's shared over the last several days about his mom, his dad, his upbringing…it's got a stranglehold on my savior complex.

He really is like an injured rat. He grosses everyone out. And I'm drawn in. I want to swoop in and bandage up his broken parts. Watch them heal.

Seeing animals, and people, heal is my catnip. It's what fills my cup. I've seen it with my friends over the last couple of years, and it never fails to make me smile.

I shouldn't want to fill my cup with Stefan.

But I do.

And now I feel like I'm drowning in a man who is only dragging me along in his game to one-up my best friend. I'm a pawn. And I'm smart enough to know better.

"So? What do you think?" Hank huffs over the sound of aluminum horseshoes clopping on the paved driveway out front.

Busted. And I'm making the old man work for it, no less, while I daydream about enemy number one.

"Just catch your breath. And then one more loop around the driveway. I think it might be up in her stifle." I was watching—sort of—but I still feel like a total asshole. "Take you for a drink after?"

Trixie is in the city working right now, so Hank is lonely sometimes. I can tell by the way he hangs around. By the way he pops into the clinic just to chat.

He flashes me one of his big grins, followed by a wink of a twinkly green eye. He has a distinct Robert Redford vibe going on that, if I were older, I would certainly appreciate. He's one of the good ones. That's for sure.

"I'm gonna need a cold one after this workout, Dr. Thorne." He turns the mare around to trot away again. But not before tossing out a casual "Try not to daydream this time!"

So busted.

I offer to drive into Ruby Creek's favorite watering hole, Neighbor's Pub. And we even manage to get my favorite table at the back near the fireplace. Spring is here in the valley, but it's damp and cool today. The weather just seems to swing back and forth this time of year, between a warm taste of summer and then a cold jolt of winter. Today is that, and I'm happy to be seated next to the crackling fire with a beer on the way.

Usually, I'm here with Billie and Violet, and sometimes they even bring Vaughn and Cole. Both of whom I like. A lot. But I feel distinctly out of place as the single friend who gets dragged along on those nights, so it's nice to hit happy hour with just Hank.

Hank folds himself into the seat across from me and looks around with a bemused smile on his face. "Love this place," he murmurs.

"Me too," I agree, picking up the plastic menu to figure out what I want, right as the waitress hustles over with our pints.

This pub is the quintessential small-town meeting spot. Stained-glass shades over the lamps, mismatched captain's chairs at every dark-stained table, and old-school burgundy carpets on the floor. There's even a jukebox in the corner.

"You eating too?" Hank asks.

"I think I might," I reply. "Cooking every night for just one person is kind of soul-sucking." I blurt it out without even considering that Hank has been doing exactly that for probably his entire life. "Sorry," I add on with a twist of my lips.

"Don't be. It's true. I'd be lying if I said I don't spend every week looking forward to Sunday night dinners with all you kids. A date at my favorite pub with Dr. Thorne isn't so bad either."

I laugh. "Maybe we should make it a regular thing. A special club for the only two people not totally shacked up on the ranch."

The waitress swings by and takes our orders. A burger for each of us.

"No men in your life?" he inquires gently.

I take a sip of the fizzy golden lager and smack my lips together. "Nope." I sound very sure when I say it, but inside I'm in turmoil. My arrangement with Stefan may not be real, but I don't like feeling like I'm lying to Hank either. "Too busy with work."

"I know how that goes." He sips his beer and nods his head. "Happy I've got Trixie in the picture now though. She's the best surprise in my life lately. You'll get one eventually too."

I grunt. "I'm not really a big fan of surprises, to be honest. I like a nicely laid-out plan. A clear path."

The older man chuckles kindly, like I've just said something desperately naive. "Oh, Mira. All the best things in my life have come as an absolute surprise. Didn't expect an eighteen-year-old girl to show up on my doorstep demanding I give her a job, but I'm glad I did. Billie is the daughter I never got to have. Didn't expect my best friend to scandalize the racing world and then die of a heart attack. But here I am, helping his grandsons run his farm." He shakes his head thoughtfully. "I mean, shit, I didn't even expect to have the job I do now. I used to bartend here, did you know that?"

I smile and rear back a tad. "I didn't. But I can totally picture it. I bet you were a real lady-killer in Ruby Creek."

A shadow of the past flits across his eyes, but he chuckles all the same.

"If Cole and Vaughn's grandfather, Dermot, hadn't waltzed in here on a wild-goose chase after a girl, I'd have never met him. I'd have never started working for him and Ada. I'd have never been out East to meet Billie. And I'd have never met Trixie at Cole's wedding in Chestnut Springs." Hank takes a swig of his beer. "Sometimes unexpected surprises change the course of our life in the most irrevocable of ways. In the best ways. Life is one big adventure, Mira. Don't let it pass you by while you're stuck on a boring old path."

I laugh, but it rings hollow. What he's just said hits a little too close to home. He didn't tell me I belong barefoot in the kitchen with a baby on my hip. He just told me to be open to new possibilities. I think he just told me to take my blinders off. But my blinders keep me safe and focused and achieving all the goals I set for myself as a younger woman.

"Thank you for sharing your wisdom, Hank," I say right as the server swings by with our burgers. "You want a good surprise?"

He nods, and his lips tip up when he winks at me. "Always."

"I hired Stefan Dalca's younger sister to work in the clinic."

His eyes go wide, and his beer goes down the wrong tube. He coughs and pounds a fist against his chest. I feel bad for making him choke, so I keep talking, trying to fill the lull. "Her name is Nadia. She's had a tough go. But I think you'll really like her. She reminds me of Billie. Well, younger Billie."

"Lord have mercy on us all," he coughs out with a laugh. And I join him too. "Listen, Mira, if you like her, I'm sure the rest of us will as well. You're a good judge of character."

God. Am I though?

We dig into our meal, and conversations about different horses on the ranch flow easily. But I'd be lying if I said my thoughts weren't constantly veering off the path. Heading in a direction that I desperately don't want them to go.

"Don't be such a baby."

Stefan has his arms wrapped around Loki's neck and is looking down at the foal like he's a stuffed animal, not a future athlete and animal that needs space to frolic and run.

"Are you serious right now?" I prod him. "I thought you were a big tough man, but you're too chicken to let this little guy romp around outside?"

"Mira. I'm not a big tough man. I'm just a dick. Remember?"

"Yeah, yeah." I wave my hand at him dismissively. Stefan is a lot of things, but the more I get to know him, the less I think a dick is one of them. "Let's go. Outside. Fresh air is good for everyone." I slip the leather halter onto Farrah's head and buckle it near her ear. She looks excited. Ready to get out of the barn.

"What if he hurts himself?"

"Can't live life that way, Stefan. Bad things happen all the time. Buck up. Let's go."

With a firm cluck, I walk Farrah out into the barn alleyway and head toward the big wide-open sliding door. Today was beautiful and sunny and dry. And now, under the quiet charm of the evening, it's the perfect time to let them take their maiden voyage outside with no tractors, no staff milling about, just calm and privacy for this colt and the mare who's taken him under her wing.

Within a few moments, I hear the clopping of Loki's hooves against the concrete and the scuff of Stefan's boots. I smile to myself. The big bad wolf has certainly developed quite the soft spot for Loki.

Out under the setting sun, we head toward the paddock that's already waiting and open. It's a big grass field on the opposite side of the lake from the willow tree where Stefan and I buried the other foal a few weeks ago. I pull Farrah's halter off, and she's through the gate. Loki follows her, like the sweet little colt he is.

Until Stefan lets him go.

Beneath the pink and orange sky, the sweet little colt blows a gasket. He's got his head down between his knees and is trying to buck. Mile-long legs fly out all over the place while Farrah takes off for a leisurely trot down the fence line. Loki goes with her but doesn't stop his antics. I shut the gate quickly and lean against the fence, chuckling.

Stefan steps up beside me and presses his elbows against the railing. "He looks like Elaine doing that godawful dance on *Seinfeld*."

I straight up cackle. That is exactly what he looks like. "He looks happy," I reply.

Stefan nods. "He does."

"You've done a great job with him, Stefan." I want him to understand what a huge difference he's made for this small horse. That even if everyone sees him one way, I see that they're all wrong. It feels like something he should know. This man is still clearly so broken up about his mother and trying so hard for the only family he has left.

His eyes flit to the side. "This is all you. I probably just made your job harder."

"Oh, you mean by using me as a pawn in your pointless war with my friends?" I joke.

Now his head turns to me. Slowly but sharply. Like a predator that's heard his prey fumbling through the forest. "Pawn?"

I roll my eyes. "Don't play stupid, Stefan. It's not cute. Making them keep Loki here rather than at Gold Rush Ranch. The three dates. I'm sure you're just desperately hoping Billie finds out about those so you can sow discord between us. I know it's all part of your plot to cut them down at the knees."

He unfolds his fingers slowly as he regards me. Turning his body to face me. And mine follows like the opposite end of a magnet, matching his movement so we stand facing each other under the golden glow of the evening sky. "You think that you're the pawn in my game?"

I scoff and roll my eyes in response. *How dumb does he think I am?*

He moves swiftly now, surely. One hand shoots out and slides between my coat and thin shirt. He palms my ribs there as he presses me back against the fence. We're supposed to be watching the horses. But suddenly, all we're watching is each other. My hands come up to push him away, but as soon as I feel the hard lines of his pecs beneath his shirt, my resolve withers.

"I'm going to tell you something, Mira." I can feel the rumble of his voice through my palms. I can't take my eyes off the sight of my hands on his chest. I'm not supposed to be touching Stefan Dalca, but my body must have missed the memo. Because my nipples rasp against my bra, and with each breath I draw, an ache coils just behind my hip bones.

"And I want you to listen very carefully." With his free hand, Stefan reaches up and drags the pad of his pointer finger over my collarbone.

My breath turns to stone in my lungs. I'm too shocked to move. And too far gone to stop him. He's standing so close I can smell his laundry detergent and the hint of pine that must be in his cologne.

"Because you are very confused."

He starts at the center of my chest, his eyes following

his finger, watching goose bumps fan out across my skin in his wake. When his finger gets close to my shoulder and the neckline of my shirt, he slips it just inside. Just under the strap of my bra. And with one flick, that strap is pushed right off my shoulder. His grip pulses on my ribs and he steps even closer, forcing me to look up and hold his gaze.

A quiet gasp escapes me when I catch sight of the expression on his face. What I see there is primal. He's not just looking at me appreciatively…he's looking at me like he wants to devour me.

I'm positive no man has ever looked at me like this before.

A sinful smile touches his mouth as he leans in close. His free hand cups the back of my skull so his thumb can brush across the sensitive part of my neck, almost at my throat.

His whisper is warm and silky. "Do I have your attention now?"

I swallow and nod, feeling chills break out over my skin. There is not a single part of my mind or body that is not entirely focused on the man who has pushed me up against the fence.

"Good. Because I want to make myself abundantly clear." We're so close. I can feel the entire length of his body covering mine. He teases me with the lightest brush of his lips against my ear as he drops his voice and holds me captive. "You are not the pawn, Mira. You are the prize."

I reel, and I feel the burn of his lips against my skin as he presses a featherlight kiss to the spot his thumb had been rubbing. My pulse hammers, and I swear all I can hear is my blood rushing through my veins. The air crackles between us. No man has ever spoken to me like this.

I should put a stop to our interaction. And yet there's nowhere else I'd rather be. My body comes to life for him in a way it shouldn't.

He steps away, and I feel alarmingly bereft, like I want to yank him back toward me. Like I want *more*. I'm the biggest traitor I know because I want him to continue. I want him to whisper more forbidden secrets against my body.

His tongue darts out over his bottom lip, followed by his teeth, in a very intentional way as his eyes peruse my body. His gaze lands on the hand I now have slung over my chest in an attempt to slow my racing heart. The other one grips the fence post behind me, possibly the only thing that's keeping me upright at this moment.

"And I love to win," he finishes with a stupidly sexy smirk, and then turns around and walks away.

Leaving me with the perfect view of his firm ass and a jumbled mess of confused feelings.

CHAPTER 13

Stefan

THE BELL RINGS, THE GATE FLIES OPEN, AND I WATCH THE new gray filly fly out with ears pricked forward. She has a sweet face, but the little demon can *run*.

She drops her head low and gets to work almost instantly. The season hasn't started yet, but she's going to be ready when it does. Jose is light in the irons, gently hovering above her, letting her stretch out and not overmanaging the way Patrick does during his rides.

Not that he ever shows up to practice days. If it's not race day, you don't find him down here at Bell Point Park. I imagine he's hanging in his mansion wearing one of those red crushed-velvet robes you see in movies, sucking on a cigar. The guy is just such a douchebag. I can't wait to bury him once and for all.

Jose and Silver thunder past where I stand, pulling my attention from my Patrick plans. And true to her name, she looks like a silver streak, a blur, as she gallops past with her dark dapples flashing under the sun. She's a beautiful mare. Although, last time I spoke to Jose, he cackled and told me that she's "a bit of a bitch" and "her attitude will win her races." Her muscled haunches push her through the turn, and I can't help but smile. I told him we could just refer to her as a "go-getter" from now on. Call her what you want, but he's not wrong—that mare has *winner* written all over her. Plus, she'll make a hell of a broodmare one day.

Happy with what I've seen, I turn and begin my walk back to the stables, wanting to have a quick chat with some of the staff down here at the track. I pass the winner's circle—a place I'd like to spend more time—and then turn toward the barns. It's quiet here this time of year; there aren't any spectators, just staff working quickly and efficiently. Which is why I'm surprised when I hear Patrick Cassel's voice filtering out of the mouth of the first barn alleyway.

"You'd look a lot prettier if you smiled more, you know."

I roll my eyes while standing around the corner, out of sight. *Total douchebag.*

"I'll smile when you show me what you're hiding in your pocket."

My blood runs cold. Another voice I'd recognize anywhere. A voice that has me leaping into action because I sure as hell am not leaving Mira alone with a pig like Patrick. And truthfully, I'd intervene no matter who was here with him. The mere fact Patrick is at the facility on a day when there aren't races is suspicious.

With my hands slung in my pockets and my neck

held tall, I turn into the wide-open end of the barn and lean a shoulder up against the frame before casually crossing an ankle over my shin. Mira's gaze finds mine almost instantly, while Patrick has no idea I tower behind him. His lack of awareness might be his most impressive quality.

"I think Dr. Thorne looks especially lovely when she's frowning." My voice comes out as a snarl, which makes perfect sense. Seeing Patrick alone in a barn with Mira has me feeling a bit feral.

He spins, cheeks reddening, lips curling into a vicious smile I don't trust at all. "Stefan, how lovely to see you."

His tone tells me he doesn't actually think it's lovely.

"Did you find your misplaced work ethic, Patrick? Putting in some extra hours? Not sure I've ever seen you here on an off day."

He sneers at me, and I see Mira worrying her lip behind him, her eyes darting down to the pockets of his bomber jacket where his hands are shoved in. It's not a stretch to say he looks like he's covering something. But I already know that.

"Fuck you, Dalca. You fired me, remember? The work I do now is none of your business."

My fingers curl into fists in my pockets. The problem with men like Patrick is they think they're much smarter than they are. He thinks he must be the smartest man in the room right now, simply because we haven't caught him.

Yet.

Mira pipes up now. "As the person in charge of these

horses' health and well-being, you trying to enter their stalls *is* my business."

He scoffs as he turns back to face her. "I was doing no such thing. Just taking a shortcut through this barn."

He's a poor liar, and the way Mira arches her brow says she thinks so too.

"You were." Her eyes narrow, and if looks could incinerate a person on the spot, Patrick would be on fire right now.

"Okay, Mira, then get a search warrant," he chuckles condescendingly. "No one is going to believe the little country bumpkin with the worst case of resting bitch fa—"

That's not happening.

My hand snakes out, fingers clamping around the back of his neck, hard enough I hope it hurts. "That's *Dr. Thorne*. And it's time for you to leave. Now." My fingers pulse, and I feel him tense.

Being the weasel that he is, he tries to leave immediately, but my grip pulls him back as I lean in toward his ear and chuckle darkly. "A gentleman like you wouldn't leave without apologizing to Dr. Thorne, would he?"

"Of course not." His voice is thin with barely contained rage bubbling beneath perfectly enunciated words. But he's also not brave enough to do anything about it. "My apologies, *Dr. Thorne*. Now get your fucking hands off me, Dalca."

He squirms around like a slippery fish, trying to escape my grasp. I almost wish I had a bat to put him out of his misery. It's just pathetic enough to make me smile before I let him go. He marches out with his head held higher than is fitting for someone who is fleeing a losing match.

"He was up to something." Mira stares at me, dark eyes searching my face like she's looking for something.

"No doubt." I shove my hands back in my pockets to ease the urge to wrap her in my arms. To assure myself that she's okay. "But he's not wrong. Short of holding him down and frisking him, it would be hard to prove."

She grunts in dissatisfaction, jutting her chin out in the way of saying goodbye. "Thanks for running interference," she adds as her eyes dart down just before she turns to saunter back through the darkened stable.

"Of course." My eyes fall to her firm ass. No one should look that irresistible in cargo pants. "And Mira?"

"Yeah?" Now facing me, she continues to step backward, putting space between us, making the pull more powerful than ever.

"Only smile when you want to."

Her full lips press down, almost certainly hiding a small smile. And she gives me that look again. The one so full of questions and confusion.

I stand and watch her leave, like she can't get away from me fast enough. Since I came clean about wanting her, she's been skittish around me.

Shaking my head, I marvel at how the more confused she is about me, the less I am about her.

I tried avoiding Mira a while back, and it didn't work. And apparently, she's trying her hand at avoiding me now. I'm supposed to attend a family reunion with her tomorrow, but I've seen neither hide nor hair of the woman since our run-in with Patrick. She's been here checking on Loki; I can see her notes and initials on his chart hanging on the front of the stall. I just don't know when she's coming because she's ignoring my messages. Calling the clinic doesn't even work anymore because the person I now have to talk to is my endlessly lippy sister.

So now I'm going to sit on the barn floor and wait for her to show up.

Was I too forward the other night? Maybe. Do I regret it? Hell no. I refuse to let a woman like Mira walk around thinking she's anything less than the queen she is. She's not a tool; she's not a pawn. I don't have it out for her friends the way she thinks I do. Did I want to buy that horse? Yes. Did I resort to a less than savory offer to make it happen? Also, yes.

But I hold no grudge. That's just business. I'm well aware Billie hates me, and that's okay. She can hate me. She has zero bearing on how I feel about Mira.

Which is determined. I feel determined to prove to her I'm not the dick she thinks I am and that I'm definitely not playing with her. That I want her.

What started out as a simple attraction morphed into a curiosity. And then into a tentative friendship, which is when she showed me the woman beneath the cocky smirk and the unimpressed looks. And that woman?

I plan to take my shot with that woman. I just need to soften her up first.

Step one: talk to her.

Step two: woo her.

Step three: win her.

Mira is closed off and actually more shy than I originally banked on. Skittish even. She comes off like this confident siren of a woman, but when I press, she turns into a deer caught in the headlights.

I'll take it slowly. I'm a patient man, and I think she'll be worth the wait.

So I wait into the night, through dinner, for two hours before she shows up, closing the door quietly behind herself before she catches sight of me and stops in her tracks.

"Hi," I venture quietly into the private barn.

"Hi," she replies sharply, propping one fist on her hip, leaning one leg out to the side. Wearing that attitude and glare like a suit of armor. "Are you waiting for me?"

"Yes." No point in lying. "You've been avoiding me."

"Ha!" She barks out a laugh. "I wonder why?"

"Am I so bad?" My cheek quirks up, but there's a part of me that doesn't want her to answer. *If she only knew.*

"No, Stefan. You're not. I'm the one who's bad. Lying to my friends about the deal we made. Sneaking away to spend time with you. Do you know how shitty that makes me feel? I already couldn't win this situation, and then you had to go say what you said and throw an even bigger wrench into my dilemma."

"Dilemma? That means you're torn by something." *Good.* There's a petty part of me that wants her to be as confused as I am.

"Ugh!" Her free hand pulses into a fist and then lets go as she storms toward the stall. "Now I have to deal with you openly wanting to fuck me too."

I tut. "Such language, Dr. Thorne."

"Oh, lucky me. Mr. Cool, Calm, and Collected is here to lecture me about how he never swears."

"I swear."

She shoots me a disbelieving look. "I have never once heard you swear."

I stand up as she approaches and drops her toolkit on the concrete alleyway with a loud clang. Loki startles on the other side of the stall door.

"I do when the situation warrants it."

"Well, I'll wait with bated fucking breath for when that situation arises."

I chuckle. I like her all snappy and worked up. I like to think she's worked up *over me*.

She's about to go into the stall when she spins on me. "Tell me the truth. Are you connected to the mafia? People say that you are, and you haven't outright denied it. One day, are you going to be calling me to stitch up some guy in a back room here?"

I laugh. Small-town gossip is vicious. And wrong.

"I'm not. I don't know why that started circulating. Probably because I waltzed into a small town with a question mark for my past, a chip on my shoulder, and more money than I really knew what to do with."

"Where is all your money from? Most people your age don't just mope around their multimillion-dollar barns all day waiting for their vet to show up so they can accost her with sexually suggestive one-liners."

Oof. She's fired up. But while we're having a no-holds-barred conversation, I might as well give her the truth.

"I took my father's multibillion-dollar shipping company and ripped it up. I sold it for parts. He spent his life building it and beating my mother. He took what I loved most, so I took what he loved most and ran it through a chop shop. I dissolved the company. I ruined his life's work and took great pleasure in its disintegration. I also signed off on his DNR with a smile on my face. It was as close to killing the bastard as I could get."

She freezes, and I wonder if I've gone too far. Only someone with a tarnished soul would take pleasure in something like that.

But I continue, filling the quiet with my reasoning. "I took all that money and bought this place, and then I took the rest and started a shelter downtown for victims of domestic violence. I fund it and am on the board." I hold my hands up and look around myself. "My mother told me on her deathbed, before she succumbed to her injuries, that she wished she'd stayed in Ruby Creek and run a racing farm. So that's what I decided I'd do."

Mira swallows audibly. I think I've poured some water on her fire. "Good." Her head bobs as though my answer pleases her. And then she moves to unlock the stall. She stops, though, before she steps down to check on the colt and looks back over her shoulder. "Are you out to hurt my friends or their business?"

Her dark eyes are almost a perfect match for her black

hair in the dim barn. Like flawlessly polished onyx. Her lips are rose-petal pink and so delectably soft. I could press her up against the wall right now and taste her. But that's not taking it slowly, and I don't want to blow this.

"No." The one word rings out between us as I hold her gaze, willing her to believe me. Willing her to see me as more than my past mistakes. "I promise."

Her lips thin as she regards me. "Okay. I'll be here at three tomorrow. Don't wear a suit."

My chest warms at the thought that we're still on for our *fake* date tomorrow. "Why not?"

"No one will believe I'd bring a guy who wears suits home. Just…" She looks me up and down. "Keep it casual. You already don't look like my type."

I almost laugh. *We'll see about that.*

As she brushes past me, I murmur conspiratorially, "Is it because I'm not purple and made of silicone?"

And I swear I see her blush.

"They're never going to buy this."

Mira is talking, but all I can focus on is her hands clamping down on the bare part of her thighs, just above her knees. She's wearing some white lacy dress with white Converse sneakers and a jean jacket. I should have my eyes on the road, but *goddamn*. Watching her hands grip her body beneath that hemline is practically pornography.

"Buy what?" I reply, forcing my eyes back to the charcoal road winding through bright-green hills.

After a rainy spring, it's an unseasonably warm day, and it feels like everything that was brown has suddenly popped into this vibrant green. I'm glad I have my sunglasses for the drive…and so I can creep on Mira discreetly.

"You. Me. That we're together. No fucking chance. I'm so screwed. And everyone will think I'm even more tragic for bringing a fake boyfriend. They're going to corner you and grill you. You have no clue what you're in for."

"Mira—"

"I'm a smart person. I was valedictorian of my graduating class at vet school. I have an IQ of one forty. People like me don't pull stunts like this and expect to get away with it."

Okay, she's really spiraling. "Mira—"

"And with you? God. What the fuck am I thinking?" Her hand closest to me jerks through her hair. "You're blond, for crying out loud. They'll know immediately. I've never batted an eye at a blond guy. Me having a type has been a running joke for years."

Yeah, joke's on you.

My hand darts out and clamps down on her thigh. Her skin is smooth and warm, and just the feel of her sends sparks up my arm.

"Mira." She stops ranting and stares down at my hand on her leg. "It's going to be *fine*. I'm good at schmoozing. I'll take care of you. I've got this. I'm not even that blond." She just sits there, frozen. Staring at my hand. The one that still hasn't let go of her leg. I could so easily slide it up her thigh and pull her panties to the side. A good orgasm would probably take the edge off. My dick twitches at the thought, and I force myself to focus on the road. "Do you trust me?"

She leans back in her seat and looks out the window. She doesn't make a move to withdraw my hand, but she goes quiet for an extended period.

If I wasn't listening carefully, if I wasn't hanging on her every breath, I might not have heard her say, "I think I do."

CHAPTER 14

Mira

WE APPROACH THE FRONT DOOR OF MY PARENTS' WHITE BI-level split house, surrounded by a sprawling yard that butts up against flat fields filled with blueberry bushes. They keep it tidy, but the house looks dated. It's not something I've ever felt self-conscious about, but with Stefan here, I feel like I might barf.

His house is so opulent in comparison, his wealth so staggering next to the small working farm I grew up on. He's so damn polished next to my family. I told him to dress casually, so he wore a white dress shirt with a pair of navy-blue chinos. And somehow, I still don't feel like he looks casual.

He's cuffed the hem and put on a pair of loafers with no socks. I suppose for him, this is dressed down. But there's something about the way he just oozes class. He looks like he belongs in a magazine shoot for casual cool. It's tripping me out. How can he be so calm about pretending to a group of perfect strangers that we're dating?

I'm *tripping*. They're going to see right through it.

My hand wraps around the door handle, and I freeze. Once I turn this handle, there's no going back. Is this one of those moments Hank was talking about? A moment that can change the path of your life forever. One simple turn of a worn brass knob.

"Are you installing important updates?" Stefan chuckles from behind me.

How is he joking at a time like this?

He steps in closer, and his hand lands at the small of my back while the other lifts my free hand. His lips press against my palm just like the time before, and my body hums—just like the time before.

I wish he'd stop touching me. And not because I don't want him touching me. It's because I do. And I shouldn't. I can still feel the shape of his hand on my bare thigh like a brand. One I hope never fades or heals.

I'm so fucked up.

"Let's go Mira-bot. It's going to be fine. I've got you." His body presses in close to mine, and I internally chastise myself for melting toward him.

I'm not sure when Dalca the Dick became a comfort to me, but I'm too stressed to fight it right now. He feels like a wall of lean muscle behind me. Tall and firm and reassuring.

I twist the handle and swing the door open.

In a matter of seconds, the smell of cumin hits me, and moments later, my mom calls out, "Mira! You're here!"

She stands at the top of the stairs. Lines of gray streak her brown hair, and she's wearing some baggy cotton dress with feather earrings and a pair of very broken-in Birkenstocks. My mom is a hippie at heart, and while we're very different women, I can't help but smile at the sight of her. Before I moved out to Gold Rush Ranch, I was still living at home, and as lame as that was for a woman in her midtwenties, I'd be lying if I said I didn't miss my parents—and my nana, who lives with them too. When you go from seeing your family every day to a couple of times a month, it's an adjustment.

"Hi, Mama."

She hustles down the stairs and wraps her arms around my neck, pulling me into a tight squeeze. "Oh, my baby. It's so nice to see you."

I feel like she's suffocating me. Or maybe I just can't breathe with Stefan standing so close. She holds me back eventually and looks over my shoulder. "And who have we got here?"

My throat constricts, and I already know I'm going to blow this.

"Mrs. Thorne, I'm Stefan. Such a pleasure to meet you." Stefan reaches around me and extends his hand to shake my mother's. His other hand falls to the small of my back, where it always does. It feels comforting having him there, propping me up. My body never fails to come alive for him.

"Oh, please." My mother *blushes*. "Call me Sylvia."

Her eyes dart down to his hand on the small of my back, and her lips tip up. "Sunny! Come meet Mira's new boyfriend, Stefan!"

Boyfriend.

The word lands like a bomb, and I stiffen at the mention. In response, Stefan's fingers slide back and forth across my skin, making my eyes flutter as I swallow what I'm pretty sure is a moan. The fabric of my dress feels altogether too thin.

His hands on my body are making me absolutely insane.

I swear my brain is melting right down into my spinal cord.

I've officially turned into *that* girl.

My dad, black beard neatly trimmed, appears at the top of the stairs with his arms crossed over his chest. His thick black hair and almost-black eyes are the perfect match for my own. He's scowling at Stefan, and it makes me smile.

Sunny is one of those men who isn't frivolous with his words. But I know by his actions that I'm the apple of his eye. When he dropped me off at college, there was no tearful goodbye. No promises to visit. He helped me unpack and snuck an envelope with a thousand dollars cash under my pillow for me to find later.

He's never babied me or treated me like I'm less capable than I am. He's never given me the "if he touches you, he's dead" talk. He's a modern man who took my mother's last name when they got married.

But looking at him now? A small giggle bubbles past my lips. Looking at him now, descending the stairs with dark eyes perfectly narrowed, I'm going to go out on a limb and say my father isn't all that wild about his little girl bringing a boy home.

"Mr. Thorne, thank you so much for inviting me to

your home." Stefan steps up to the stairs and sticks his hand out.

My dad just grunts and says, "Pretty sure Mira invited you," as he clasps his hand back in a death grip.

This is off to a great start.

"I'm sure glad she did." Stefan grins at my father, completely unperturbed.

We remove our shoes and head into the house together. Straight into the hustle and bustle of my father's family all together under one roof. He's a second-generation Canadian, and his siblings have spread out all over the country, which is why this annual get-together happens. Mostly, everyone convenes to see Nana.

At the kitchen table, my grandmother is folding samosas with a bored expression on her face. I'm pretty sure she could do this in her sleep.

"Hi, Nana." I bend down and drop a kiss to the top of her head and whisper, "Are you making enough that I can take some home with me?"

She shakes her head. "You think I'm so old I've forgotten you hoard these like a squirrel preparing for winter?"

I laugh. She's right. I always have them stocked in my freezer. "Nana. This is Stefan." Stefan is standing across the table, his eyes on her hands. "He's my…"

I don't know if I can lie to her about this.

"I'm her boyfriend," he says, like he's not concerned about pretending to be my boyfriend at all.

Nana looks him over and smirks. "He's blond."

Oh god. She totally knows. "He's not *that* blond," I reply, parroting what Stefan said earlier and trying to be casual as my eyes bulge out at him. Stefan just chuckles at me, shaking his head like I'm nuts.

"Can I help?" He pulls out a chair and sits down across from my grandmother, sincerity lining his every movement.

She shrugs but pushes a stack of the wrappers across the table and moves the bowl of filling into the middle. She doesn't give him any instructions; she just keeps going and expects him to pick it up.

I watch Stefan's keen eyes observing her closely, studying her movements. After watching her make a couple, he reaches into the bowl and takes a spoonful of the filling and then gets started on his first samosa. His gaze darts up and down when his fingers move. He mimics everything she does. Rises to the challenge. And makes a pretty damn fine-looking samosa.

I catch Nana assess it as she reaches forward to start her next one. She doesn't compliment him; instead, she just says, "He's fine, Mira. You can go."

Stefan doesn't even look up at me, already engrossed in making his next one. He looks so earnest about learning this, it warms my heart to him. The look of concentration on his face, the way he captures the tip of his tongue between his lips make my stomach flip.

But I've been dismissed.

I turn and grab two beers from the fridge and drop one in front of Stefan. As I walk away, I drag my hand across the broad expanse of his shoulders with my free hand.

I can't explain why I did it. I just felt the overwhelming need to touch him back. To thank him for doing this for me.

I still can't quite figure out why he's doing this for me.

You are not the pawn, Mira. You are the prize.

Try as I might, I've been unable to scrub that sentence from my mind. I feel like he went and carved it into my brain like teenagers carve their initials into a picnic table. There's no erasing it. The rut is there. And I'm stuck in it.

I walk into the living room and am met with a chorus of hellos, hugs, and backslaps. My cousins, my uncles, my aunts—it's nice to see everyone, but it's always so overwhelming. So loud and busy. I prefer to socialize one-on-one or in a small group. It's more relaxing, more intimate—less chaotic.

The get-together moves around me, and I chat when necessary from where I lean against the wall. But my eyes keep finding Stefan, hunched over a table, working quietly with my grandmother.

It makes my chest ache in a foreign way. And I give up all pretense of looking elsewhere and allow myself to watch his hands moving deftly, his toned forearms flexing below the cuffs of his dress shirt, which he's now rolled up. He really looks into it. And I'm finding myself entranced. It's right up there with watching him kiss Loki square on the nose. Or stroke Farrah's forehead with so much love and respect.

What if I've been wrong about him this entire time?

"Honey, you're staring." My mom nudges me with her elbow, shaking me out of my daydream.

My cheeks pink at once. "Oh shit. Sorry."

"Don't be sorry. It's nice to see."

I roll my eyes and take a swig of my beer, peeking at the table again. Which is right when Stefan looks up and catches me staring. A slow grin spreads across his face, and he lets his eyes trace my body. Heat pours through my bones, and I feel like they might melt entirely when he looks at me like that. Like he's undressing me with his eyes and plans to devour me.

He finishes his perusal with a sly wink, and I'm almost positive my panties combust on the spot. *Wink. Poof. Gone.*

I look away, blinking and swigging pointlessly at my empty beer bottle.

"No shortage of chemistry between you two. I bet the sex is sensational."

Here comes the free-spirit, Kama Sutra side of my mother. A couple glasses of wine and this is what comes out to play.

"Mom. Please, don't."

She turns to face me, and I see Stefan behind her, being dismissed by Nana with a wave of her hand. With only a few steps, he's closing in on us. Which is right when my mother adds, "Listen to me, Mira. Your father looked at me like that too. And guess what? The sex was sensational. It still is. A marriage is hard work, but great sex makes it easier."

Someone dig me a fucking hole.

"Wise words," Stefan says, folding himself into the spot right beside me. His arm snakes around my waist, hand splaying across my rib cage possessively as he presses a casual kiss to my temple. Like this is perfectly normal. Like this is real.

It's feeling pretty authentic right now. In my family home. Where he's being nice and polite and charming.

It's unnerving.

My mother grins and moves on to the next group of people, completely undeterred. In fact, I'm pretty sure in her mind, Stefan just promised her grandchildren.

"What are you doing?" I whisper-shout through gritted teeth.

He pulls me tight to his side and whispers against my hair, "Pretending to be your boyfriend. Like you asked me to. You do realize people in relationships touch each other?"

I scoff. "I wouldn't know."

I chance a look up at him to find blatant confusion on his face.

"Excuse me?"

"You heard me."

"Are you implying you've never been in a relationship?"

I try to drink more out of the empty beer bottle. I'm like a nervous toddler sucking on a soother for comfort. I absently wonder if beer bottles are the adult equivalent.

"Wrapping those pretty lips around a bottle like that isn't an answer, Mira."

On a gasp, I inhale whatever backwash I left in the bottle and end up coughing while he gently pats my back.

"You can't just keep saying things like that."

"Answer the question." His thumb swipes across my cheek, wiping away the tear my coughing fit elicited.

I take a deep breath. "I'm not implying anything. I'm *telling* you I've never been in a relationship."

"Why?"

"Because it's never served me."

His chuckle is dark and low. "Why is that?"

"Because the idea of being beholden to a man annoys me. I don't like having to report what I'm doing or why I'm doing it or where I am. They always have all these expectations, and I don't like feeling like I can't do whatever I want without running it past someone else."

"Why else?" His breath is warm as it pours down the side of my neck. If I turned my head, I could press my lips against his and get whatever this is out of my system.

God. Why are we having this conversation in the middle of my family living room?

To throw him off, I turn and whisper, "Because I can fuck myself better with Mr. Purple than any man ever has."

I don't know why I thought that would throw him off. The man is relentless. Like a dog with a bone.

The way his tongue presses into the side of his cheek thoughtfully drives me to distraction. I turn my head away, wanting to see if anyone can tell what's going on in our corner of the living room. But no one seems to be watching. They're all lost in their own conversations, happy and relaxed.

Unlike me. My feet go heavy, and a weight lurches through my gut when Stefan murmurs, "Challenge accepted. But I'm not going to fuck you until you're *begging* for it."

And then he saunters away to work the room, like he didn't just knock me into a complete tailspin.

CHAPTER 15

Stefan

THIS IS FUN. NOT ONLY AM I HAVING AN ABSOLUTE BALL teasing Mira, but being in a house full of happy, loving family is making me feel like I'm living in a TV show or something. The space is loud, but it's full of laughter and camaraderie. It's the polar opposite from the house I grew up in, and I am reveling in it. It doesn't hurt that the food smells amazing.

I'm so hungry.

And based on the less than stealthy looks Mira is shooting me from across the room, she is too.

She's been dancing around the house and keeping her distance from me since I told her I was going to make her beg. The way her eyes widened—damn—that's a look I want to see, but from above her while I slide myself between her legs.

Her cheeks are pink, and she's smiling. She is stunning, and I'm spellbound. I'm trying to talk to her father about the nitty-gritty details of being a blueberry farmer, but my focus keeps slipping to his daughter.

The things I want to do to her.

If he could read my mind, he wouldn't be tolerating my presence in his home, I'm sure. He's gruff and intelligent and gives clipped answers. His eyes remind me of Mira's in color and the way they flash with a keen cleverness. I would be a fool to underestimate this man, but I am softening him up to me.

Over the music and hum of conversation, Sylvia shouts, "Dinner is ready!" from the kitchen and waves toward the huge family table they have set up for everyone.

I follow the crowd of people. I've met them all now, but I'd be lying if I said I can remember every name or relation. It's overwhelming.

Gravy dishes, fresh naan bread, and the samosas I'm super proud of making all look sensational. When I'm done staring at the food, I notice Mira is pulling a chair out at the opposite end of the table from me. Retreating like she usually does. Backing down. I like her when she fights back. She's a tough cookie when she's working, but this shy, softer side in her personal life is a new facet.

I suppose the fact that she's never been in a relationship could be part of that. I'm thinking her awkwardness around me can be chalked up to lack of experience. She's just mature enough to come off like she has more than she does. Either way, I'm happy to sit by Nana—I like the old crone.

"Mira, you're not really going to leave Stefan over there by himself?" her mother exclaims in front of everyone, and I wish she'd just left it.

The good news for Mira is that if she wants a man who is happy for her to go on having her own life and goals and ideas—I'm that guy. I couldn't care less if she wants to sit at the opposite end of the table. I saw how she's been looking at me all night. I'm pretty sure that where she wants to be sitting is on my cock.

"She can sit wherever she wants," I say, but Mira is already walking toward me with a tight set to her jaw. I pull out the chair next to me, and she sits down like she's made of wood. She's clearly annoyed. She's got that look on her face like she might gut someone.

I secretly love this side of her. The resting bitch face. Even when she looks at me like *that*, her fierceness is exciting. She's not afraid to let her claws out, and I'm not afraid to get scratched.

I tuck my chair in next to her, and she leans incrementally toward me. "Thanks."

She mumbles it tersely, and I offer her a gentle nudge of my elbow against hers. The meal carries on, and I get lost in the flavors. I answer the odd question about what I do—run a racing business. What my accent is—Romanian-ish. If the food is too spicy for me—no.

I love the whole thing. I only wish Nadia were here to see it. It might soften up that very jaded side of her. She grew up too fast, and I'm not sure how to slow her down now. A worry for another day.

"So, Mira, any plans to get married soon?" a woman from across the table asks. Her aunt, I think. Her father's sister-in-law. She smiles, but I can see what Mira mentioned.

There's a level of judgment, and it makes me roll my shoulders back and sit up straight.

"Can you pass the naan bread, please?" I try to interrupt.

The woman hands it over as Mira leans into me. "Naan."

"That's what I said." I take the platter with a kind smile.

"No, you said naan *bread*. It's obviously bread. Like chai, you don't need to call it chai tea," she whispers to me, keeping the conversation between us with an amused curve to her lips.

"So, Mira? You never answered my question?" the woman cuts in, not taking the out I tried to provide her.

Mira rips off a bite of her *naan* and chews angrily. "Nope," she says through a full mouth. Like if she shoves enough food in there, she won't say something that she'll regret.

"That's a shame." The woman's eyes dart to mine before turning back on Mira. And I can already tell that what's going to come out next will be unnecessarily cruel. I slide a hand between us and take a hold of her thigh again. I'm pretty sure my hands belong on her thighs.

"You're so focused on your job, and you aren't getting any younger."

Mira goes completely rigid, and I let my thumb rub gentle circles on her inner thigh in an attempt to soothe her.

"You need to think about having babies at some point. You won't experience that fulfillment until you have one for yourself."

Mira's eyes narrow, and her mouth opens, but I cut her off. The part of me that has failed at protecting the women in my life up until this point rears its ugly head. "You know what's wild?" I announce to the entire table. "I've answered a lot of questions tonight. And it's been an absolute pleasure meeting every one of you. But not a single person has inquired about my family planning agenda or implied that I might be close to my expiration date on becoming a father."

The room is so quiet you could probably hear a pin drop. Have I gone too far? Some might think so. Others might think…not far enough. I smile and shovel a mouthful of lentils past my lips and chew thoughtfully, making sure I take a moment to meet the eyes of every single person who is staring at me.

My thumb never stops stroking Mira's inner thigh.

"I find it fascinating that no one has ever asked me that as a man, but somehow it's polite dinner conversation for a young woman with lofty career goals and an enviable level of focus."

No one says anything, but I see Sunny's lips twitch as he eats again.

I look back at the woman who started this whole conversation. She looks properly chastised, but I can't find it in myself to care. I have a vicious side too. A protective side. And just because I haven't been able to protect the people I care about in the past doesn't mean I can't start now.

"Maybe you can ask her about the premature foal she saved this month instead?"

I keep eating and feel Nana pat my leg gingerly before she gets back to her food. But it appears I was so busy glaring at everyone else that I missed looking at the beautiful woman beside me. The one who is currently boiling over. Tears glisten across the surface of her wide eyes, taking me completely by surprise. With a loud screech, her chair shoots back.

"Excuse me," she bites out before storming away from the table and heading toward the front door.

With her gone, I can let my fangs out. I can't help it— wolves raised me.

I dab at my mouth with the cloth napkin before placing it on the tabletop. "The next person to make that woman cry will wish they hadn't." I push my chair back calmly and turn to Nana. "Thank you for the beautiful meal. I look forward to meeting you again." Then I turn to Mr. and Mrs. Thorne. "Thank you so much for hosting me in your home. I had a lovely time."

I say nothing more because I'm spitting mad. I don't think I can come up with any additional nice things to say at this current juncture. Mira's father stands on my way past and shoves his hand into mine, shaking it with a firm nod. Sylvia looks like she might cry too.

It's almost exactly like Mira said. Lovely people, but so averse to confrontation they sit by for garbage like that.

Lucky for her, I'm not so lovely.

I stride to the front door and slip my feet into my soft brown loafers before heading into the humid spring air. It's sunny and warm, but it's raining. Fat drops of water fall from the sky, and I expect Mira to be waiting in my SUV, but she's not.

I scan the driveway, feeling the rain soaking in through my thin shirt. The urge to snap on someone is powerful right

ELSIE SILVER

now. The look on Mira's face when that woman just kept going, even though she was clearly upsetting her niece…

Fiery rage burns through my bones as I recall it.

Never again.

A flash of white catches my eye on the far side of the yard. Mira is standing in the rain staring out across a field of low-growing shrubs. She looks tiny from this far away, fragile even. My feet move toward her before my brain even has time to catch up. All I want to do is talk to her. I want to whisk her away to the floor of a stall in my barn and stay up all night talking to her. Hearing about her hopes and dreams. I want to tell her everything.

I want my hands on her body. My skin on her skin.

"Hey," I murmur once I'm close enough I'm sure she'll hear me over the patter of the rain. Looking up above us, I see dark clouds circling the valley and the bright rays of sun stretching down through them, bathing us in their light.

"Stefan, please. Not right now."

"Mira—"

"Can you just not?" Her voice is tearful, and from behind, I can see her hands shoot up so she can press the palms of her hands into her eye sockets. She's trying not to cry.

She's so strong.

I step closer and touch her midback, right over the indent there. I can't explain why I find this part of her body so erotic, but I can't stop resting my hand on this indent. I trail my fingers up the column of her spine until they glide across the wet skin exposed between her shoulder blades.

156

"Stefan." Her voice sounds rusty when it breaks over the sound of my name. "You can't keep doing this."

"Doing what?"

The rain falls around us, muting any other sounds like a veil. A protective layer from the rest of the world. I watch a droplet of rain roll down the slender slope of her neck, tracing her body the way I wish I could.

"Making me want things I can't have."

My heart thunders against my rib cage. That's not the answer I was expecting. "I'm not."

She shrugs my hand off her body, but she doesn't step away or turn around. Instead, she groans and tips her head up to sky, loose locks of dark hair plastered to her face. She closes her eyes and lets the rain wash over her face.

"You are. You embody it. With you here charming everyone and then burning the place down to defend me...I feel like I could have it all. The career, the family—I could have someone like you. But that's not real. *This* isn't real. I can't have that."

"Mira, listen to me." I step closer to her. She smells like honey and fresh rain. "You can have that."

"People wouldn't understand. They wouldn't forgive me." Her chin drops to her chest now.

With the wild mass of black hair pulled over her shoulder, I'm stuck staring at the rain shimmering on her bare skin.

"Who cares?" My hands itch to touch her, and I don't fight it. I reach forward and grip her hips from behind as I drop my lips to the bone at the base of her neck. My tongue darts out over the droplets of water there, and she whimpers the second it does.

I pull away momentarily to watch goose bumps race out over her arms. A dead giveaway. "Tell me that's not real, Mira."

Her chest heaves under the weight of her breathing. With our height difference, I can see the globes of her breasts from over her shoulder. Full and round and covered in water. I can't take my eyes off her, and when she turns to look at me over her shoulder, her dark eyes aren't shrink-wrapped anymore. They are living fire, dancing with every shade of amber and burgundy and black. She looks almost otherworldly.

Her rose-petal lips part slightly as she scours my face, and I wonder if my eyes are the same. I wonder if I look like I'm starving the way she does.

"It's real." Her voice is thick and sultry, and I reach across her body and twist her toward me.

My eyes are fixed on her puffy lips. The way they moved as she said "It's real." I know in my heart, in my soul, that it is too. And I'm about done with pretending it's not.

I cup her neck and press my thumb against her jaw as my mouth crashes down onto hers. Her lips open for me instantly, and she goes soft in my arms. She discards all the resistance in her body like a piece of dirty laundry, dropped and forgotten on the floor.

We melt into each other. In a lush green field, covered in fresh spring rain, we give in to the pull between us.

I stroke my tongue against hers, and she matches my fervor as her hands roam my body. One shoots straight under my shirt, and her long fingers splay across the lines of my abs while she moans into my mouth. The other hand grasps at the fabric on my chest frantically, like she can't get a grip. Like she can't get close enough.

The world swirls around us, but we stand still, lost in each other. And, damn, it feels good. I knew we'd be explosive, but this is mind-altering. This is like a drug.

This is the best kiss of my life.

Frantic kisses turn languid and exploratory. I run my hands over her, luxuriating in the way they glide across her wet skin, and she wraps her hands around my neck like she never wants to let go.

I hope she never does.

I move my mouth over her cheek as I grip her head in my hands. The full length of her body presses against mine as she tries to move in closer. I pepper soft kisses up to her hairline and feel not an ounce of guilt over the scene I made at the dinner table.

This woman is about to be my undoing.

And I'll do almost anything to prove to her I'm deserving. I'll burn it all down to make it happen.

"We shouldn't be doing this." She leans her cheek into my lips with need. "Someone might catch us."

I kiss her forehead and slide my lips down the bridge of her nose, cupping her jaw with both my hands as I tip her head up. "Good. Let them catch us." And then I take her lips again, swallowing the tiny whimpering sound she makes and committing it to memory.

I never want to forget this kiss. The feel, the smell,

the sound of rain pattering while Mira whimpers into my mouth. It's one for the record books.

But then her hand slides down my back and disappears under my shirt. The tips of her fingertips trace the top of my boxers, sneaking just beneath the elastic.

This isn't one for the record books.

This *is* the record book.

CHAPTER 16

Mira

I want to grab his ass so bad.

How I went from wanting to get as far away from him as possible to now standing here, soaked, in a field, weighing the merits of grabbing the town bad guy's ass, I'll never know. It's a *great* ass, and I'm already drowning in a dunk tank of poor decision-making, so why the hell not?

I slide a couple fingers in between the buttons of his shirt to draw him closer. My other hand has been tracing the line of his boxers, but now I let my lizard brain take over and push it down between the back of his pants and the smooth fabric of his boxers. When I splay my fingers out and squeeze, he follows suit, fisting my loose hair and giving it a gentle tug. His ensuing chuckle is dark and velvety—thoroughly amused—like he knows I just bit off more than I can chew. I feel it rumble across my lips, and the corresponding shot zings through my core.

Our foreheads rest together as we breathe the same air. Suspended in the moment.

A shiver races down my spine, and he pulls me into a hug, muscular arms wrapping around me like a shield. "You're cold. Let's grab your jacket and get out of here."

"God. I really don't want to go back in there." The thought of facing everyone after pitching a fit and running out of the house feels like too much right now. Plus, I'm awfully comfortable where I am, and as soon as the cold seeps in from where we've spent the last several minutes plastered against each other, so will reality.

And I don't want to face the reality of making out with Stefan Dalca right now.

His hand strokes my back in soothing circles, and I almost want to purr under his ministrations. Because I am now basically a cat in heat.

"I'll go in and get it for you. Let's get you in the car."

When he steps back, I'm cold, just like I knew I would be. The damp air and cool water chill me to my core, and I wrap my arms around myself to conserve the warmth that Stefan's firm body left behind.

I want him to hold me again. It's a bad idea. We both know that it's a bad idea. That's why we walk in silence across the soggy grass toward the driveway. He opens the passenger-side door of his silver SUV, and I crawl into the seat. He doesn't even put his hand on the small of my back, nor should he. But my inner cat-in-heat wants him to. I love the way he touches me so casually. The way his hands linger on my body like I'm a piece of art worth savoring.

Before going to the house, he comes to the driver's side and starts the vehicle. He cranks the heat and shoots me a panty-melting grin before darting back into my parents' white rectangular house. His hand grips the wrought-iron railing on the front steps as he takes every second stair. His pants are wet and tight against his round ass.

I grabbed that ass.

It really is a great ass. And his upper body ain't bad either. Especially with a wet shirt clinging to every indent and hugging his broad shoulders in the most alluring way. I momentarily wish I was his shirt before scrubbing my hands over my face.

What am I doing?

When I drop my hands, I look down at myself and laugh into the quiet vehicle. I thought Stefan's clothes were leaving little to the imagination, but my white eyelet dress looks like a translucent slip. It's suctioned onto my body, and I'm pretty sure I can see my nipples through the fabric. And not because they're still pebbled from the way he devoured me. I thought this dress didn't require a bra, but I didn't account for the wet T-shirt contest we just had.

My head snaps up when the door across from me swings open.

"Got it."

I instantly grab the denim jacket out of Stefan's hand and cover my tits with it. He grins at me knowingly and shoots me a wink.

"Dick," I mutter as I turn to the window.

"What? I'm only human. Am I supposed to complain

about my smoke-show fake date wearing a wet white dress? Because I refuse."

"Yeah. Yeah. Save it for the spank bank, Stefan."

His hand reaches across the back of my seat as he checks behind us before pulling out. "Oh, no doubt." He pushes the stick into drive and smiles. "I imagine you and Mr. Purple will have quite the time tonight."

Dick.

My cheeks heat, and I wish they didn't. I'm accustomed to acting one way around my girlfriends, but coming face-to-face with a man and talking about sex so blatantly is kind of new to me. There are things I want to do, want to try, but I've had such sparse and mediocre sex, I've never found someone I'm comfortable enough to try them with. Basically, my cool, confident exterior is a farce when it comes to that topic.

If I study anything hard enough, I can master it, and that's exactly what I've done. But I'm worried that Stefan is going to call my bluff.

"Are we going to talk about the kiss?"

"Nope."

"Dr. Mira Thorne caught kissing enemy number one in the middle of a field." He tuts me jokingly. "What would the girl gang say?"

I shoot him a dirty look because I don't need him rubbing my nose in that mess. I'll beat myself up about it enough later.

"How was it in there?" I ask as we turn onto the road and head back out to Ruby Creek.

"Fine."

I snort. "Very believable."

"It was. It was as fine as any of them deserve after that episode."

"Ugh. I'm sorry I put you through that."

He shrugs, eyes on the darkening road. "Don't be. I had a good time."

"Ha. No, you didn't."

"I did. Your parents are very welcoming, and I'm pretty sure I love your nana. The food was excellent. And the dessert was even better."

I laugh. I can't help it. He looks so damn pleased with himself.

"You have to understand, Mira," he continues. "The house I was raised in wasn't filled with laughter. I didn't grow up having family gatherings. There weren't relatives who cared about where my life was going. Are yours overbearing? Yup. Out of line? Absolutely. But they all care about you. If they didn't, they wouldn't say anything. I know because that's what I got."

Well, shit. When he puts it like that? "I'm sorry. My family problems must feel very trivial to you."

His hawkish eyes shoot over to me, glinting like emeralds. "Definitely not. Anyone who thinks they can speak that way to you in front of me is in for a rude awakening."

I swallow. For some reason, that sentence sounds very long-term to me. Like there will be future opportunities for someone to speak to me out of line with him in my presence.

"I know my mom loved me," he continues quietly. "She used to sneak into my room in the dead of night and wake me up to talk with her. Partly because that's when he'd be drunk enough to not notice or too asleep to care. It was also because under the cover of darkness, I couldn't see the bruises on her body."

My chest aches at his admission. That feeling where a crack fractures itself right down your sternum. What must that be like? To not have your mom there laughing and making inappropriate sexual jokes while making moon eyes at your dad. When I was younger, I thought it was gross. Now I think it's kind of inspiring.

I want to be making moon eyes at someone after thirty years of marriage.

"It always felt like a special time for us. A time when I could tell her anything while we huddled beneath my duvet. I felt safe with her on those nights. I felt like there were no secrets between us on those nights. It was in those moments she could be the mom I always wanted her to be."

My lashes flutter over full eyes. Stefan is confiding in me right now, and it's pulling at my heartstrings. "That's a beautiful and terribly sad memory all at once."

He laughs, but it's a bitter laugh. "It was." He shakes his head and presses his lips together. "Until she ruined it."

A part of me knows I shouldn't press him on this—it sounds intensely personal. But the scientist in me is constantly solving equations, and Stefan has quickly become the most challenging one of my life. "How did she do that?"

His eyes dart to me, and a look of vulnerability flashes across his face. He looks younger, more human, with a lock of golden hair plastered to his forehead and a pink flush to his sharp cheekbones.

"You don't need to answer tha—"

"No. It's fine. I trust you to not blab my history all over Ruby Creek."

I offer him a firm nod in response.

His chest heaves under the weight of a ragged sigh before he launches in. "He mostly ignored Nadia and me. There were moments when I remember thinking he was kind to us—as kind as someone like him can be. But one day, he turned on me. It had to have been the day it all came out. I don't remember when it started, but I remember the last time it ever happened. My mother threw herself in front of me while I ran out to the barn and hid at the bottom of my horse's stall with my eyes squeezed shut. But not before he broke my nose. And when he found me cowered there, he promised to sell my horse. The stable hands marched the only thing that was truly mine onto a trailer that very day, and he was gone."

Stefan clears his throat and looks out the driver's-side window. "The next day, I packed a bag and started school in Switzerland. I was thirteen."

"Jesus." My hand falls across my mouth. "I didn't know you had a horse."

"He was mostly a pet. But he was *mine*. He was my best friend. My heart horse. My reprieve from my life. I could spend all day out in a field with that horse, pretending I was anyone in the world. A knight, a traveler—the options were endless so long as I didn't have to be a boy stuck in a violent home. On the bad nights, I curled up and slept on the floor of his stall in the small barn we had. When Constantin sold him to teach me a lesson…well, the only lesson I learned was that when a heart breaks, the pain never stops."

It's quiet in the vehicle as I absorb what he just said. I try to imagine a small blond boy sleeping on a stall floor, and in my mind, that boy morphs into the man I've seen over the past couple weeks. The one who will still sleep on a stall floor. The one who will hold my hand on a stall floor.

Stefan speaks again. "So I left at my mother's insistence. I left my baby sister behind in that house. Bandaged nose and suitcase in hand. At that point, it felt like a punishment. It felt like I was unwanted. And I suppose, in a lot of ways, I was. But now I can see it for what it was: a kindness. A way to save me."

His Adam's apple bobs in his throat as he stares out the windshield. I scan his profile, the subtle bump in his nose, and try to imagine him without it but can't.

"She met *him* when she was young and vulnerable. Naive and traveling for the experience of it. He was wealthy and alluring, and I imagine he put on a good show to lure her in. He excelled at manufacturing the perfect facade. She married him quickly. It was a whirlwind romance. She told me in her last hours he seemed wonderful until she signed the wedding contract. She told me…"

Stefan clears his throat, and his fingers pulse on the steering wheel, making the skin around his knuckles whiten.

"She told me she was already pregnant with me when she met him."

"Oh, shit."

He smiles ruefully. "*Oh, shit* is right. He needed a pretty young wife for appearance's sake, and she needed someone to take care of her. Pregnant out of wedlock, uneducated, and from a small town on the other side of the world. She did what she needed to do, I suppose. But it backfired when he found out I wasn't really his."

My god. How fucking sad is this? It sounds almost unreal. Like one of the daytime soap operas I would curl up and watch with my mom when I got home from high school. Stefan was hiding in a stall alone, and I was watching trash TV and laughing with my mom.

The world is a cruel place.

"And she didn't tell me any of this until she was on her deathbed, hooked up to wires and machines. That's actually part of the reason I came back here."

My head tilts. "What is?" I ask as the dark fields whip past us. We're almost home.

"She told me she wished she never left this small town. That she should have stayed and trained racehorses. I don't know… She wasn't making much sense at the end. It was whispers and broken sentences. Maybe I'm on a wild-goose chase." He huffs out a small disbelieving breath. "Just before she died, she told me my biological father used to be the bartender in Ruby Creek."

CHAPTER 17

Mira

"Listen." Nadia's tone is so condescending that I flinch.

I'm jumpy today. I've barely slept for the past two nights. All the coffee in the world hasn't helped—in fact, I'm fairly certain it's making me worse.

"I can't read whatever kind of sign language these dirty looks are," I hear her say. "You're going to have to *talk* to me. Or write it down or something. Wait, let me grab my *crystal ball*."

I shove the swinging door open from the back room to stop her there. Nadia has been excellent her first week. She's a hard worker, a fast learner, and she has just enough of a backbone that the good ol' boy farmers and ranchers in the area don't walk all over her. Doesn't hurt that they're all too busy trying to impress her.

The girl is a looker.

But her charm appears to be lost on Griff. He's glaring at her from beneath his signature black cap. The man can wear a pair of Wranglers and cowboy boots like no one's business, but he's not chatty. He's a different dude, for sure. He trailers his horses to the clinic now and then for some work, spends a few days, and then heads back up to his cabin in the woods.

He's a mountain man recluse personified.

"Griff! Good to see ya. You got those samples we talked about?"

The man just nods at me, places a paper bag on the front desk countertop, and then struts back out the front door like he owns the place.

"Piece of work," Nadia mutters, rolling her brown eyes.

Brown.

It's all I can focus on for a moment. Stefan's eyes are green. Vibrant green. Like emeralds and bright spring grass and like…Hank's.

Fuck me. Now that I've seen it, I can't unsee it. Every time I close my eyes, I compare the two men on the backs of my eyelids. If it weren't for the bump in his nose, Stefan would be a dead ringer for a younger Hank.

Maybe I'm imagining it. No doubt, there have been many a bartender in Ruby Creek. But the horse-racing clue? I don't know. It just seems like too big of a coincidence.

"Do I have something on my face?" Nadia rubs at the corners of her mouth self-consciously.

"No. No. Sorry. Just tired. I zoned out."

"What the hell is wrong with that guy? He walked in here like he's some sort of celebrity, like I should know him.

Wouldn't say a goddamn word. Manners leave something to be desired." She huffs out the last part like she's taking personal offense.

"Griff? He used to live around here."

There are lots of stories about Griffin, none of which I feel are verified enough to share. Small-town gossip can be unnecessarily cruel.

Nadia bristles and mutters, "Still a dick," before turning back to the computer.

She's been an immense help with organizing my schedule and keeping people paid up. It makes my life so much easier, and it doesn't hurt that I enjoy her company. Sometimes, I have to remind myself that she's only nineteen.

Stefan's nineteen-year-old *half* sister. Does she know? Man. I thought my family was fucked up. But my drama is minor league compared to the bomb Stefan dropped on me the other night.

And then there's the kiss.

This is why I keep to myself. Why I don't date. I dip my toe in the shallows, and suddenly I'm flung into the goddamn deep end. I'm at a loss for how to navigate this situation. What I know. My feelings. My body's memory of Stefan owning me the way he did.

I'm fucked up.

"I need to go check on Loki," I blurt out. Nadia looks at me like she doesn't understand why I'm running my schedule past her. "I, uh, won't be back. Can you lock up?"

"Of course." Her pale-gold curls shake with her head like I've asked her to do the most mundane thing in the world.

"Thanks." I grab my favorite brown coat off the hanger and shove my arms through as I head out the front door.

On the drive over to Cascade Acres, I mull over my best plan of action. For both problems: the kiss and what I think I might know.

The kiss needs to never happen again. I'll have to tell him that much. I can't handle it, and it's not fair to get involved with my best friend's nemesis. Perceived or not. Stefan and I can be friends. In secret. And he can be my client in public. That's what I'll offer him.

The next problem is less clear-cut. I could find out his mother's name and ask Hank. But that feels intrusive. He asked me not to share his story with anyone, and I won't betray his trust. I don't want to get his hopes up for nothing because I could be very wrong, and I don't want to drag Hank into something that might be nothing.

I think I just need to ask him more questions. Feel him out. Maybe we can chat in the barn. I'll make coffee, and we can sit on the floor.

I look forward to our barn floor dates. *Meetings?* Barn floor *meetings*.

When I pull through the gates, from the bottom of the hill I see his SUV parked at the house, so that's where I go. My palms slip on the steering wheel as the nerves creep in my stomach. I'm accustomed to having difficult conversations with people. It's part of my job description. But this know-ing-and-keeping-secrets thing is killing me.

Having to keep him at arm's length is killing me too.

I pull up at his sprawling house up on the hill, and right

as I step out of my truck, the front door opens and I'm met with the sight of a tall shapely blond in a tight pencil skirt and expensive heels, leaning in to kiss Stefan on the cheek. My stomach flips and threatens to push itself up my throat.

She's gorgeous. Standing next to Stefan in his expensive clothes, she's the perfect match. My baggy canvas coat and ponytail look downright grubby in comparison. I realize I know nothing about Stephan's dating history. Less than nothing, actually.

But this is perfect because I was drawing a line in the sand. *Right?* And I refuse to be the type of woman who lets this bother her. I'm good enough for him to kiss in a field, but in any other setting, we're completely mismatched.

"Just don't make me drive out to the boonies again. You can come to me next time," the woman says with a genuine smile.

My throat thickens, and my stomach churns. *I really am naive.*

"Thanks, Jules." Stefan chuckles and gives her a wave as she walks down the stairs before his eyes fall on me. "Dr. Thorne." His voice is warm and gooey, and I want to punch him for thinking he can use that tone on me after having another woman over to his house.

And then I want to punch myself for even caring. Maybe it isn't even what I think. Deep down, I have a hard time believing Stefan would do that to me. But I'm just far enough out of my league with him to feel insecure about it anyway.

"Hi. I'll only be a minute." I walk toward the front step and smile as I pass Jules. She smiles back kindly and gives a subtle dip of her chin. I don't have it in me to hate other women, so I tell her exactly what I'm thinking. "Killer shoes." There's one wide buckle across her foot and a matching one that wraps around her delicate ankle in a sensual-looking cuff. They really are hot. If I didn't work in a small town and spend most of my days covered in horse shit, I'd rock the hell out of a pair.

Her perfectly white teeth flash back. "Thanks! Just got them."

I reply with a small thumbs-up and continue my beeline for Stefan while she heads over to her sporty BMW parked around the corner. Of course she drives a BMW.

The sooner I can get this over with and get out of here, the better.

"Come in?"

"No. I can't. I need to check on Loki and then get back to the clinic," I lie.

He nods but can't hide the disappointment that takes over his features for a moment.

"Listen…I don't know how to phrase this gently, so I'm just going to say it. You can't kiss me anymore."

One brow quirks up as his arms cross, and he leans against the doorjamb. "Is that so?"

"It's inappropriate. I shouldn't have let that happen."

His jaw ticks, but he doesn't say anything. He just glares at me. Haunting me with those clear green eyes.

"I'm good with continuing whatever sort of friendship we've forged. But it needs to stay under wraps. And I'll honor my end of the deal. One more date."

"Mm-hmm." He sounds and looks pissed.

"You're not my type. And I'm not yours. And it will be better this way."

God. I'm rambling like an idiot.

"You're not *my* type?" Tension lines his body even though he casually crosses his foot across his shin.

"No."

"And I'm not yours?"

"Exactly." My voice comes out clear and concise despite the fact that I'm rambling inside. This feels *wrong.*

"And I'm not allowed to kiss you?"

"Really glad we cleared this up." I wave my hand with my truck keys and turn to leave.

He projects his voice across the driveway before I can hide in the safety of my truck. "Guess I'll be waiting for *you* to kiss *me* then."

Stefan Dalca is relentless.

The package Stefan had delivered to my apartment for our date tonight essentially gave me two things to do. And I'm not wild about people telling me what to do. Just ask my family.

But when I opened the shoebox, he put me between a rock and a hard place.

I already felt guilty because I didn't tell him my hunch about Hank. Instead, I turned and ran like the chicken I am. I was so unnerved by seeing a woman at his house and by his reaction to me dialing things back between us that my mind went blank. And now it's been a week, and I still haven't said shit.

The guilt is eating me alive.

It just feels like me sticking my nose where it doesn't belong. I'm good at listening, and I hear it all in this job. But I don't run around flapping my gums about it—especially when I don't know something *for sure*. I could hurt many people over an unverified hunch. It's just a hypothesis. I've done no research, and that's what I need to do. Find more information before I make a claim like that.

And then he bought me *the* shoes. The ones the woman leaving his house had on her feet. Hers were a nude color that matched her pretty flaxen hair. But these are black—a perfect match for mine.

I love the buckles. They're gold and chunky and feel so rich next to the soft leather. My inner teenager who wore heavy black eyeliner loves the classy punk style. I have no idea how he knew my size, but they fit perfectly.

A note accompanied the shoes.

Dr. Thorne,

My car will pick you up at 5 p.m. on Saturday to attend the Next Chapter Thoroughbred Rescue Fundraiser. Our final "fake" date. It's a black-tie event. Wear the shoes.

—S

The defiant devil who lives on my shoulder says to send them back.

But I can't.

I'm going to enjoy the shoes. Because the only person I'm punishing by getting rid of them is myself. If I'm taking the shoes, I'm sure as hell not following his instructions to wait around like some sappy lovestruck date. This is *fake*. I'm more than capable of showing up at his place on my own.

So that's what I do. I hop in my truck and drive to Cascade Acres. Do I feel out of place driving my dusty work truck wearing expensive heels and an evening dress? Yes. But it makes me smile. Somehow, I feel very much like myself, a woman of contradictions.

When I arrive at Cascade Acres, heels clicking delicately on the rough concrete alleyway, the staff give me a few funny looks, but they continue with their tasks. It's almost quitting time for them, and I've become a regular fixture around here, so they wave and go about finishing up.

"Hello, little Mister Loki." I swing the stall door open and take in the two chestnut horses. "And you, sweet mama. How are you?"

Farrah bobs her head under my palm when I rub it across her forehead. She really is a sweet mare. And truth be told, I barely need to check on Loki anymore. I want to say he's out of the woods. But it's become part of my schedule. A habit.

What I don't want to admit is that I like coming here. The thrill of running into Stefan has become an addiction. I told him to stay away, and now I'm the one loitering around.

Stefan has stayed out of my way this week. I haven't seen him since that day on his front step when I told him we can't kiss anymore but can continue to be friends. Judging by the way his jaw ticked and his arms crossed over his chest like a shield, he wasn't happy.

But he also didn't seem deterred.

He hasn't been since that first day he asked me out, so I guess I don't know why he'd start now. He's been jokingly asking me out every opportunity he's gotten, and I've laughed and brushed him off. It's a running joke at this point. But it didn't feel like a joke last weekend. It felt like it could be the start of something with the power to knock me right off my track. Right off my wobbly high heels.

It's better this way, even if I secretly listen for his footsteps in the barn every day and my eyes dart up to the house every time I go to leave. I should be happy he's giving me the space I asked for, but I wish he'd go back to being completely relentless.

I think I might miss him.

Which is why the sound of dress shoes clacking against the barn alleyway sets my heart to racing. It doesn't sound like work boots or sneakers. It sounds almost like my heels sounded. I both dread and long coming face-to-face with him tonight.

My poker-face game is strong though. I just need to keep myself in a professional frame of mind, and I should be able to handle whatever Stefan Dalca makes me feel.

I set to work on checking Loki over, keeping my back toward the stall door so I don't have to face him when he gets here. I hear the stall door swing open even though the buds of my stethoscope are in my ears.

He doesn't say anything. I can feel him standing behind me. I can feel his eyes on my body, searing their way over my bare skin. Having him stare at me uninterrupted is unnerving. His presence is heavy. It presses on my chest and threatens to steal my breath.

And my heart.

I somehow count the heartbeats, even with the tall glass of distraction standing behind me. But when I turn to take him in, my mind goes completely blank. He's leaning against the frame of the stall door, hands shoved in the pockets of his bespoke midnight-blue tuxedo, doing that thing he does where his tongue runs across the inside of his cheek. His hair is slicked back perfectly, totally tidy, not a single strand out of place.

But his eyes are chaos. Brambles in the wind. Darker than their usual bright tone.

"You wore the shoes."

His voice is deep and sure—authoritative. Something I like about him. I don't have to be tough and independent around Stefan one hundred percent of the time. He doesn't think less of me for getting tired of being strong all the time. Last weekend in the rain was proof of that. He kissed me senseless and then still treated me like I was perfectly capable and not in need of excessive coddling.

"How could I not? They're beautiful. Thank you."

"At least you're walking through wood shavings and manure in them and showed up here all on your own. I'm not entirely disappointed. I fully expected you to wear a pair of sneakers just to put me in my place. But I still thought you'd maybe wear them one day."

One side of his lips tip up suggestively.

"Ah, yes. For all the fancy events this small-town veterinarian attends."

"Who said anything about an event?" He smirks. And then he winks. *Is he implying what I think he's implying?*

Loki chooses this moment to shove past me. With a small nicker he approaches Stefan and snuggles his head in between his body and his arm and rests there.

"Is he...snuggling you?"

Stefan smiles as he pulls his opposite hand out of his pocket and slides it up and down the young colt's neck. "Horses are an excellent judge of character, didn't you know?"

Loki nuzzles in farther. It's fucking adorable. Especially now that Stefan has confided in me about his horse as a child.

"We've become buddies over the last several weeks. Sometimes I sit out by his paddock with my laptop and work. He's so innocent, you know? My first foray into breeding wasn't exactly a success. I just want to soak this up with him while he's still here."

I swallow audibly. Stefan is so fucking misunderstood. Anger flares in me over how hard on him my friends are. If they could just see this side of him—the one who comes to my defense and snuggles baby horses—I just know they'd see him in a different light. It would be impossible not to.

He looks up just in time to catch me gawking, his eyes glowing in the most captivating way. "You are beautiful, Mira."

I glance down at myself, feeling like I could almost purr at his compliment. The way he looks at me makes my pulse beat in my throat. The wine-red slip-like dress does me an awful lot of favors. Slim-cut silk, it ends midcalf, and the cowl neckline gives me coverage where I need it—over my boobs, since a bra is a no-go in this dress.

I hold my hands over my stomach to still the lurching sensation. "Thank you. You don't look so shabby yourself." Which is to say, he looks fucking edible. Mr. Purple is going to get a hell of a workout tonight. "For a fake date."

His lips thin, and his jaw pops as he steps back from the stall, opening the door to usher me out. With one last pat for mom and baby, I step through the door into the quiet barn. The staff have now cleared out, leaving just the two of us standing facing each other in the stable.

Stefan's eyes coast down my body and pause at the floor. "Your buckle is undone."

I look down at the beautiful new shoes, grateful for the excuse he's just given me to stare at the ground and catch my breath.

"Oh, thanks," I breathe out. I definitely should not be breathless over a man who spent the night with another woman after kissing me the way he did.

"I've got it." With two long steps Stefan is right in front of me, one knee down and reaching for the strap. The sight of him kneeling before me unexpectedly takes my breath away.

His warm hand wraps around my ankle, and I shiver. His movement pauses, but his head stays down. I watch his fingers move deftly, gently tucking the strap back through the gold buckle. When it's back in place, he continues holding my ankle like he's entranced by the sight of my dark-red toenail polish.

But then his hand slides up the back of my calf, and he looks up at me, green eyes boring into mine with so many unsaid words, looking at me like I'm the most incredible thing he's ever seen. So much overflowing emotion.

My lungs seize, and I don't try to stop myself from getting lost in his emerald gaze. The seconds tick by as the pads of his fingers slide along the back of my calf. I feel the softest contact so intensely. The warm hum of electricity races up my inner thigh. I clench my core against the growing heat and roll my lips together to stifle a moan.

With a simple clearing of his throat, he stands, leaving my body begging for him to return his hands to my bare skin.

His fingers encircle my wrist like a bracelet. His lips press against my palm tenderly, and my stomach drops. Like it always does around him. "We should go," he says, letting go of my arm and walking toward the door looking completely unaffected. But me? I still need a few seconds to come back down to earth.

Something between us just shifted. I just can't tell for the life of me what it is or what it means.

All I know is that I wanted his hand on my leg to keep going.

I wanted his lips on my skin.

CHAPTER 18

Stefan

THE LONG RIDE DOWNTOWN TO THE VANCOUVER CLUB, some ritzy private hangout, is filled with tension so thick you can feel it in the town car. My intense attraction to Mira, paired with the lance of agitation I felt when she referred to our date as fake, makes me want to shove her flimsy silky dress up around her waist and bury my face between her legs—driver be damned.

I'd love to ask her how fake we feel after I make her come so hard she can't see straight.

But I won't. I said I'd make her beg. I said I wouldn't kiss her. Despite what she might think of me, I'm a man of my word. An honest man.

So we ride in tense silence on opposite sides of the black leather seat. At one point, the driver turns up the music to fill the space. I'm sure he thinks we're some couple who'd just had it out and hate each other's guts.

Little does he know the tension between us is because we both want to rip each other's clothes off. But Mira is pretending to be completely oblivious to our chemistry. She's smart enough to recognize what's going on between us; she's also masterful at avoiding it.

Maybe after tonight, it will be clearer to her what type of man I really am.

I tip the driver when he pulls up to the old stone building, and he beats me to Mira's door to open it for her. The man smiles at her and scowls at me, like I've been a prick—and I guess I have. Truthfully, I rage-played Mario Kart on my phone the entire way here rather than attempt to make small talk with her.

Mira just stared out the window.

I wish she'd tell me what she's thinking, but I know she's not the type of woman who spills all her deepest thoughts and feelings at the drop of a hat. That's part of what I like about her. She's like a vault, and once I figure out the code, I'll get that side of her.

I could keep her secrets. She could be soft with me. She could let loose with me, and I'd still stand back and let her be the fiercely independent woman she is. I don't want to tame her; I just want a front-row seat to watch her win the race.

She steps out of the car and thanks the driver with a gentle smile. I'm instantly jealous. I want her smiling at me, not ignoring me. I want her looking at me the way she did when I ran my hand up her leg.

I settle for letting my hand fall against the small of her back as we walk up the front steps of the opulent club. A small gasp spills from her lips when I touch her exposed skin. I'm accustomed to doing this when she has a shirt on, not a backless dress. And with nothing between us, my hand tingles and my thumb strokes the dip at the column of her spine of its own volition.

I can't help myself around her.

It's probably too cold outside for what she's wearing, and she presses into my side incrementally. I slide my hand farther, cupping her hip. The dress is so thin I can feel the lace strap of her panties through it.

We enter through the front door into the heritage building and take another small set of stairs toward the ballroom. Creams and golds line the crown moldings on every wall, and tall windows boast red-velvet drapes. Chandeliers drip with crystals and beads. The place screams money.

We stop at the door, and she looks up at me, slightly wide-eyed. Her makeup is heavier than usual tonight. Her hair is silky and shiny, like polished onyx. Whether she realizes it or not, she's the most beautiful woman in the room, and it's not even close.

"Let's go. Might as well enjoy this last fake date. There will be lots of familiar faces." The words are bitter in my mouth, and I try not to let the distaste show on my face.

Mira nods and gazes back into the room. "Then we need to keep a professional distance." I want to protest because I don't give a damn about these people. I want her right here, tucked into my side for everyone to see. But before I can say anything, she steps away, turning heads as she makes a beeline for the bar.

I watch the sway of her rounded hips, the swell of her firm ass, her dainty ankles in those heels. I want them propped up over my shoulders while I slam into her.

I roll my shoulders back and will my growing erection away. Something that's become a constant battle around Dr. Mira Thorne. I come to stand beside her at the bar in the corner, and the steady hum of conversation wraps around us, the quiet clinking of glasses, the odd round of raucous laughter.

People here are trying too hard. Unlike at Mira's family's house, where everyone was exactly how they are—even if that was meddling and overbearing. Every time I attend an event, it's a reminder of why I left this lifestyle behind me. Sure, I put a suit on for race days or for sponsorship meetings for the shelter, but generally, I live in jeans and sweaters so I can tinker around the farm. I feel safe there—like the version of myself I want to be.

Already I feel my youth kicking in. The schmoozing. The wheeling and dealing. The "I'll scratch your back if you scratch mine" chatter. Wealth impresses some people.

But I know better.

I'm here for one thing only. And I can see him across the room telling a story with animated hand gestures to a group of people who are pretending to be interested. A foot shorter than everyone here and a notch or two more obnoxious. The man is a predatory snake in the grass—precisely the type of man I have zero patience for in my life.

He plays checkers.

But I play chess.

A lesson Patrick Cassel is about to learn the hard way.

Mira steps up to the bar when the people ahead of us get their drinks. "I'll have a beer in a champagne flute."

The bartender, his brow knitting together, looks at her like she has two heads.

Her head tilts. "Did I stutter?"

The man jumps into action, shaking his head as he does, like he's offended by her request. A crack of a bottle later and Mira is reaching for her glass with a fake smile.

The bartender turns in my direction. "What can I get you, sir?"

I rub my stubble as I look over the fully stocked bar. "I'll have what the lady's having."

I swear the man rolls his eyes. Mira fails to stifle a giggle, and I find I don't care at all what the bartender thinks when she makes noises like that. When my eyes dart to her, amusement is written all over her face.

"Very classy, Mr. Dalca."

"I guess that makes two of us, Dr. Thorne."

I wink at her, and she can't help but smile as she looks around the packed room, taking in the women in fancy dresses and men in tuxedos, not missing a single thing.

"Lots of people I know here."

"Figured as much." I grab the glass off the bar and toss a tip down before taking a sip of my beer.

"It's kind of funny," Mira begins, though she doesn't look very amused. "There are several people here who aren't all that great to their horses. In fact, I'd say they're part of the problem with this industry. The reason so many young thoroughbreds end up injured and unusable. And yet here they are, opening their checkbooks like it absolves them of that responsibility."

She sounds so fierce. She isn't wrong. There is no shortage of questionable people in this industry.

"You must get tired of seeing that."

She takes a quick swig of her drink, chocolate eyes dancing with intelligence. "You have no idea." But now she's staring at Patrick across the room. For such a small man, he sure can project his voice.

I wrap my arm back around her, wanting to feel the line of her panties again, and usher her out into the crowd. My index finger absently slides across the thin strap. *Good god.* These panties must be barely anything at all.

When I rub down the line again, unable to stop myself, she leans into me. "Hands off. I'm not interested in joining your rotation."

She looks smug, but I'm downright confused.

"My rotation?"

She scoffs. "You know. Me on Saturday nights. The hot blond on Sunday nights."

"Hot blond?" I stop us in our tracks and, with a firm grip, spin her to face me.

Her eyes roll. "The one with the shoes." She points down at her feet. "Who was leaving on Monday morning?"

Her eyes dart behind me, and I turn to look at what she's signaling toward. Juliette Monroe. If Mira's assumption wasn't so absurd, I would laugh out loud. I stare back down at her fierce face. "Jules is my *lawyer.*"

"Your…lawyer." She takes a huge swig of her beer and shakes her head as she looks out across the room. "You fucking idiot," she whispers to herself as her cheeks flare to match her dress. Although part of me wants to laugh, the other part wants to shake her.

I step in close to clear a few things up about us. About me and my intentions where she's concerned, but I'm cut off by one of the most annoying voices in the world.

"Well, well, well. Look what the cat dragged in. How's the offseason treating you, Dalca?"

I take a deep breath, eyes flitting to Mira's. She looks uncertain, but now it's go time. I turn and take one step ahead of her, trying to keep Patrick as far away from her as possible.

I smile, but it doesn't touch my eyes. This is the face I mastered as a child. "Patrick. Life is good. How are you?"

Patrick grins. His teeth are too white, and his hair too greasy. I can't for the life of me remember why I hired him. A winning record, I guess. *Too winning.* I've beat myself up about that enough.

Now I know what kind of man Patrick is, and I have no intention of letting him get away with it.

"Just great. Living the dream. Riding much nicer horses than yours these days. Guys like us always land on our feet. You bangin' the vet now?" He nods at Mira and grins at me, like he's begging for me to give him a nosebleed the old-fashioned way. A nice bump to match my own.

Mira moves beside me, her face calm and her head tilted at him like she's sizing him up and finds him entirely lacking.

Condescension drips off her in waves. "Did you know that I can castrate a pig just as easily as a horse, Patrick? Even a little one like you."

Now there's something I'd like to see. I glance behind myself at where I saw Jules chatting someone up before. She's already looking in my direction and nods once.

I smile, except this time it's real. I'm going to enjoy this.

"Who are *guys like us*, Patrick?"

He chuckles like I'm being intentionally obtuse, but the truth is I hate the idea of being lumped with men like Patrick. It makes my skin crawl.

I roll my shoulders back and tug at the cuff links on my shirt before staring down my nose at the man. "I've often thought the best way to judge a man is by his actions rather than his words." Patrick's eyebrows knit together as people around us start to watch. "You talk like you've got it all. But the fact of the matter is you harass women with unwanted advances and drug horses to keep yourself in the winner's circle." His face goes white, and Mira's head snaps toward me.

Hushed murmurs break out around us. These people thrive on drama, and I'm about to feed the beast.

"Get a grip, Dalca." His tone goes frigid, and his watery eyes narrow, taking on a vicious facial expression.

"You're a disease, Patrick. A blight. And I've got all the documentation to prove it." A couple of officers appear from a back hallway. Just how Jules and I planned it. "You drug my horses, you face the music."

Patrick sputters but is cut off by the officer stepping in front of him. "Patrick Cassel?"

191

The officer explains the situation to him, reading his rights, suggesting an attorney. Probably a good plan. I'm going to love wasting my stepfather's money on burying this rat.

Patrick looks grim. White as a sheet. And then spitting mad when he meets my eyes. "This isn't over, Dalca."

"I trust it's not." I slide my hands into my pockets and smirk. "I'm just getting started with ruining you."

Patrick turns beet red as the officers lead him away in a shiny set of cuffs. They suit him so well.

"Unbelievable," Mira murmurs, mouth hanging open. "I was right?" She places her drink on a tall cocktail table and walks after him toward a darkened hallway at the back of the ballroom. A neon emergency exit sign lights the door at the very end of it. She looks stunned, entranced.

"You going to go to the station with him?" I joke. "Never took you for a rubbernecker."

"Are you kidding me?" She keeps walking down the hall, head craned to listen to the excuses falling from Patrick's twisted tongue. "You think I signed up for blood and gore as a career without being a rubbernecker? This is too fucking good. You don't even know how hard I'm trying to refrain from pulling my phone out to record. This is *gold*. I want to remember this night for the rest of my life. Best date ever."

When the door slams shut behind them, she flops against the wall with a satisfied sigh. And I don't miss that she didn't call it a *fake* date this time. "How did you pull this off?"

I smirk and puff my chest out, feeling proud of myself for how smoothly that went off. "The day you told me your suspicions, I had another vet draw blood from each horse I had living down at Bell Point Park. When they came back positive for performance-enhancing steroids, I hired a PI to find me the proof."

"Why didn't you have me do the tests? I could have helped!"

"Because I needed to have an impartial third party do the testing. You're too connected to Patrick to stand up in court. No chance was I getting you embroiled in this."

She rolls her eyes. "How honorable."

I take a step closer to her, knowing we're perfectly obscured at the very end of a dark hallway. "You know I'm right."

Mira looks at me, her eyes clear, with something like wonder painted on her face. "I think I might have been wrong about you. I think everyone might be."

Her head tilts back to keep eye contact as I take another step, leaving only a few inches between the tips of our toes.

"I think you've been wrong about me on a few counts, Dr. Thorne." I place one hand against the wall on each side of her, effectively caging her in. "The only reason my lawyer has been around so much is because she helped me organize this whole show."

"Oh." She breathes out.

"Yes, *oh*. But I do rather enjoy your jealous side. Do you think I've been asking you to let me take you on a date for the past several months just so I could pursue another woman after finally tasting your lips? Do you think I'd give up that easily?"

"No, I thought you were teasing me. I thought it was all a big joke. A game."

I lean down to whisper in her ear. "Absolutely nothing about the way I feel for you is a joke. And I'll keep telling you that until you believe me."

Her breathing quickens, and the silk covering her voluptuous breasts heaves beneath the weight of her gasp.

I lift my index finger and trace the spaghetti strap where it caresses her collarbone. "I'm just very, very patient. I know what I want, and I'm willing to wait for it. I don't mind biding my time until you catch up." My finger slides over the crest of her shoulder, and I feel her warm breath against my jaw as she tips her chin to follow. She's watching my every move, her eyes locked onto my finger. "It's a shame I'm not allowed to kiss you anymore. Because you look positively edible right now, Mira."

With one quick grab, her fingers twist into my dress shirt, and she yanks me toward her. Free hand wrapped around the back of my neck, she pulls my face to hers and kisses me with so much longing that my stomach drops.

The kiss isn't frantic. It's hard, and her mouth clamps onto mine like she's trying to steal my soul. It almost feels like an apology.

Apology accepted.

I use my tongue to trace the seam of her lips, and she moans. Her mouth falls open, and our tongues meet instantly. She jerks me closer still, and I revel in it. The event hums at the opposite end of the dim hallway, but here in the shadows, I feel like we're in our own little world.

Just the two of us.

Her soft breasts press against my chest, and I imagine sliding my dick between them one day, watching her round eyes go wide while her tits glisten. I let my hands trail down over them, featherlight. A tease. Her nipples harden through the thin silk while her soft lips move against mine.

Nothing about this feels fake. Our bodies. Our minds. Our hearts. Absolutely everything about being with Mira feels like one of the most real things I've ever had in my life. And I won't let her slip between my fingers now.

I'm going to make her come on them instead.

I pull away to nip at the lobe of her ear, and she whimpers in protest. "Do you remember what I said I was going to do to you if I had you up against a wall, Dr. Thorne?"

"What?" Her voice is pure lust, almost slurred.

"I told you that you'd be the meal."

CHAPTER 19

Mira

ALL THE AIR EMPTIES FROM MY LUNGS. THE SOUND OF MY ragged exhale rushes through my ears, blocking out the sound of polite conversation and classical music playing in the ballroom. Stefan is smirking at me, like he knows something I don't.

And for the first time in my life, I think that might be true.

I wrack my brain, trying to think of the first time he asked me on a date. It's been so long that I can't even remember. It's become an ongoing part of our relationship, comic relief for the awkward tension that comes with doing work for my best friend's enemy.

Unprofessional? Maybe. Necessary icebreaker? Definitely.

I don't know why it never occurred to me that it might have been real. The way he looks at me. The way he touches me. The way he defends me. And now every interaction between us is hitting me upside the head like an awkward teenager with a dodgeball she never saw coming.

I've been dodging and deflecting for *years*, only to find out I was playing the wrong goddamn game all along.

The heat of Stefan's lips moves against my neck. Goose bumps spread across my arms, and I squeeze my thighs together.

"What do you say, Mira? Are you going to give me a taste? Would you like that?"

His mouth moves down over my sternum, a quick nip at the top of one breast before he crouches. My mouth dries at the sight of this perfect man working his way down my body. I usually have a quick quip or snarky comment at the ready, but right now, all the blood has rushed away from my brain to somewhere between my legs.

Every reason not to do this grows wings and flies right down the hallway.

"Yes," I say, throwing caution to the wind.

His teeth find my nipple through the thin silk of my dress, biting down gently before sucking, and a moan erupts from my throat.

"Quiet, Kitten," he murmurs, dropping to one knee. "I don't want to be interrupted."

My chin falls to my chest just as his second knee hits the ground. "Right here?"

He presses a firm kiss to my stomach before dragging his teeth across my hip bone. "I think I've waited long enough, don't you?"

My clit aches, and I buck my hips toward him. Stefan Dalca is kneeling before me, hands on my thighs, still looking so proud and polished—but just a bit undone. He yearns for me. I see it in his eyes. He does nothing to conceal his longing. And that feeling must be contagious. Or maybe seeing this man on his knees for me twice in one night is just too much to take.

"What if someone walks down here?"

He reaches forward playfully and undoes the buckle on my ankle. "Oh, look at that. Your shoe needs fixing. *Again.*"

Biting down on my lip, I check down the hallway one last time. We're fairly hidden here. And I'm already not feeling like myself tonight. My concern for the consequences slips away as I murmur, "Yeah, fuck waiting." And then I gather the silk of my dress in my hands, like I can't get it lifted fast enough.

And it must not be quick enough for Stefan either because he lifts what's left and disappears beneath a curtain of red fabric. Immediately, he pulls one leg over his shoulder and wraps his strong arm around it to pin me in place against the wall. His face is so close to my pussy that I feel the dampness of his breath against the front of my panties as his teeth graze my inner thigh. He clamps down, taking a quick bite that borders on painful but mostly drives me to tip my hips toward him again.

"That's what you get for making me wait so long."

"I'm sorry" spills from my lips, and I don't even care how out of character the words are for me. All I want is for him to keep going.

His spare hand trails up my thigh, and his deep chuckle vibrates across my core. "No, I'm sorry."

"For what?" I pant.

"For this." His top hand grips the waistband of my skimpy lace thong, and the other one reaches right toward the damp strip of fabric and pulls down. Hard.

The sound of my panties tearing echoes through the hallway, followed by my startled gasp.

"What the f—" The scolding dies on parted lips because Stefan doesn't waste any time putting his mouth on me. My head tips back against the wall, and the ceiling opens up in blackness and bright stars.

I'm officially having an out-of-body experience.

He starts slowly, keeping his tongue wide as he laps at me. There's no protecting myself from him with one leg slung over his shoulder. Every nerve ending fires, and I moan loudly before clamping one hand over my mouth and dropping the other onto the back of his head. Even the silk of my dress in my palm feels sensual. A match for the feel of his tongue sliding across my pussy.

"Delicious," he murmurs before gently nipping at one lip.

"Oh my god." My palm muffles my voice, and my eyes flutter shut at the feel of his lips and tongue and teeth between my legs.

He's a master, and I'm so far gone that my wanton hips keep swiveling, riding his face. All I can think about is how good this feels and how I don't want it to stop.

Which is right when he pulls away and trails his thumb

over my seam with an appreciative groan. He presses down on my clit with firm, even pressure, and suddenly, all I want is to see his face. I pull my skirt the rest of the way up, grasping it at my hip, and watch Stefan's green eyes staring at me greedily. His fingers press into my thigh hard enough they might leave marks, while his opposite hand plays with my pussy like it's his to use as he sees fit.

I feel the heat from my cheeks clawing its way down my throat and across my chest.

His hair is disheveled, and his lips are glistening when he asks, "Are you always this wet for me, Mira?"

Good god. I don't think I've ever hooked up with someone so talkative. Maybe that's why every hookup so far has sucked. Maybe that's why I'm soaked.

"I don't think I've *ever* been this wet for *anyone*," I whisper back.

One side of Stefan's mouth tips up seductively as his thumb slides over to spread me open. He liked that answer.

Part of me wants to crumble because no one has ever looked at me like Stefan. So closely. But the other part of me wants to open my legs wider and give him all the access he wants. He doesn't give me time to think about it. His head tips down, and two fingers glide inside me.

"Fuck." My voice doesn't even sound like my own.

With Stefan's lips on me, I feel like a completely different woman. I feel like the woman I pretend to be, free of nerves and shyness. With his hands on me, I come alive, like I'm soaking up every spark that sizzles between us.

And right now, riding his fingers while he tortures me with his tongue, there is no shortage of sparks.

A familiar tugging sensation takes root at the base of my spine, and my legs shake. His fingers slide in and out of me rhythmically as his tongue works circles around my clit.

"Stefan," I whisper. "Stefan…I'm going to—"

He looks up at me abruptly and presses his thumb down over the bundle of nerves where his tongue had been. "Come for me, Mira."

One quick circle with his thumb and I'm gone. All the tension between us snaps as my orgasm overtakes me in a wave that crashes over my body. Stefan watches me. His fingers continue to torture me, but his eyes scour my face, my body, my every movement.

It's unsettling the way he's looking at me with so much pleasure. Like my climax was just as enjoyable for him as it was for me.

Shyness overtakes me, and I throw one arm over my face. My other arm hangs limp beside me, my dress still twisted between my fingers. "Stop staring at me!" I half laugh. I sound out of breath.

"I can't," he growls. Butterflies swarm my stomach as he leans forward and presses a soft kiss to my aching core, sending aftershocks through my body.

This man is going to be the death of me.

His fingers soften on my thigh and stroke soothingly before he removes it from his shoulder and leans away. His hand closes around my fisted one, softly, loosening my grip so the fabric falls back over my bare thighs and ripped panties.

"You owe me a pair of panties."

"I'll buy you an entire shipping container of them if it means I get to keep ripping them off you."

I roll my eyes and laugh. The nerves, the tension, it all leaves me in a girlish giggle. A sound I'm almost certain I've never made. "Maybe."

"Maybe?" He smooths the silk back down over my thighs and straightens my dress from where he still kneels before me.

"I mean, I guess I see what all the fuss is about now."

He rises, towering over me like usual, looking concerned. "Have you never had a man do that for you?"

My lips roll together, and my cheeks heat. He just put his mouth on the most personal part of my body, and I can barely look him in the eye or talk about sex like a normal adult. "No. No, I have. It was always just *okay*. Awkward. Even sex. You know? Not a lot of it. Here and there. I tried hard to love it. But it just always felt okay. Mechanical maybe. Just not that exciting. Kind of boring."

Fuck, I'm totally doing an awkward ramble. He killed my brain cells like I knew he would.

His serious face slowly morphs into a cocky, panty-melting smile, and my words die in my throat as my eyes go wide. He looks almost predatory with that grin on his face. He leans in and kisses me slowly, softly, expertly. And I melt into him. I can taste myself on his lips, and it wakes something primal in me. When he pulls away, I try to move closer for more, but he chuckles and presses his lips to the shell of my ear.

"Boring? Dr. Thorne, haven't you learned by now that I love a challenge?"

No, it has definitely never been like this before.

"Let's get out of here." I grab his hand and tug him toward the emergency exit.

"What? You don't feel like networking out there?" His voice is thick with amusement and something more seductive.

"Do you?"

"No." He comes to stand beside me and drops his hand to the small of my back like he always does. I clench at the feel. It drove me to distraction before, and now it just straight up makes me crazy.

"Did I mention that this is a good look for you?" He chuckles and snaps the elastic waistband against my skin before leaning back to get a good look. The scraps of my ruined panties have apparently ridden up so they butt up against his hand. With a low growl, he tucks them back down and gives my ass a squeeze.

Perv.

I smile anyway. Reveling in his admiration.

"The only reason I brought you here tonight was so you could watch Patrick take a tumble off his glass throne."

A small laugh bubbles up out of me as we take the stairs down with a sense of urgency I can't explain. "How thoughtful of you to include me in your scheme."

"I've told you before...I'm not the villain you think I am."

"Or maybe you're exactly who I think you are and I like it."

His eyes sparkle and his grin turns wolfish as we hit the bottom landing and push out into the cool night air. "Maybe."

With our fingers intertwined, we search the pull-through for our town car. Something I can say I've honestly never done. Yellow taxi? Uber? For sure. Personal driver? It's kind of weird.

Especially when we find him and get in the car. Things between us were so tense before that the guy is shooting me skeptical looks through his rearview mirror, like he's worried about me—or my sanity.

I guess I can't blame him. We left the event early, and now I'm wedged up against Stefan in the middle seat rather than leaned against the opposite door staring out the window while he played Mario Kart. Yeah, I saw that. And he's fucking terrible. He obviously needed the practice, so I just left him to it so I could disappear inside my head for a bit.

We speed through the dark city, lights a blur outside the window. Twists and turns and bridges pass us by, but all I can feel are Stefan's fingers combing through my hair. His firm thigh pressed tight and warm against mine. The side of my breast against his suit jacket and the sticky remnants of our torrid hookup in that hallway between my legs.

The drive back to Ruby Creek is far too long for what I'm feeling right now. I thought it would cool the heat simmering in my veins. I thought I might come to my senses and change my mind about hooking up with my best friend's enemy, but the closer to home we get, the less in control I feel.

I drape my hand over his knee, fingers twirling nervously.

If I could wish away all the fabric between us, I would. I want his skin on mine. His shoulders over me. His hands gripping my hips. I've never been so physically worked up over a person in my life.

Without even thinking of it, my hand glides up his inner thigh. My body knows exactly where it wants to go—where I want to be. The tips of my fingers trace the inner seam of his slacks. I can feel the hem of his boxer briefs beneath the expensive fabric, and I can totally understand how he felt the need to rip my panties the way he did.

How have I gone so long without realizing we weren't just business associates? It's so on-brand for me, immersed in books and work and taking care of everyone that I missed something just for myself.

No more. I deserve fun in my life too.

"Mira." Stefan's hushed voice is gravelly as his lips move against my hair. "If you don't watch that hand, I'm going to pull you onto my lap and fuck you right here in this car."

My lips part, and I suck in a harsh breath. I don't think I've ever heard him swear before, and I didn't expect it to make me instantly wet when he did. I peek down and am met with the impressive outline of his cock pressing against the front of his pants.

I'm definitely not going to be bored when Stefan Dalca finally fucks me.

CHAPTER 20

Stefan

MIRA IS DRIVING ME ABSOLUTELY INSANE TRAILING HER FINGERS up my leg.

The fields hurtling past the window of the town car are dark, and if we didn't have company, I'm pretty sure my inner caveman would come out to play and I'd take her on the spot. But I promised her I wouldn't fuck her unless she begged, and that's a promise I intend to keep.

"My place or yours?" I murmur against her hair. I can't stop touching it, so soft and thick.

"What about Nadia?"

"She told me she'd be out for the night, so she won't be able to hear you screaming while you ride my cock later." Her fingers pulse at my words. I love how flustered she gets when I say things like that.

"What if she comes home? She's my employee."

"Okay, then. Your place."

"We can't go to my place."

My muscles tense. "Why not?"

She shifts in her seat, shimmying her shoulders more upright rather than leaned in against me.

"It just doesn't seem right. What if someone sees you there?"

My eyes narrow. "Yes, how embarrassing for you."

She turns her wide chocolate eyes on me with a grimace. "I just don't know if I'm ready for that."

The practical part of me knows what she's saying is rational, and I'm not here to coerce her into sleeping with me. But the unwanted little boy who lives inside me feels a bit different about that sentiment. It feels like she's embarrassed. Like I'm a dirty little secret—and I don't like that.

Following suit, I straighten up and lean away. "Okay. Of course."

"I'm sorry," she whispers, turmoil flickering in her eyes.

I smile at her and weave our fingers together the way she did that night on the floor of a dirty stall. "Never be sorry for setting your own boundaries."

She nods and rests her head against my shoulder. "Thank you."

"For what?"

"For the best date of my life."

My chest warms, and I lean into her again, pressing a kiss against the top of her head as we pull in between the large gates at Cascade Acres.

"Just pull up next to that truck there. I'll walk up to the house."

The driver nods and does as I ask with a quiet "Yes, sir."

This time I beat him out of the car to open Mira's door for her. I feel like a dork for how quickly I rounded the car, but I'm not letting this guy get his hands on her a second time. His sneaky looks through the rearview mirror happened just a few *too* many times on the drive to be merely coincidental. I'm not an idiot. I'm familiar with what's running through his head. I almost told him to keep his goddamn eyes on the road. A surge of possessiveness overtook me that signals how royally fucked I am where Mira Thorne is concerned.

Mira slips her hand into mine as she steps out of the black town car, and keeping her tucked close, I walk her toward her truck. She looks hilariously dainty and dolled up to be stepping into such a beast of a vehicle, but Mira is full of contradictions.

I don't want the night to end here—it feels unresolved—but I also know she doesn't need a man clinging on to her with a death grip. The crunching of tires on gravel filters in from behind us as the town car pulls away into the darkness. The floodlights on the barn are the only reason we can see anything as the clock nears midnight. Ambient light isn't a thing in Ruby Creek.

I look up at the sky while Mira digs through her small purse to find her keys. Every star is so bright against the blackness of the night, the constellations so clear, it almost feels like I could reach up and touch them. When Mira catches me staring at the sky, her head tips back, and I watch the ethereal shadows play across her features.

"Beautiful," she murmurs.

"Very," I say back. Except I'm not looking at the sky anymore. I'm looking at her, visually tracing the elegant slope of her throat. Her deep eyes, her full lips, and her glowing skin. She's downright enchanting. I've always thought so, but spending this much time with her and Loki has tossed me into turbulent waters I didn't see coming. I'm completely adrift with Mira. About to drown in her. And I'm not sure I have enough of a survival instinct to save myself. I'm not sure I want to.

I'm thinking I might be more than just enchanted with her.

My dick twitches, and I shake my head at myself. I've got a date with my palm in T minus about five minutes.

She smiles at me now. I used to think it was a smirk, like there was something high and mighty about her smile, but now I recognize it as a defense. A facade.

I lean forward and kiss her cheek. "Thank you for the best fake date of my entire life," I say before winking and shoving my wandering hands into my pockets. Then I turn and take a quiet stroll up the driveway to my big empty house before I turn into the one begging her to give me a chance.

Still, I refuse to be dissuaded. I can handle hurt feelings, but I'm not easily deterred.

I know she's worth it.

CHAPTER 21

Mira

I AM STUNNED.

Did he seriously just call what happened between us tonight a *fake date* and then walk away like it was nothing? After I said it was the best *date* ever?

Fuck him.

His head shoved between my legs definitely did not feel fake. That line has been crossed. That line has been absolutely wiped off the playing board. And him lobbing that term at me like a grenade stung.

It stung worse than it should have.

I slam my truck door shut and fire it up. I need to get out of here before I kill someone. There are too many things in this truck I could use to commit a crime. And Stefan is far too close and unsuspecting to escape.

It's hard to make me angry. But when I do finally get there, I find it hard to come back down. My hands shake as

I wrap my fingers around the steering wheel. Through the window, I can see his dark figure swaggering up the driveway to his McMansion.

Looking completely unaffected, I might add.

Fucking prick.

Here I sit barely able to contain my rage, and he's all calm and polite. And I hate it. I feel like a fool, and I especially hate that.

I hit the gas and peel out of the driveway, sneaking one final peek before I turn out onto the road, and I swear his shoulders droop, his head tips forward. I'm not sure he meant for me to see that change in body language. Or the smirk slipping off his face.

But I did.

On the way home, my mind keeps wandering back to the sight of Stefan walking up the sloped driveway, the way his proud shoulders fell. The way he stiffened beside me when I said we couldn't go back to my place. The way he asked if he embarrassed me.

The ranch's circle driveway comes into view, and then it hits me.

I hurt him.

So he went on the defensive. And in his attempt to protect himself, he pissed me off too. All because we're both treading so damn carefully around each other, trying to keep things *fake* when they clearly aren't anymore.

For two smart people, we sure can be stupid.

He sure can be stupid. Too polite. Too patient. Too fucking perfect. It's annoying.

I take one loop around the driveway at the ranch and drive right back out into the dark. The back roads between Cascade Acres and Gold Rush Ranch aren't well lit, but I've been driving them so much over the last month that I feel like I could probably do it with my eyes closed. I speed. My lead foot presses against the gas like my heart thunders against my ribs as I pass through his front gates. This time, I drive right past his barn and straight up to his house. I jump out and pound my fist on his stately front door. It's cold now, but my adrenaline is pumping so hard I don't feel it.

The door doesn't open fast enough, so I bang on it again. I'm about to slam my palm down on it impatiently when all I'm met with is air. The door swings open, and Stefan stands there, brows knit together with a frown on his lips. He's so fucking hot I almost can't handle it. His cheeks are flushed, and his shirt is untucked. I almost just straight up maul him—but first I have some things I need to get off my chest.

His mouth opens to say something, but I cut him off. "You know what? Fuck you." His brows shoot up, and he rears back. "That date was not fake, and we both know it. So fuck you for saying that."

I'm worked up, and my chest rises and falls heavily. "And also fuck you for walking away like a perfect gentleman. Weeks of blatant sexual promises, and you walk away? You should have bent me over the hood of my truck and fucked me on the spot." I watch his bright-green eyes go dark. "Stop treating me like you'll break me. If I wanted someone to court me and bore me to death, I wouldn't be wasting all my free time with you." I stomp my heel-clad foot and feel completely juvenile as I demand, "Stop dicking around and show me what you've been promising."

His eyes roam the full length of my body, licking over me like a flame. And he definitely doesn't look confused now. He looks like he might incinerate me on the spot.

Stefan crosses his arms over his chest. "Is that your idea of begging, Dr. Thorne? Why would I sign up to be your dirty little secret?"

My tongue darts out over my lips. "You won't be."

His head quirks. "Doesn't seem that way to me. I thought I wasn't your type," he spits out, betraying his otherwise unaffected persona.

"Okay. You're mad."

His gaze flits between my eyes and my mouth. "I'm not mad. I'm…too invested."

The words hit me like a battering ram to the chest. "I'm sorry."

"Stop apologizing." His head shakes. "It's unnecessary."

I step forward. "I'm sorry I made you feel that way."

His jaw ticks, but he doesn't move, continuing to stand in the doorway like a sentinel.

"I'm sorry I took so long to figure this out."

I take another step, unable to resist his appeal. I've been moving toward him slowly this entire time. Since the first time I laid eyes on Stefan, I've been in his orbit. And suddenly, the pull is more than I can bear.

Right now, he's too close, and I'm too weak.

"I'm sorry you're too invested."

He grunts as I move into the entryway of his house. Mere

inches separate us now. My teeth dig into my bottom lip as I weigh my next words. My fingers itch to touch him, and I follow their lead, reaching up under the tails of his dress shirt to his hastily buttoned slacks. The zipper is still open, and there's no doubt in my mind what I interrupted him doing by charging back up here.

I pop the button open and slide my hand down over his firm stomach and the front of his tight boxers where I can feel the swell of his rock-hard cock. "But not that sorry." I squeeze and feel my cheeks heat when he jumps. I meet his eyes now, but they give away nothing. He put himself on the line, and I turned him away, so I guess it's my turn to make it up to him. "Because I'm a little too invested myself."

I drop to my knees, feeling the smooth hardwood and the silk of my dress beneath them. "Let me show you."

With one firm tug, his pants and boxers slide down around his legs, and his dick springs free, bobbing in front of me.

"Mira. Get up," he growls.

"No." I palm his bare length, relishing the feel of his smooth skin against my hand. "I'm not done apologizing yet."

"I told you to stop apologizing."

I stare at him from beneath my lashes, feeling a strange type of power coursing through me as I kneel before him. *Is this how he felt on his knees for me?* Because all I want is for him to be thrusting into my mouth and whispering my name.

With one hand on each of his toned thighs, I let my tongue graze the drop of arousal glistening on the tip of his cock. He groans and tips his head back.

"Should I stop?" I ask with feigned innocence.

One broad palm strokes my head as he stares down at me. The night air is cool against my back through the open door, but the energy between us runs hot, crackling with electricity.

"No." His voice is so raspy, I almost don't hear his simple response.

But with that one word, I pounce, opening my jaw wide and taking him into my mouth. My tongue swirls and my cheeks hollow out as I suck. Stefan's hand is gentle against my hair while I bob in front of him, hoping to show him with my mouth how real this is. How badly I want this.

How badly I want *him*.

My hands roam his body. Fingers tracing the defined lines of his abs before reaching behind him to squeeze his ass. The ass I've been staring at far too much.

As I increase my pace, his fingers tangle in my hair, and his opposite hand scoops up my loose hair in a fist.

"Hard to have a good view of your apology with all this hair in the way, Mira." His fingers tense, tugging lightly at the roots, and my core vibrates.

I hum in pleasure at his corresponding moan. I tilt my head back and peer up into his eyes through my thick lashes, feeling his length bump up against the back of my throat and gagging slightly as I do. Heat flashes in his green irises, and I brace my palms against his thighs again before going soft in his hands.

He must feel the shift because he takes over, fingers gripping my hair to move my head in a rhythm that suits him, and I submit, loving the feel of him taking charge.

And excited about the way my body tingles, the way my dress feels too restrictive. Excited about the open door behind us—the thought that anyone could pull up to his house and catch me on my knees with his dick in my mouth.

Excited in a way I've never been until tonight.

His stomach and the loose ends of his dress shirt bump against my nose as he pumps into me, and my jaw aches in the most delicious way.

"You are so fucking beautiful, Mira. Down on your knees for me. Dark-red lips wrapped around my cock." I moan on his length, feeling myself melt for him, practically purring at the compliment and how undone he sounds. His fingers tug my head back, forcing me to look into his eyes. "But this is no apology." His eyes dance between mine as he stills in my mouth and brushes my cheek with his thumb. "This isn't even you begging. This is just you taking what you want." He leans forward, and his voice goes quiet. "This is instinct. This is *real*. And *you* want *me*."

I blink a couple times but don't make a move. *I want him so badly.*

"I guess you're a lucky girl because I want you too. I have since the first day I laid eyes on you."

And then he moves, hips thrusting between my lips as his deft fingers cup the back of my head. My fist wraps around the base of his cock, and my opposite hand cups his balls, squeezing gently as we move together.

I press my knees down onto the floor, really leaning into him, wanting him deeper, even though it borders on feeling like too much. Too overwhelming. Like pretty much every-thing about Stefan Dalca already is.

His movements turn frantic, and within moments, he says, "Mira, I'm going to come." He tries to pull away, but I clamp a hand down on his ass and pull him closer. No chance is he pulling out now.

"Jesus Christ," he grunts, and then, with one hard jerk, he throws his head back and spills himself into my mouth. I feel every twitch, hear every garbled moan as he holds my head close to his body, and all it does is wind me up more. Is this what he felt like after what happened in that dark hallway?

Because this is addictive. Blow jobs have always felt like a chore, but that one felt like a drug.

I pull away and stare at his cock, feeling mindless with lust. "I want to do that again," I say without even thinking about it. I *need* to do it again.

The familiar sound of Stefan's responding chuckle makes my chest pinch as my gaze flits up to his face.

In one smooth movement, he drops to his knees, meet-ing my eyes and cupping my jaw lovingly. "No. Now it's my turn to take what I want."

He reaches behind me and slams the front door shut. The click of the latch sends a shiver down my spine.

It's the sound of going all in on whatever this thing is between us.

CHAPTER 22

Stefan

BEING ALONE TOGETHER IN A QUIET HOUSE, WITH NO PRE-tense of work separating us, feels intensely intimate. Mira's eyes widen slightly when the door slams shut. We're on our knees facing each other, and it's like she just realized she's in for one very long night. Sex has been boring for her?

Challenge fucking accepted.

I drop my mouth onto her puffy lips and kiss her. I taste myself, and I don't even care. It makes me feel like she's mine. I want her smelling like me, tasting like me, and looking at me with those round saucer eyes while I move inside her. I want her to be *mine*. Period.

The way she looks constantly surprised by our chemistry is such a turn-on. I hope she never stops looking at me like that.

Shocked awe. Lips slightly parted. Cheeks stained a pretty pink.

Her mouth moves against mine as our tongues tangle, and I slide one hand down over her ribs to where the dainty zipper holds her dress closed. I was happy to rip the panties, but this backless dress is going to make more appearances in our life. I'll find fancy places to take her just so she keeps wearing it.

Because she and I? We're just getting started.

Mira's fingers move against the buttons down the front of my shirt as we both undress each other. When I tug the dress off her shoulders, I lean back to get a better look. I always knew she had incredible tits, but seeing them bare right in front of me is a gift.

"Fuck," I murmur, tracing the feminine curve of her heavy breasts and the deep-brown nipples that are pointing straight back at me.

"Yeah," she says breathlessly, eyes roaming my upper body just as appreciatively.

I reach forward and palm one, squeezing gently as I flick a thumb across her nipple. "I'm going to fuck these one day."

"What?" There's the shy girl I've come to know.

I lean close again, kissing her neck and covering both of her breasts with my palms. "I'm going to watch you rub oil all over them." A ragged moan breaks out of her throat as I continue kissing along her jawline. "And then I'm going to slide my cock between them. Watch your gorgeous eyes go wide while I do." She whimpers, fingers shaking as they trail up over my chest, nails scratching slightly as she does. "And then I'll leave you with a pretty pearl necklace before I settle in for another taste of what's between these thighs. You'll never be bored with me, Mira. I can promise you that."

"Jesus Christ," she breathes out with a small tremble in her voice.

"I don't really care what you call me while I do it, sweetheart. So long as you spread those legs and let me worship between them."

She jerks back now, fisting my hair. "Stefan, so help me. If you don't shut up and get naked with me right here and now, I'm going to lose it."

A sly smile takes over my face. "Are you hungry, Kitten? I like it when your claws come out."

She shimmies the rest of the silk down over her hips, moving just enough to discard the dress on the floor, and sits back on her heels. Now she's kneeling in my fully lit foyer, wearing nothing but a pair of torn panties around her waist.

"I thought I liked the dress on you," I say, devouring the sight of dark hair tumbling over her shoulders and wild eyes boring into mine with so much hunger it almost knocks me over. "But now I think I might like it better on the floor."

"Lose the clothes, Stefan." There's an edge to her voice, an urgency.

I slowly remove my shirt, dropping it behind myself. "Is this your version of begging, Mira?"

She licks her lips and looks down at her hard nipples, the blush on her chest, the raised gooseflesh on her arms. Her voice is quiet when she looks up at me shyly and replies, "Yes."

My pants are torn off in a flurry, and I'm too ravenous to

leave the hardwood floor of my entryway. Does she deserve better than being fucked on the floor? Definitely. But I'll make that up to her later.

I sit down and reach forward, yanking her into my lap, feeling her wet lips slide across the length of my erection. Her hips buck, rubbing against me again, and we moan in unison. My lips latch onto one nipple, and I suck.

"There's a condom in my wallet. Pants pocket." Then I dive back down onto the opposite nipple, sucking hard, swirling my tongue and then squeezing with my teeth. She's grappling with my pants, fumbling around with my wallet, chucking cards and cash all over the floor in a rush to find the aluminum wrapper while I feast on her breasts like a man starved.

"These are delectable," I murmur, wrapping my hands around her waist as the tearing sound fills the room.

"There," she breathes out as she pulls the condom out triumphantly.

I lean back onto my hands and watch her. She looks downright erotic, her heart-shaped lips all puffy and glistening, her eye makeup slightly smudged. And all I want to do is make more of a mess with her. She's a canvas, and I'm about to paint.

"You put it on."

"Me?" Her hands tremble as she looks around the room, but I don't think it's nerves. Mira's not a nervous woman.

"Who else would I want to put it on?"

The tip of her tongue peeks out between her lips, and she nods. Her hands are sure when she wraps them around my length and edges back a bit, carefully rolling the condom over my cock. Her hands look delicate, but with all those hours of professional training, she moves with confidence.

When she looks up, her long hair makes a curtain around her face. "Now what?"

The contrast of her vulnerability and confidence is such a goddamn turn-on. I can barely handle it. I reach out and grab her. Hands back on her waist, I move her onto my lap, my dick right up against the front of her pussy, resting on her stomach, giving us the perfect visual for how much room I'll be taking up inside her.

And both of us are watching. It seems like neither of us can look away.

I lift her slightly, feeling her nails digging into my bare shoulders, lining the head of my cock up with her slick entrance before I stare into her beautiful face. "Now you sit on it."

A small smile touches her lips as she eases herself down. What was frantic before suddenly feels in slow motion. She pauses after every inch with a small gasp. I've never seen anything sexier than the look of pure lust on her face as she takes me. At first, I watch her pussy, the way it stretches around me, but now all I can see is her face and the way her focus is fully on where we're joined.

Her lips are slightly parted, her eyes glazed with pleasure, and she looks downright fascinated. I'm not going to last if she keeps looking at *us* like *that*.

When she drops to fully seated, we groan in unison. I feel her pulse and clench around me. My head tips back and hers tips forward, her lips moving across my chest reverently.

Her hips swivel, and she moans. "Stefan." Her breath breezes against my nipple as her hands travel up the back of my head, and I can't keep my hands off her any longer.

Sitting up tall, I wrap my arms around her and drag her mouth into a gentle kiss. Mira's hips move in a soft twisting motion, and my vision blurs. I can't pinpoint what it is. The angle, the snug fit, the tense lead-up? All I know is that sex—two people coming together—has never felt so absolutely necessary as it does right now.

I've known I'm attracted to Mira for a long time, but my head is spinning with the way this feels like something else entirely. Her lips on mine, her hands gripping me at the same time as her cunt. Our kiss turns into just breathing each other's air while her hips pick up the pace. She rises and drops herself down onto me with abandon.

"Stefan, you feel…" She trails off, head back and fingers knitting around the back of my neck while she continues to ride me.

And for once, I'm speechless.

The sensual curve of her throat entrances me, the light sheen of sweat on her chest distracts me, and the way her tits bounce while she fucks me is my undoing.

In one swift motion, I pull her close and flip her over onto her back so I can be on top. "How do I feel, Mira?" My hand trails over her chest reverently as I push up above her. "Tell me."

I expect her to need some time to think about that. I

expect her to balk. But her lust-drenched voice takes my breath away when she says, "You feel like this is how it's supposed to be."

I drop my head into the crook of her neck. The smell of her perfume is strongest here. It's intoxicating, something with licorice and honey. My tongue darts out as I pump slowly into her. "You are fucking delicious. And you are fucking right. Stuffed full of my cock is exactly how you're supposed to be."

A quiet chuckle filters into my awareness. "All that scolding about language, and you talk like this as soon as the clothes come off."

I smile against her collarbone and nip at her soft skin again. "You love it. And Mira?"

"Yeah?" she breathes, impatiently writhing against me.

I pull up, catching her gaze again, feeling the bite of the hardwood against my knees and the squeeze of her thighs around my waist, those hot-as-fuck spiky heels scratching at my back. "You feel like this is how it's supposed to be too."

She nods and rolls her lips together, but that movement blends into the shaking of her body as I thrust in hard. I rest one elbow by her head so I can watch her face while I drive into her. My other hand finds her clit and circles.

"Oh god," she cries out as I press down and continue with slow, hard strokes. Her pussy flutters around me. Soon, her legs shake. She's close.

Her legs clench, keeping me close, and I throw one leg up over my shoulder, needing to feel her deeper. My hand wraps around her ankle, brushing against the cuff of her stiletto. I turn my head and press a kiss to the delicate bone there. "I knew these would look good propped up on my shoulders."

Her top teeth bite down into her pillowy bottom lip as I slam into her, making her tits bounce with the force of it.

"Good girl, Mira. Come on my cock now." I give her clit one firm squeeze and she tenses, rearing up beneath me before dissolving into a tangle of trembling limbs and incoherent words. I can make out "holy fuck" and "so good," and it makes me smile as I brace myself above her and chase my own release.

Her hips move to meet mine even as she mewls and goes soft beneath me.

She's so wet and so warm, and I tell her as much. "You feel like heaven," I say as I slide into her body one last time.

And then it hits, and I drop my head onto her heaving chest as I spill inside her.

We're both sweaty and breathless as her hands circle around the back of my head to hold me close.

"Is sex always like that for you?" she pants out, awe bleeding into her voice.

And because I pride myself on being honest, I tell her the truth.

"No. It's never been like that. Not even fucking close."

CHAPTER 23

Mira

SORE AND GUILTY. THAT'S WHAT I AM.

My entire body aches in the best way. I've always seen that on shows or read it in smutty books—someone talking about being sore from having their brains fucked out all night. I thought it was fiction.

It is not fiction.

Stefan lies beside me in his spacious king-size bed looking exhausted after taking me over and over again until we ran out of condoms. Being a sex expert must be exhausting. The man is a fucking god. I'm a girl who lives inside animal science textbooks and peer-reviewed papers and uses a big purple dildo when the fancy strikes because I honestly don't think about sex that often.

Until him. Until his whispered words and searing glances. Now all I can think about is sex. This is a disease a condom can't save me from.

Obsession.

My eyes flit over his face. His cheekbones and defined nose. His dark dirty-blond hair all disheveled from where my hands spent hours hanging on for dear life. His lips swollen from me latching on to his face like a goddamn succubus. Or maybe they're swollen from the words that spill from them.

The man has a filthy mouth. His accent gets stronger, more sensual, when his walls come down. I'm pretty sure he could talk me into an orgasm if he tried, if he looked at me in the special way he does. Yeah, I'm almost positive I could orgasm on the spot from that alone.

Maybe if he played with my nipples too. The way he rolls them. I had no idea he'd be *so* into my tits or that covering up the way I do would drive him crazy the way he confessed to me last night.

He sighs and pulls me into his chest. Nothing about Stefan is simply what meets the eye. He's complicated and fascinating, and god, he's really not boring. He's beautiful— I've always thought so. The accent, the smirk, the mysterious background. Nobody prepared me for the fact he'd be equally alluring and beautiful on the inside.

He's addictive.

I snuggle in close, the smell of his mint soap from the shower last night wrapping around us as I try to escape the sense of looming guilt closing in on me. Not guilt for sleeping with him. I truly cannot bring myself to feel bad about that. Though I'm not looking forward to everyone inevitably finding out. That's probably something I'll put off for a while yet. I need to wait and see where this goes.

I feel the light dusting of hair on his chest against my cheek as I close my eyes. I can see his face above mine last night while he moved over me, giving me more pleasure than I've ever experienced.

I was mindless in the moment. But the memory haunts me. The green eyes. The knowledge he's looking for his biological father. Knowing I have a hunch and haven't disclosed it makes my stomach burn. I need to figure this out, and fast. It's a terrible secret to keep. But blowing up multiple people's lives when I could be wrong isn't ideal either. I need to stick to my plan, my hypothesis followed by a proper inquiry so I don't make an ass of myself.

He'll never forgive me if I'm wrong. Too many people in his life have let him down, lied to him. He talks about protecting the people around him, but it sounds to me like no one has ever protected *him*. I don't want to cause him pain. When I tell him about this, I want to be sure. And after lying here for the past hour mulling it over, I don't think anything less than sure is a risk I'm willing to take. Anything less is not what he deserves.

I need to play it safe with Stefan Dalca because I don't want to lose whatever it is that we've just found.

"Stop squirming or you'll force me to fuck you again." Stefan's voice is sleepy against the top of my head, and his legs tangle with mine, clamping them down into the memory-foam mattress.

I giggle quietly and feel his hips grind forward, his erection rubbing against my stomach. "You're out of condoms, remember?"

"Careful handing me a challenge like that, Mira. I'm full of ideas that don't require a condom at all. That's hardly a deterrent."

His fingers trail down my arm, and my skin pebbles beneath his touch. "Tell me about this tattoo." His voice is all gruff and sleepy, and butterflies erupt in my stomach. "What does it mean?"

I giggle quietly, watching his finger trace the outline of the black floral design on the inside of my forearm. "It doesn't mean anything. My parents told me I couldn't get a tattoo when I asked for one, so I went out and found someone who would give me one without their permission anyway."

He hums thoughtfully before lifting my hand and pressing a quick kiss to my palm before resting it against his cheek. "Fascinating that you still think it means nothing."

"What do you mean?" I look up at him, and his eyes glow with such intensity, his beauty is consuming—it steals my breath just to look at him this closely. This intimately.

That signature devil-may-care grin graces his lips, and then his mouth is against the ornate ink on my arm, lips and tongue tracing the lines in a way that has me squeezing my thighs together. "This right here is proof that you are your own woman," he says against my skin. "No one tells Dr. Mira Thorne what she can and can't do."

I try to change the direction of our conversation, feeling suddenly jumpy in the presence of someone who can turn me to putty in his hands while also reading me so damn easily. Someone whose vision is like a laser through every shield I've erected. Someone who appreciates my rebellious streak—encourages it even.

"What's with you always kissing my palm?"

His eyes meet mine once again, and his responding smile is soft and vulnerable; completely oblivious to my inner turmoil. Instead of replying right away, he runs his fingers over top of mine, still watching his skin slide against my own with a look of quiet awe on his face.

"You have beautiful hands. Almost as beautiful as your mind and heart. Sometimes I find myself staring at them while you work, so elegant and strong all at once. Hands that heal. Hands that save lives." His voice drops. "Hands that belong in mine."

My heart races, and my body heats. I swear it's like he uncovered some secret button on me and knows exactly how to push it. He makes me feel treasured. I get this indulgent side of him that no one else sees. I feel like I'm in on a secret. One that I want to keep for myself—to revel in.

"See? You like that plan. I can tell by the little sigh you just made," he grumbles, lifting my palm to press a reverent kiss right to the center, his lashes fluttering shut as he does.

I didn't even notice the sigh. I must sound like a lovesick teenager.

"It's true. You promised me I wouldn't be bored, and I'm not."

One eye flicks open as he looks down at me. "You really thought sex was boring?"

"It was always…fine? Like…nice? But not something I felt like I couldn't go without. My mind would always wander somewhere else. Like a diagnosis I couldn't figure out or what was going to happen on the next *Grey's Anatomy*. It just wasn't a priority. I'm too busy to worry about sex. Still am."

He chuckles like he doesn't believe me. "Okay, Dr. Thorne."

"What?" I bristle. "I am. Better sex doesn't make me any less busy."

"Better? Is that all?" He lifts up to rest his head in his palm and smirks down at me.

If I were wearing panties, they would melt for a smile like that. Instead, we're both tangled up in each other, completely naked, and now I'm feeling like that was a colossally stupid idea. Even a single layer of protection would have kept his hand from gliding across my bare skin, from cupping my ass and sliding a finger through my slick core.

"You're awfully wet for someone who is just barely better than bored."

I say nothing as his fingers continue their exploration, spreading my wetness over my lips as proof of how completely full of lies I am.

"Do you often get this wet for men who aren't your type, Dr. Thorne?"

My head snaps to him. "Stop saying that." I don't like him saying that. I meant it to push him away, and now it's not true. It's so damn far from the truth. And I'm done pushing this beautiful, complex man away.

"Why?" His green eyes glitter as they move between mine knowingly.

"You know why." I roll my eyes, body wound tight.

Stefan flips me flat onto my back. "I don't think I do. You're like a safe, and I think I'm close to figuring out the combination. So don't worry, Mira. I'm going to get in there and learn all your secrets. I'll keep them for you, too. Especially the one about me being *exactly* your type."

And with that, he winks and disappears beneath the covers.

★★★

My walks of shame usually just refer to drunkenness. Smudged makeup. Maybe a broken heel on my shoe due to said inebriation.

A fancy backless dress and missing panties just slap a little differently, and I pray no one sees me as I race up the stairs to my apartment above the barn with my fancy stilettos in hand. Stefan offered some spare clothes or to "borrow" something from Nadia. Both options seemed even more obvious to my sex-addled mind.

I fumble with my keys, cursing under my breath as they drop to the landing. "Motherfucker." I don't even risk looking around myself. I pick up the keys and get through the door before slamming it behind me and leaning up against it. A deep sigh leaves my chest, and I let my eyes close as I lean my head back.

Once I get my bearings, I open my eyes and look around the tiny apartment. I'm home, but it feels very empty and very quiet. A bit lonely even. My friends are paired off, connected at the hip to their men and loving it, and I just left the house of the only man who has ever made me feel something for no reason other than I needed some goddamn space. Tearing myself away from him after one night of mind-blowing sex was already hard enough.

I need *space.* And to think.

My phone pings, and I pick it up.

Violet: Don't forget it's girls' night!

Goddammit. How did I forget? And why does it have to be after pulling an all-night sex-a-thon with the man they all hate?

Violet: I invited Nadia too. Hope that's okay!

Fuck. This is going to be awkward. My thumbs fly across the screen.

Mira: Of course that's okay. We going to Neighbor's?

The pub is our go-to hangout.

Violet: Nah. The Paddock. Nadia said she doesn't really drink, and I thought that might be more low-key. I'm tired, but I need a break. 7 p.m.? I won't last late.

I'm not sad that we're going to our favorite field to drink and chat. It's honestly my favorite meeting spot.

Mira: See you then, hot mama.

Violet: It's cute that you call me hot when we both
    know I just look eternally exhausted.

Violet loves this new chapter of her life. But being a full-time jockey and mom to a baby is hard work. She's lucky she has Cole, who might be the most attentive husband and father of all time. I absently wonder what type of father Stefan would be as I let my dress fall to the floor, shaking my head at myself. *Pathetic.* I crawl into bed, determined to catch some hours of actual sleep before I make an appearance and try not to seem super guilty around my closest friends. But when I close my lids, all I see is Stefan and his beautiful green eyes.

My new favorite color.

When I wake up, I'm distracted. Not feeling like myself. The problem is…I don't want to go to girls' night. I want to go to Stefan's house. I want to fall into his bed. I want him to wrap his arms around me so I can disappear into him. I feel like a child who's just gone through a developmental leap. I can firmly say I have *never* felt like this about a guy before.

Especially not one I shouldn't be tangling myself up with.

Especially one I'm keeping secrets from. Or whom I'm keeping secret.

It feels dirty. It feels like an injustice to a man who has done nothing but go out of his way to help me, to defend me, to soothe me.

It's a fucking trip, is what it is.

I lock the door behind me and jog down the narrow set

of stairs to the ground floor. The ranch is quiet, the horses are in safely for the night, the ones who are prepping for the upcoming season are living down at the track for their training regimen, and all the staff have gone home for the day.

There's still a spring nip in the air this close to the mountains. I pull my oversize canvas coat tightly around my body and consider going back for an extra blanket, but when I round the corner of the barn and look down the grass pathway to the paddock where we meet up sometimes, a bright fire catches my eye. The three girls are already there, and it's looking like they've got a pretty cozy setup, which is new.

This whole thing started when Billie was hired as the trainer here at Gold Rush Ranch. According to her, she spent her first night on the farm lying on a blanket by her new project horse's paddock with a bottle of wine, a loaf of bread, and a wheel of cheese.

Now we just keep the tradition going. It's cozy, and as someone who hasn't had a lot of friends, I love the simplicity of it. Just good people and simple food under the open air of Ruby Creek. I hope we're still lying here drinking wine out of the bottle when we're old and gray.

Assuming they don't hate me when they find out I've been fucking the enemy.

"What have we got here?" I ask as I approach the group.

Violet smiles softly and runs her fingers through her hair. "I said I was cold when Cole walked me down here. A few minutes later, he pulled up to the barn with lawn chairs and a fire bowl."

Good lord. Cole Harding is such a goner.

"He carried this all down here for us?"

Billie laughs as she cracks open a bottle of wine. "Have you seen the guy? He's built like a tank. I think he enjoys carrying heavy stuff for fun in his free time. He's also totally pussy-whipped."

Chuckles erupt, and Violet's cheeks go pink as she rolls her eyes. "Vaughn is no better. Care to tell the class what he's doing tonight?"

I drop into the empty chair and wink at Nadia, who looks happy but a little out of place. "Let's hear it, B."

She takes a swig of wine straight from the bottle because according to her it "tastes better that way." With a deep sigh, she passes it over to me and says, "He's planning our wedding."

I almost spray wine out my nose. "He what?"

Trying to avoid eye contact, she rifles through the backpack at her feet and pulls out a loaf of French bread. "You heard me. He's planning the wedding because I don't care about our wedding and my parents and Vaughn do. So I told them to plan it and tell me where to be when the day comes."

My brow furrows. "Billie, I'm well aware you're not a weddings-and-babies type of person, but don't let other people tell you what your day should be like."

"I'm not." She shrugs as she rips a chunk of bread off before topping it with a slice of cheese from the plate in her lap. "I just don't care. I'd marry Vaughn tomorrow, right here in this field. And he knows that, but he has a better sense of duty than I do. He's also my mother's dream. Listening to them talk to each other makes me wish I could have fallen in love with someone who would have been a disappointment to them." Violet snorts, and Billie hits her with a grin. "Either way, he can handle her, and I can't. So he can taste the cakes and worry over invite fonts. I'd rather be here, doing this."

"Cheers to that." I hold the bottle of red wine up and then go to hand it to Violet.

She just shakes her head with a shy smile. I check to see that everyone is distracted with their food before quirking one brow at her. She nods and looks away, cheeks and chest going crimson.

Dang. Another baby Harding on the way already.

I give Violet's knee a quick squeeze before whispering, "I'm so happy for you."

She smiles so hard I think her face might crack open. No wonder Cole was out here setting up a whole fire and chairs for her. Papa Bear is feeling protective.

I hand the wine back to Billie since Vi obviously doesn't want this announced. "How about you, Nadia? How's life in Ruby Creek treating you now that we got that pesky principal off your back?"

She gives me a conspiratorial, pleased look. Her golden tresses pulled up in a messy bun make her appear younger than when her wild curls flow down to her shoulders. "That was fun."

"It was."

"What did you guys do?" Violet asks, leaning forward from under her blanket, looking all wide-eyed and innocent.

"We, uh…" I glance over at Nadia, and she shrugs. I

figure if we were going to get in trouble for this, we would have by now. "We egged her principal's car."

Violet gasps, and Billie cackles before asking, "Why?"

"Because he's a sexist pig," Nadia bites out, clearly still miffed about her humiliating ordeal.

"Yes! I knew I liked you, Nadia," Billie says before holding her bottle of wine up over the fire in a cheer. "Here's to taking out all the sexist pigs."

Nadia raises her soda in response.

"Here, here!" I call as we all dissolve into a fit of giggles.

Silence descends as we all work on getting some food in us. Chugging wine on an empty stomach is a rookie move. And we're all too old for that shit.

"Speaking of sexist pigs...I was at the second-chance fundraiser last night," I tell them. "Patrick Cassel was arrested."

"What?" Billie drops her food onto the plate and stares at me, mouth agape. "What for?"

"Doping horses without their owners' consent or knowledge, among other things, I assume."

A low whistle erupts from Billie's lips. "Goddamn. I knew that guy was a piece of shit, but that's really just the cherry on top, isn't it?"

"Yeah. My brother has been slaving over taking that guy down for months," Nadia mumbles over a mouth full of food.

My eyes go wide, and Billie's head whips to her. "Stefan?"

She nods right as Violet pipes up, "You make him out

to be a lot worse than he is, B. Your grudge-holding ability is next level."

All I can hear is my heart pounding in my ears. This is toeing the line awfully close to my secrets spilling out. And with a warm buzz coursing through me, I wonder if it would be so bad to just get it off my chest. Just blurt it out and get it out in the open.

"I hate that fucking guy," Billie grumbles as she rips at her bread again.

"Hey, hey, hey now, that's my big brother you're talking about," Nadia chimes in just as Violet scolds her with a whisper-shout, "Billie!"

I take a contemplative swig of wine. A really big one. "You realize he saved your horse, right?"

She scoffs, agitation lining her every movement. Billie *is* a championship grudge holder. Ask her parents. I appreciate that she's got her baggage, her reasons, but I'm feeling protective of Stefan. The Stefan I know doesn't deserve that kind of treatment.

"We'd have figured something out," she says. "The guy is a slimy fucking snake in the grass."

My cheeks heat with indignance. "No. That foal would have died."

She rolls her eyes and chuckles, trying to lighten the mood. "Okay, Mira. When you're done fondling Dalca's balls for doing us one little favor, let me know."

I take another large swig and then rest my head back on the chair, looking up at the darkening sky, feeling the heat of the fire soak into my bones. "I did a lot more than fondle his balls."

Violet spews water all over herself.

Nadia groans and shakes her head with a small smile. "Fucking gross. I knew it."

Billie stares at me, shock painting her pretty features. "Please tell me you're joking."

"Sorry, B. No joke."

"Okay…" She settles back in her chair, pressing her lips together. Clearly mulling over what to say next. She steeples her hands in front of her face, tapping her fingers on her nose before pointing them back at me. "Is this you going deep cover? Like when a CIA agent bangs the bad guy to uncover enemy secrets? Because I could probably admire your commitment."

I tilt my head to the side and smile at her with sadness. I recognize she's not going to like this, but when have I ever done things the way other people wanted me to? "No, B. It's…"

I worry my bottom lip between my teeth as I search for the right label for Stefan and me.

"It's real."

CHAPTER 24

Mira

I FEEL LIGHTER WALKING BACK TO MY LOFT APARTMENT above the barn. Actually, I feel almost giddy. Part of that is the wine, and part of that is just the general feeling of relief at ditching one of the secrets that's been weighing on me. I didn't like lying to my friends, and I didn't like treating a man who's been nothing but incredible to me like I was ashamed of him.

The fact of the matter is, I'm not ashamed of Stefan Dalca. *At all.*

Luckily, Billie sort of let it go after I dropped that atomic bomb on girls' night.

She tossed out a joking "Well, you know what they say: love is blind!" and then dropped the topic altogether. She probably needs to sleep on it. The conversation moved on easily after that, though I didn't miss the curious smiles Violet was shooting my way or the way Nadia chuckled and shook her head when she hugged me goodbye.

Everyone had something to say, but no one said a thing. And now I'm back in my apartment. Alone and all amped up. Positively fixated on how badly I want to see Stefan.

Before I talk myself out of it, I pull my phone out and fire off a text to him. I'm tired of holding myself back.

Mira: What are you doing?

Text dots roll across the screen almost instantly.

Stefan: Plotting evil ways to ruin your friends' lives.
You?

I snort.

Mira: Dork. Come visit me.
Stefan: At your place?

I scan the small space. Cat's out of the bag where my friends are concerned, so why the hell not?

Mira: Yes.
Stefan: Why?

Why? That's not exactly the response I was going for. Now I feel uncertain. Out of my depth.

Mira: Okay, don't. I'll be there to check on Loki tomorrow.

I toss my phone down on my bed, feeling a tad huffy. I'm terrible at asserting myself with Stefan. I'm too inexperienced. I take things too personally. I want him to pick up on all my innuendo so I don't have to admit out loud I want him more than I care to admit. Like a total sucker, I pick up my phone to check if he's said anything.

Stefan: Do you miss me, Dr. Thorne?

Groaning, I scrub a hand across my face. *Do I miss him?* It's been about twelve hours since I saw him. Missing him already would be so fucking lame.

My eyes spring open.

I am so fucking lame.

I reel with the realization. I've spent so much time at his farm, working with him, going on fake dates with him, he's become a staple in my day without me even realizing it. A nervous breath shudders through me as I type back my response.

Mira: Yes.

And then I sit and stare at the screen. The blank screen. No dots roll. No messages come through. My throat burns, and I squeeze my hand on it to stem the flow of embarrassment. I shouldn't have been so straight with him. He must think I'm fucking nuts.

I get up and walk across the hall to the small bathroom where I aggressively brush my teeth.

Yes. Why did I have to say yes? I'm officially that girl who had sex with a guy once and is acting like a clingy psycho. No wonder he didn't respond.

As I wash my face, I realize I wouldn't respond to me either. If a guy told me that after one night, I would run in the opposite direction with my career and independence clutched in my fists. So I can't blame him.

A loud banging on the door startles me, and I instantly dread the thought that Billie is here to tell me off for hooking up with the enemy. I'll have to tell her she was right. That I'm nuts and he was a bad idea.

But when I swing the door open, the person standing there is Stefan.

"Hi—"

The crash of his lips against mine cuts off anything I was about to say. He steals my breath and commands my body. His muscular arms wrap around me the exact way I wanted them to, his day-old stubble scratching against my face as he devours me.

His hands palm my ass, and he lifts me up, hiking my legs around him as he takes a few steps into the space before kicking the door shut behind us, and then turns to press me against it. My arms close around his neck as I kiss him back, all the worry from mere moments before disappearing with the way he's holding me—owning me.

I moan when he pulls his sinful lips away and presses his forehead to mine. "Hi." His breath tickles my damp lips, and I wish he'd just shut up and keep kissing me.

"Hi," I say back, *again*, letting my fingers trace the soft hair at the nape of his neck.

"You missed me?" His eyes are soft, wide—uncertain

almost. A look I don't see on him often. And something about that look undoes me a little.

"Yeah," I breathe back quietly, feeling like we're in our private universe again.

Somehow, when his arms close around me, the world melts away. Everything that mattered two minutes ago ceases to exist now because he looks at me like I'm the only thing he sees.

His lips tug up at one side as he stares at me with so much warmth. "I missed you too."

My heart jumps in my chest, rattling against my ribs. The man with the shiny veneer, the mysterious past, and the impenetrable smirk *misses me.* Hearing him, of all people, say that to me feels like so much more.

I kiss his cheek, appreciating the feel of his stubble. I kiss his nose, right on the bump I've come to love so much. His eyebrow, the one that quirks up just after he says something inappropriate.

I rake my hands through the sides of his dark-gold locks, knowing exactly what I want from him at this moment. "Take me to bed, Stefan."

He hits me with a cocky smirk, and my core jumps in response. "Whatever you want, Kitten."

Within moments, I'm tossed on the bed and feel the crush of his body on top of me, caging me in. The only light is what filters in from the hallway. His arms frame my face as he pauses, watching me as I watch him. Our eyes connect, and I don't even try to look away.

This man. This look. It makes me want to dive deeper.

I want to get lost in this connection, disappear into it, and never come back out.

I have never felt so desired.

And Stefan doesn't ruin it with words. Instead, his thumb traces the lobe of my ear, and his stern features soften. I love the way he's always touching me. A hand pressed here, a thumb grazing there. It's like he can't help himself where I'm concerned. Like he can't keep his hands off me even if he wanted to.

His lips find mine, searing my soul with their reverence. I'm not sure what's changed between us tonight. But where last night felt like fucking, like two people working out some tension and having some fun, tonight feels almost thoughtful. More profound. There's a shift in the air, in his eyes, in the way sparks dance across my skin when he touches me.

Kneeling above me, he strips me bare, working every piece of clothing off my body, gentle hands moving over every square inch of my body. We don't speak, the dirty talk doesn't come, we just watch, lost in each other's eyes. The gold flecks, the mossy hues, the dark forest greens. There are just as many facets to his irises as there are to him, and I want every one. I want to explore them all. I want to see them all, even the darkest ones—the questionable ones. Stefan doesn't scare me. I don't see him as a threat. He's not my enemy. And he looks at me the same way. He looks at me like I'm a dream come true.

Words aren't even necessary when a man looks at you like *that*.

His clothes fall in a pile around him. T-shirt, soft gray

joggers…no underwear. My neediness obviously pulled him straight out of some downtime. But watching his cock bob before me, fully erect already, the lines that cut down from his toned abs, right over his hip bones—like arrows for where I want to go—I don't feel an ounce bad about pulling him away.

"You are so beautiful." My voice is breathy, almost desperate sounding. "Inside and out. Every last piece of you."

He crawls back on top of me, skin sliding against skin, and I can't keep the tips of my fingers from tracing the shapes of his defined muscles. Every curve, every sharp corner, they're almost like a map.

The winding road that brought us together.

Because who the hell would have guessed.

"No one has ever told me that before," he replies as he strokes my hair, eyes devouring my every feature.

My heart squeezes, and I rear up to taste his lips. He kisses me senseless while our hands roam each other's nude bodies. We learn each other, each hollow and dip. I want to memorize it all. There's something so innocent about it, something exploratory rather than rushed.

It's also stoking my inner fire, driving me absolutely insane.

"Condom. Bedside table," I breathe out between kisses.

Needing no further urging, Stefan pushes up and reaches beyond my head, into the drawer. But rather than grabbing for a condom right away, he pauses. I watch his lips take on a mischievous curl before a hand darts out. When his focus switches back to me, he smirks, looking suddenly playful.

ELSIE SILVER

And then he holds up…

"Look who I found."

Mr. Purple.

"Oh." The sight of him holding the big purple vibrator sets my heart to racing.

"I wonder who can make you come harder?" Stefan muses. "He is my top competition, is he not?" His head quirks in challenge.

I can't help but smile. "He is."

"Challenge accepted, Dr. Thorne." And with a cocky smile he clicks the bedside lamp on and slides down my body until he's braced between my spread thighs. "This is something I want to watch."

My top teeth bite down on my bottom lip to stifle a moan.

I fail miserably.

I arch my back as the low buzzing sound fills the quiet room. I feel the tip of the vibrator as he drags it through my folds with an appreciative grunt. I am *soaked*, something he has a perfectly clear view of.

The vibrator swirls around my clit, and my eyes flutter shut, hips bucking desperately. I am going to come fast playing this game with Stefan.

"Are you always this wet for him? Or is it me?" His voice is low and gravelly as he plays with my body.

"It's you." The words tumble off my tongue, almost a plea.

"Fucking right, it is." He pushes an inch of the length into me slowly, and my legs fall open wider. I love the way his crass side comes out to play in private. The rude words stoke my inner fire in a way I never knew they could.

"Oh god!" Another inch in, and it feels so tight; the vibrations feel so intense. It's an entirely different experience having someone else control the pace and the pressure.

"Sit up, Mira. I want you to see how pretty you look right now."

I groan. How such a simple request can seem so filthy is beyond me, and it sends arousal coursing through my veins. Most of my sexual experience has happened in the dark, an added layer of protection, with me squeezing my eyes shut and imagining things that might make it more exciting.

But Stefan Dalca has laid me completely bare with the lights on and has turned my mind to mush. I push up on my elbows and gaze down the valley between my heaving breasts. Stefan stays focused on my pussy, pushing the vibrator into me slowly, and I almost fall apart on the spot. His disheveled hair, his flushed cheeks, his eyes devouring me. It's too much.

"Jesus Christ," I pant as he slides it home. The vibrations rattle through my core, and my legs shake. The visual of him between my legs, completely engrossed—entranced—is more than I can take.

"No, Mira. It's just me." He smirks, eyes flitting up to mine, as he slides the vibe all the way out before pushing the length back in.

"Stefan." His name is a prayer on my lips. He's my new religion. Heat prickles out over my skin, and I'm ready to combust.

"You are fucking incredible." He pumps it in and out of me slowly, eyes getting hotter by the second. He looks like he might set me on fire with his gaze alone. "Do you have any idea how utterly irresistible you are?"

My entire body quakes under his ministrations. My fists clench the sheets, holding on for dear life, and I can feel my wetness coating my lips. He's making an absolute mess of me.

"I'm—"

The words die on my lips when he pulls the vibrator out and presses it to my clit. It's instant fireworks. They crackle across my skin, shooting down my inner thighs all the way to my toes. The arches of my feet cramp. My vision blanks.

I have never come so hard in my life. But I get barely any time to consider it before he tosses the vibrator across the bed and the tearing sound of a condom wrapper filters in through my jumbled consciousness.

I'm flat on my back when Stefan edges up beside me, peppering kisses along my shoulder as he twists me over and lifts my leg. From behind me, he wedges his rock-hard length between my legs and pulls me flush against his firm body.

"I can see why you like him so much." His voice is ragged against the shell of my ear as he lines us up, hand gripping my inner thigh possessively. "But I think you'll like this even better." He shoves his cock into me to the hilt, filling me so deliciously. "Or maybe we can work together more often?"

"Yes."

"You like that?" he growls.

"I love it."

That seems to be all the urging he needs as his hips piston into me, hitting a spot I've only ever been able to reach with a toy. The blunt head of his cock tantalizes the sensitive spot as he drives in. Our skin is slick, and I grind my ass back into him.

"More."

He fucks me harder, his moans echoing my own.

"Harder," I beg, feeling that telltale coiling sensation at the base of my spine. The one that swirls out around my hip bones and yanks on every nerve ending.

"Mira," he pants. "How do we feel this good together?"

The tension crescendos under the weight of his words.

He turns my head back toward him to claim my mouth as he pounds into me. "Who fucks you better?"

I don't even need to think about it. "You do. Always you."

His hips slap hard against my ass as I push back at him, and I snap. I tumble. I fall hard. "Stefan!" I cry out.

I feel him twitch and throb, spilling his release inside me as my entire body shakes. Our lips clamp together, like an anchor holding us together as we set each other adrift on a stormy sea. We clutch at each other desperately, perspiration mixing, limbs tangling. Joined in every way imaginable.

And I am so far gone I barely recognize myself.

CHAPTER 25

Stefan

"TELL ME ABOUT YOUR MOM."

Talk about a buzzkill. We just had the best sex of my life. The woman of my dreams is sprawled naked on my chest, and she wants to talk about my dead mom? The fingers I've been trailing down the indent of her spine stop in their tracks.

"If you want," she adds. "I'm just curious. You don't have to."

"Mira, take a breath. It's fine. You never need to feel like there's something you can't ask me or tell me. After what I've been through, honesty is important to me."

She stiffens, so I keep rubbing her back, wanting to go back to that blissful state of relaxation we were in just a moment ago.

"Nora was…" I'm at a loss for what to say about my mother actually. "Naive. Quick to fall in love. Starved for attention and constantly looking for more. And sometimes in all the wrong places. She grew up in a small town but had a wanderer's soul. I suppose that's why she started traveling." I try to imagine my mother living in Ruby Creek, and I can't. She doesn't fit here.

Mira drags a nail over the lines of my abs tenderly. My cock thickens, but I can take her again in a bit. I'm kind of enjoying the quiet solitude of talking with her, even about something I never say out loud. She has this way of making me feel safe, like she's really listening, not just humoring me to achieve some end. She genuinely enjoys our conversations, and somehow that's more flattering than anything else she's said or done. Her attention is healing.

"She was also strong and driven. Curious. She would pack up and hit different countries for a few months at a time. Traveling on a budget. Hitchhiking. Working odd jobs to make ends meet. And then when she depleted her bank account, she'd come back here and work whatever jobs she could find to replenish her account before taking off on another adventure. Until she went to Romania and met Constantin. Then her travels stopped, and that's when she was pregnant with me. He essentially locked her up and threw away the key. She should have hated him for it; instead she loved him to her dying day. Even against her better judgment."

"It's sad, you know?" Mira muses. "She sounds like a fascinating woman—a free spirit—the way you describe her. It seems a real shame to tie her down that way. I wonder what she could have done with her life under different circumstances?"

I take a deep swallow. I've been so angry at her for so long, so busy wallowing in my pity, that I haven't let myself consider how truly sad her story is. "I've never quite thought of it that way. Mostly I think about how badly they fucked up Nadia and me."

"I think your experiences have shaped you in ways you don't even see."

"Yeah, yeah. Morally gray. I know." I roll my eyes up at the ceiling and sigh, feeling tired of always being labeled the bad guy. "And they've shaped a crooked nose."

"I like your nose."

My heart seizes in my chest. "You do?"

I've left my nose as a sort of reminder. I could have had it fixed by now, but then I wouldn't be able to beat myself up over not keeping my mom and sister safe every time I look in the mirror.

Mira clambers her naked body on top of mine, looking straight down into my eyes. "I do," she says before delicately kissing the bridge of my nose. Her finger trails down in its wake, making me feel more self-conscious than I have in years. "I've always thought you were devastatingly handsome. Alluring." She kisses me again, more slowly this time. "The nose. The accent. The quick tongue. I've always been drawn to you. Even when I barely knew you."

I bask in her attention, soaking up her sweet words like medicine. Loving that this attraction wasn't one-sided.

She tips her head and presses a kiss to the center of my chest. "You're not morally gray. You walk the line of being intensely supportive without being overbearing perfectly.

254

Look at Nadia. Look at me. Life gave you some sour fucking lemons, and you added the sugar and made yourself some lemonade. You love so fiercely. I think she'd be proud of you. Just like I am."

Love.

The word bounces around in my head. A perilous word to be sure. I love Nadia, absolutely. But the way Mira lumped herself in there felt a little too natural. My heart says she belongs on that list, but my head says it's too soon. My head says that everyone I love ends up hurt. Or dead.

Could I love Mira that way? Fiercely? I stare down at her elegant fingers, still skating across my skin. I think I probably could.

Possibly already do.

I grunt and palm her skull, silky hair sliding beneath my skin as I kiss the crown of her head. I pull her closer and chide myself. For a guy who claims that honesty is an import-ant quality to him, I'm a fantastic liar. I shouldn't love Mira. Because everything I touch turns to shit. And when I love something too much, the universe takes it away from me.

"Good morning."

I turn around from the coffee maker to see Nadia sliding onto a stool at the island in the kitchen. This is my favorite room in the house. I love cooking. I especially love cooking for other people. It's an easy way for me to show affection without having to talk about my feelings.

When Nadia moved in with me, she looked me in the

eye and told me to stop apologizing to her. My guilt over leaving her behind as a teenager is heavy, and the regret over not going back as an adult is possibly even worse.

So I cook for her. It's my way of saying sorry without uttering the words. Homemade fine dining. I slide a plate of smoked salmon eggs Benedict across the island toward her, followed by a cup of piping-hot coffee.

"Fuck yes." Her eyes light up, and she runs her finger through the hollandaise sauce before sucking it off with an exaggerated moan. My sister has no shame.

"You've been hanging out with those Gold Rush girls too much."

She laughs. "So have you."

I ignore the comment. I know Mira wants to keep us under wraps. And as much as I hate the feelings of inadequacy that come with it, I respect her decision. No matter how badly I'd like to shout it from the rooftops and not feel like I have to sneak over to her house under the cover of darkness. She asked me to stay last night after our heart-to-heart, but I knew she'd regret it in the morning when I would inevitably have to walk out to my vehicle amid a bustling farm filled with her friends and colleagues.

I put her on all fours and fucked her hard one more time—just the way she likes—and kissed her senseless before driving home in a haze of memories and complicated feelings.

Plus, I have work to do around the farm this morning. Racing season is almost upon us, and I've got some young horses that really need to get started training. Something I know nothing about. But luckily, Griffin does.

"Ready?" I ask as he rounds the corner after using the washroom.

He lifts his chin and grunts, hiding beneath the brim of his baseball cap. Nadia whips around, startled by the strange man standing in our house.

"Sorry, Nadia. This is Griffin. The guy I bought this place from."

She takes one look at him and places her fork down. "*That* is Griffin?"

My brow furrows as I load my and Griffin's coffee mugs into the dishwasher. We've already eaten and had coffee and are ready to go. The guy gets up at the crack of dawn, and I don't mind getting him acquainted with his new projects nice and early.

"Yeah."

"Your *best friend* Griffin?" Her eyes bulge in their sockets.

"Relax, Nadia. Adults don't have *best friends*."

Griffin snorts, rubs his beard, and walks to the front door to shove his feet into a pair of worn cowboy boots.

"I've already told you. He sold me this place, and we've just stayed in touch."

Okay, that might downplay it. I like Griffin, and he probably *is* my best friend. He's not invasive or annoying, but he's also the only person in this valley who didn't treat me like a leper when I got here. He moved up into the mountains once I took over. His new property is pretty remote, but I've been up a couple times. He's a private guy, but he's invited me hunting—a new experience for me—and I've helped him with some repairs to his cottage.

Which is why he's here repaying me the favor. As a former bronc rider, he assures me he can get a few youngsters started up for me, and that's not a gift horse I'm about to look in the mouth.

My sister's face scrunches up in confusion as she whispers, "But…he's a total dick."

I bark out a laugh as I round the bar top toward the front entryway. "I'm glad you think so." I wink at her. "Then I won't have to worry about you scaring him off with your antics while he's here."

I swear I can almost hear Nadia roll her eyes. That girl has an attitude the size of Texas. And to be honest, it's part of what I love about her.

And Mira.

Fuck.

Not love. *Like.*

I toss a coat on and step into my work boots, shaking my head at myself as I head out the front to catch up with Griffin. It takes about an hour to get him all set. I show him the three youngsters that need a start, and I feel suddenly very overwhelmed by running the farm.

Needing the sunshine, I walk out to the paddock where Loki and Farrah now spend their days soaking up the rays and rolling in mud. His shrill whinny greets me as he trots across the pen with a real prance to his step, knees coming up higher than necessary just to show off. The older he's gotten, the more hilarious he's become. He's going to be a handful, that much is clear. He's smart and playful…and mischievous. I frequently catch him trying to undo the chain around his gate. He bucks and leaps around his pen like he's a world champion bucking horse.

Yeah. I don't envy the poor sucker who has to get on him for the first time. This horse will probably be reading full sentences by then. Either way, I'm beyond relieved to see him turning a corner. He's a healthy colt. No one would ever guess the shape he was in a couple months ago.

I've come to love him. There are a lot of horses on this farm and at the track in the city that belong to me, so leave it to the one horse that money can't buy to weasel his way into my heart. I haven't loved a horse like this since I lived in Romania.

"Hey, bud." I stroke the broad white blaze down his forehead, and he snorts his contentment. Wild as he might be, we've forged a special friendship. I told Billie once that DD was her heart horse, a horse she could understand like no one else can. A term I learned from the villagers in my hometown.

Looking into Loki's wide black eyes now, watching his soft lips nip at the button on my jacket—trying to pull it off, I might add—I wonder if I've met a second heart horse.

The thought of him leaving in only a few months makes my chest ache and my nose tingle. He's a pain-in-the-ass little horse. But he's *my* pain-in-the-ass little horse. The only reassurance I give myself is knowing at Gold Rush Ranch he will get the absolute best shot to live up to his potential. He'll receive top-of-the-line care. And he might even get to dump Billie Black in the dirt a couple of times.

I chuckle, scratching at his ears. "She's stubborn, but I think you might have her beat in that department."

With that, I grab a pitchfork and start picking out his paddock, tossing manure and loose hay into a wheelbarrow. I have paperwork I should do, registrations, endless emails to answer, but I'd rather hide out here with Loki, trying to avoid his snappy lips as I clean out his field. Physical labor is therapeutic in a way I never imagined. I never really did any until I bought this place. It was part of how I chose to recreate myself.

I didn't get my MBA so I could do farm chores, but I didn't get it to run a horse-racing empire either. I watch Mira, an absolute force to be reckoned with, going after everything she wants. Refusing to be deterred. And I'm just…adrift. Everything is so unresolved for me. I have so many questions about my background that are just *blank*. There's no one to ask because there's no one who knows.

I spent most of my life working my ass off to not become Constantin, to not give in to that part of my genetic makeup. A wife or family felt like a curse I wouldn't ever place on another person, least of all one I professed to love. After all, what if I became him?

And then I found out not a single part of me belongs to him, and my world unexpectedly unlocked. I wasn't beholden to that dark legacy anymore. It was freeing but also confusing. Without that vendetta, I knew nothing about what I wanted out of life.

The older I get, the more I ache for a family, for a connection, in a way I never knew I would. I'm a well-put-together facade. I'm a lost little boy, living his life based on a crusade. A promise I made to no one but myself.

And for what?

There are days where I have no clue what the hell I'm doing with my life—where I wonder if it matters. But most of all, there are days where it feels like I don't know where I'm going because I have no idea where I came from.

The only thing that's certain about where I'm going is that Mira will be with me when I get there. I'll make sure of it. I'm playing for keeps.

CHAPTER 26

Mira

My fingers twist together as I wring my hands and stare at Stefan's door. I haven't seen him in over a day, and I've had too much time to think.

Too much time to overthink.

On top of that, I'm meeting Hank for dinner tonight to do some further research. Questions and confusion are riddling my brain.

How is this all happening so fast? How is *he* interested in *me*? I mean, god. How am *I* interested in *him*? Am I about to ruin my life over a guy? Are we exclusive now? After years of having my nose stuck in a textbook and then throwing myself into a career, sex has always been just sex. I now know that I never experienced a true intimate connection when I fell into bed with a guy just because I felt like that was something I should be doing. Especially now that I realize what I've been missing.

And now Stefan Dalca has orgasmed me into confusion.

Confusion about what we are, where we're going, and what this all means. Because it feels like it means more than just sex.

My phone vibrates in my pocket, and I pull it out, grateful for the distraction. Until I see that it's Stefan texting me.

> **Stefan:** You planning on coming in? Or are you just
> going to stand out there and rub your hands raw?

I look around, trying to see if he's watching me out a window or something. When I see nothing, I text back, figuring he has some sort of security camera app on his phone.

> **Mira:** You're creepy.
> **Stefan:** Part of my charm. You love it.

Anxiety coils in my gut at the mention of the *L* word. The only thing I've loved in recent memory is my job. And my girlfriends at the ranch. Maybe the odd horse. Loving something is a distraction, a time commitment, a risk. And I'm not a big risk taker—especially not when everything I've worked my ass off for is in jeopardy. My career, my independence, my *sanity.*

I take a deep, centering breath and text back.

> **Mira:** I'm coming in.

> **Stefan:** Door's open. I'm in my office. Take a right at the
> kitchen.

With a small shake of my head, I twist the knob and step into the impressive house. I kick my boots off and walk back toward Stefan's office, which I peeked at last time I was over. My mouth goes dry when I enter his space.

He's leaned back in his chair, one foot casually slung over his knee as he looks through the contents of a brown folder with a wall full of books behind him. He's sexy wearing a simple white dress shirt with cuff links that glint in the light, the veins in his hands bulging in the most mouthwatering way. I sometimes get lost staring at his hands when he's fucking me, the way they flex when he grips the sheets and drives into me harder. I never knew such a generic part of a man's body could be so distracting.

I hear a low rumble, a chuckle, and my eyes snap up to his face. Which is honestly no less hot. He studies me with head quirked and his fingers in a loose fist pressed against his soft lips. And he's wearing those fucking glasses. Like he knows the whole hot professor thing has been an ongoing fantasy for me.

I'm instantly wet. I'm thoroughly ruined. I should tell him it's been nice knowing him and get the hell out of here before I spontaneously combust like the sex-crazed maniac I've become.

"What's going through that beautiful head of yours right now, Mira?"

"I haven't heard from you in almost two days."

"I had meetings at the track today. Was there something you needed me for?" One side of his mouth tips up knowingly. *Fucker.*

"No."

I engage him in some sort of staring contest. I refuse to drop his gaze, but it's doing funny things to my insides standing here, staring at him in the quiet office. Especially when he looks like *that*.

"Okay. So you're here because?"

"Are you serious?" I hiss at him, stepping close enough that my thighs butt up against the wide oak desk. "You fucked my brains out. Like, I am literally brainless now. You told me my hands belong in yours, for crying out loud. I can't stop thinking about it. And about you. And it's all driving me crazy. What am I supposed to do now? I haven't heard from you at all. And I just need to know what this is so I can organize my life accordingly. And that's what I came here to ask you, but you're sitting there looking like Professor Pornstar."

Stefan's face slowly transforms from amused to serious, his gaze turning heated toward the end of my rant.

"You've made it abundantly clear you don't want a clingy man-child in your life. Which is perfect because I don't want to be that. I love how fiercely independent you are. You were working these past two days, and so was I. I fully intended to call you when I finished what I was doing here."

I sniff, feeling foolish and realizing he's right. I have said that. I do want that kind of relationship. *Did* want.

But he ruined my brain. And now I'm obsessed.

"Well." I roll my eyes. "You don't have to go radio silent. Especially after everything that happened over the weekend. How am I supposed to discern what that means? How am I supposed to know you're not off dating other women?" I sigh and stare up at the ceiling, hating how completely inexperienced I sound. "This is fucking annoying. You've put a curse on me. You're all I think about."

He laughs and leans forward, elbows propped on the edge of his desk. "Mira."

I press my lips together, not wanting to look at him. But the silence stretches between us. He's waiting for eye contact. I give in, dropping my gaze to his. He's back to looking amused. Which honestly kind of pisses me off.

"What?"

"When? When on earth am I supposed to see all these other women? I've spent almost every free moment I have for the last several weeks with you."

I blink at him.

"I sleep. I work. I work out. I run the farm. I obsessively check on Loki. I try to keep my sister on the straight and narrow. And then I spend my free time either with you or thinking about you. You've put a *spell* on me. *You're* all *I* think about."

My heart lurches in my chest.

"I…I didn't think of it like that. Everything just feels so uncertain."

His grin turns wicked. Knowing.

"That's because I fucked your brains out."

I clench, not fully understanding why hearing him talk this way does it to me. The dirty words drive me crazy. The way he switches from all proper and businesslike to scorching hot and foul-mouthed. It's the dichotomy that gets me off. He pulls it off so well.

He stands and tugs open the top button of his shirt before turning his attention to the cuff links at his wrists. He rotates them slowly, his calloused fingers moving so deftly, it's almost distracting. The plunk of the metal as he sets each one on the desktop sounds loud in the otherwise quiet office.

The silence stretches between us before he says, "And now I'm going to pull those tight jeans down and fuck the uncertainty right out of you."

A small gasp erupts from my lips, and my heart rate crescendos as he ambles around the desk.

"You look pleased. I thought I wasn't your type."

I roll my eyes. "Men who gloat aren't."

Amusement rumbles in his chest as he rolls up his sleeves like he's about to get to work. "But are you bored?"

I wish he'd stop rubbing that in my face. He knows damn well I'm not bored. I'm not sure how any woman in the world's history could be bored with Stefan Dalca. Or how any of them had him and then let him go.

"Do you fantasize about your professor, Mira?"

My head snaps up as he adjusts the glasses on his face. *Fuck. Looking that good should not be allowed.* The forearms. The dress shirt. The glasses. Just…fuck.

My eyes widen as he draws closer. "My professor?"

"Yes." He comes toe to toe with me, forcing me to look up at him. This conversation doesn't make him the least bit uncomfortable, but I'm glowing pink. "You brought that up like it's something you've thought about before. Did you? While you were still in school? Do you now?"

What the hell? Was he taught to be some sort of psychic in Romania?

"It—" I roll my shoulders back. I will not be ashamed of this ongoing fantasy of mine. I refuse. I dig the dynamic, so what? "It is. So yes, I have."

The smile that takes over his face is far too greedy. A smarter woman would run with a man looking at her like this, but all it does is make my stomach drop and my heart race. I realize I trust Stefan. With my heart and with my body. So instead of running, I bite down on my bottom lip and hit him with my best wide-eyed look.

He picks up on the change instantly.

Hand darting behind me to grip my ponytail, he asks, "Care to tell me why you came to my office today, Miss Thorne?" He leans close, voice vibrating across the sensitive spot below my ear. "Are you concerned about your most recent grade?"

A small part of me wants to laugh. This is *so* unlike me. So out of character, it feels almost silly. But when he tugs at my ponytail, forcing my head up farther, I catch sight of his glowing green eyes. All traces of humor melt away. I'm not good at dirty talk, but I love listening to his. So here goes nothing.

"Yes," I whisper.

"Do you have any suggestions for how you'd like to make it up to me?"

I pant as his lips slide down the side of my neck and across my chest, the cool plastic corner of his glasses scraping against my throat.

"I was hoping you could tell me what it would take."

"Dangerous choice, Miss Thorne."

The change is subtle, but he's not calling me Dr. Thorne right now. I love his intelligence. Even during sex, Stefan is thinking. In one swift motion, he turns me toward the desk and bends me over it, my ponytail still wrapped around his hand.

He gently presses my cheek against the cool surface as his free hand roams the center of my back, all the way down so he can grab a handful of my ass. "How hard are you willing to work?"

"As hard as you want me to." My fingertips slide over the polished desktop as I try to get some purchase. I feel like I'm free-falling. Completely out of control. Completely out of my element.

"Fuck, you're perfect." His body looms over mine as he presses a gentle kiss to the back of my neck. "Now stay right where you are. If you move, there won't be any extra credit."

All I can muster is a whimper as I feel the heat of his torso leave my back. His hands glide down my sides, savoring every curve with reverence I've never felt before. When he reaches my hips, his arms encircle me while his hands do away with the button and zipper at the front of my jeans. He drags my skintight jeans down, savoring every rasp of fabric and inch of exposed skin. He unwraps me like a present he's always wanted and will never forget. He uses one dress-shoe-clad foot to nudge my feet into a wider stance, and then my panties are slid down, stretched between my thighs while I'm bent over and bared to him.

"You were made for me."

The statement is like an anvil to my chest. It feels an awful lot like that's true. Like we were made for each other.

I peer over my shoulder at him. The air between us is thick. I can feel it, the way it vibrates, the way it heats as his eyes scour my body. Bright and sparking with…

Love?

"I need to get a condom. I'll be back. Don't move."

I swallow audibly and nod, body humming with anticipation.

He leaves, and I do as he asked. I feel myself getting wetter and more worked up with each passing second I wait for him. The longer he's gone, the more I want him. When he returns, his control has frayed beyond being patient. The jangle of his belt blends into the rip of the condom wrapper.

He steps up behind my bare ass and drags himself between my cheeks. "Next time you need to fix an assignment, I'm going to take you here."

My body trembles with need. I'm at the point where I don't care where he takes me. I just want him inside me.

Now.

"Okay," I murmur, looking over my shoulder again as he notches himself at my slippery entrance.

We lock eyes for only a moment, and I feel like the look we share says it all. It answers every question I've been wrestling with for the past forty-eight hours. A promise is made in that look, and then he impales me with one rough thrust and sends me reeling. His hands grip my hips hard enough I'm certain there will be bruises tomorrow. And I bask in the raw passion. The intense need. I love the way we bring out each other's most base instincts. The way we're both so proper in public and so improper behind closed doors.

"Take it like a good girl, Miss Thorne," he says, before his control snaps completely and his voice becomes a harsh growl. "Every. Inch."

The wet slapping noises of Stefan taking me forcefully fill the room, mingling only with his heavy breaths and my quiet, desperate moans. He eventually leans over my body and reaches beneath me, finding my clit with his fingers.

He rubs firmly while continuing to drive into me wildly, panting in my ear. "If there was any uncertainty in your mind about where we stand, let me clear that up for you now." He slows his thrusts, pulling out and then driving in hard, rattling my body with the force of his claim. "You are mine." My hands slip on the desk, and my legs shake. "And I am yours."

And as I fall apart beneath his firm body, feeling him move inside me, I know I'm exactly where I need to be.

There's no uncertainty now.

CHAPTER 27

Stefan

I'M SITTING AT THE KITCHEN ISLAND STARING OFF INTO space, trying to pull all the thoughts running through my head together. Trying to pull *myself* together.

I wanted to go for another round. I wanted Mira upstairs, spread out on my bed, begging for more. I wanted my skin on hers and her moans in my ear. I wanted to live between her thighs.

Unfortunately, she had other plans. Something with Hank, their farm manager over at Gold Rush Ranch. So I let her go, as badly as I wanted to beg her to stay. Her independence is one of my favorite things about her. She's not clingy or obsessed despite how she might feel right now. She's just excited, and I am too. This thing between us feels new—like it's going somewhere. I don't have to worry about cramming our time together in because we have all the time in the world.

I have a feeling about her.

A smile tugs at the corner of my lips, and I lean my elbows onto the counter before me. Getting lost in the dark lines weaving across the marbled stone countertop, I replay our conversation. The one that took place almost immediately after I'd bent her over my desk and claimed her the way she needed.

As I tugged her pants up over her deliciously round ass, she asked me quietly if we were exclusive now. Vulnerability written all over her beautiful body.

I pulled her into my arms and assured her. "Absolutely."

"Are we dating? What do you call this?"

I laughed. She scowled.

"I don't give a fuck what you call it so long as you're mine."

That's what I'd told her. And I'd meant it. Because it was all so obvious to me.

Sitting here now, it hits me that I'm putting it all on the line for her. Pushing past all my fears about caring too much for another person. Trying to let go of my deep-rooted fear of betrayal. Ignoring the fact that the people I've loved the most in life have been ripped away from me. Acknowledging I have a terrible track record for protecting those very people.

But the look she gave me when I told her she was *mine* was worth the risk.

Over and over again. Worth it.

Because she looked at me like I was *her* prize as much as she is mine.

I feel like it's too soon to be in love. I feel childish even entertaining the thought. But maybe that's just it; maybe a child knows what they're feeling and freely admits it. They don't have years of baggage telling them to ignore what they already know to be true.

With a shake of my head, I pivot and opt to distract myself by showering the other woman in my life with some attention.

"Nadia!" I call up the stairs.

She came home shortly after Mira left, and I momentarily scolded myself for fucking her so publicly. Sometimes, it's hard to remember I'm living with another person. Nadia leads her own life. She is loving working at the clinic and doing her schoolwork in whatever free time she has left. In fact, I'd go so far as to say she's happier than I've seen her, well, ever.

I know she's out with boys. Possibly even *many* boys. But as her older brother who doesn't have a super close and personal relationship with her, I'm never sure what to say about that. I just hope she's being safe. I hope she's making good decisions. Because whether she recognizes it or not, she's a fucking catch. And I suppose that's one area I can find solace. The women at Gold Rush Ranch are an excellent influence—they don't take any shit. And that's the exact type of women Nadia needs in her life.

Strong women.

Something she hasn't had and something I can't do for her no matter how badly I'd like to.

"Yeah?" She jogs down the stairs, looking like a spitting image of our mother.

I'm always glad she didn't take after *him*. I don't really look like either of them, and my chest aches from the questions swirling in my head about whom I *do* look like.

"Wanna grab a bite?"

Her brow furrows. "Why? What's wrong?"

I bark out a loud laugh. "Nothing. I just want to hang out with my little sister. Is that a crime?"

She smiles back, looking amused. "Let me change real quick. I'll be right back."

Twenty minutes later, we walk through the grungy front door of Neighbor's Pub. Nadia's pick, not mine. Apparently, this is where the "coolest" people in town hang out. I eye the place suspiciously and wonder if we have wildly different definitions of cool. The place smells like stale beer, deep-fried chicken, and butter. The smell of popcorn wafts off the self-serve popcorn machine in the corner. The thought of shoving my hand in there to take a bowl full of cold popcorn that everyone else has touched holds zero appeal.

Nadia looks completely at home, and I realize this is probably where she's spent several of her nights lately. Even though she doesn't drink.

I can see a bit of the place's charm. Locals stooped over pints of frothy golden beer line the bar, and "Hotel California" blares through the speakers, mixing with the clacking sound of someone breaking a set of pool balls. It belongs in a movie. I guess I've never felt welcome enough in Ruby Creek to make my way in here. I constantly feel like the outsider and haven't gone out of my way to change that.

"Isn't this place great? So Canadian." Nadia smiles wide as she slides onto a stool at a high top beside a pool table. "Any chance you want to play?"

I marvel at my little sister, no longer the sullen young woman who stepped off a plane. She's strong, so fucking strong. My chest pinches at the thought of how she had to pull herself up by the bootstraps. About how I left her hanging to serve my own ends.

I hope she can forgive me one day.

"Yeah. Yeah, I'd love to." I shake my head and smile back, trying to clear the guilt of walking down memory lane.

"Great. I'll be right back. Drink?"

"Yeah, I'll have…"

"Don't say wine, Stef. I know you're a wine guy, but this isn't a wine place." She grins at me, ribbing me. Not treating me like the bore of an older brother I sometimes feel like with the age gap between us. *This is what I want with her.*

"How about a cosmopolitan?"

"Dear god," she huffs. "You are such a priss."

A deep laugh rumbles in my chest. "I'm joking. I'll take a beer."

"Are you though?" She quirks a brow at me before strutting away, laughing.

I watch her walk up to the bar, cringing at the way heads turn as she passes. I could take off a few heads for looking at my baby sister the way they are right now, but I haven't held that kind of role in her life, and it would be weird to start now. So I won't.

Instead, I glance away, scanning the rest of the bar.

Taking it all in, until my eyes snag on an ass I'd recognize anywhere. An ass cupped by the denim I pulled down mere hours ago.

Mira is digging through that godforsaken popcorn machine with a scoop in one hand and a basket in the other.

I'll be happy to take care of her when she inevitably gets sick after this. That's how much I like this girl. I'm looking forward to holding her hair back while she hurls.

I find myself peering around the bar, wondering why the hell she's here when she said she had a meeting with Hank. She wouldn't be here with someone else, would she? After everything we've done together? Everything we've shared?

I can't imagine it, but it doesn't stop my gut from churning and my heart rate from ratcheting up. If Mira wasn't with me, what kind of guy would she be with? My eyes scan the bar, hoping upon hope that she wouldn't lie to me.

There's a lot I can tolerate. But lying isn't it. After my life, it's a hard line for me. Anxiety creeps up over my sternum as I let my paranoia run away with me. *Something* feels off. I just can't pinpoint what.

But then I find Hank sitting alone at a cozy two-person table beside a roaring fireplace in the back. My body relaxes as I watch Mira smile in his direction and head back that way.

She's almost at the table when she's intercepted by Nadia. Her body tenses. I see her lips moving, asking whom Nadia is here with, as she looks around nervously.

Something is definitely off.

Nadia greets Hank, and he smiles back with a quick wink. And then when Nadia points at me, Mira's eyes shoot in my direction. She smiles, but it's tentative. She waves, but it's small.

Not one to back down from an awkward situation, I stand and walk across the room, approaching the small table and watching Mira's eyes go more round with every step I take in her direction.

She has *never* looked at me like that. I feel like I'm watching my own life play out before me.

"Stefan. Hi." She pushes the loose strands from her ponytail behind her ears as she takes a seat. Across from Hank.

"Sir." I reach toward the man and offer my open hand.

He grins, looking between Mira and me as he shakes my hand.

"Oh, please. No need to call me sir, son. We owe you a big thank-you for taking on our little guy the way you have. Mira tells me you've named him Loki?"

The apples of Mira's cheeks pop up as she looks away shyly. Sounds like someone has been talking about me.

"Yeah. The name fits him well. He's a mischief maker. You're going to have your hands full with this one."

Hank shakes his head. "Not me. Billie. I'm too old for projects like that. She can play bucking bronco on her own." He grins. "Loki. The god of mischief. I like it. The funny part is…I think Billie will too."

We all chuckle, and then Mira says, "Hank and I have something of a standing date here on Tuesday nights. You know…as the two unattached people at the ranch." I don't know why she's acting so nervous. Like I'd be mad about her going out for dinner with a man old enough to be her father. "I've missed a couple times, so here I am. Making it up to him."

"You brought him to this dive to make it up to him?"

Mira's cheeks pink as she lifts her pint of beer to take a long swig.

My brow furrows as I take her in. Something passes between us, and I get the sense she wants me to leave. But before I can go, Hank pipes up.

"Aw, nah. I love this place. Did Mira tell you I used to bartend here?"

Mira freezes, pint glass held high as her eyes bore into mine over the rim. All the sounds around us blur to white noise as I drag my eyes off the woman I thought I trusted to take in the man sitting across from her.

His features hit me rapid-fire. Like bugs against a windshield. Eyes. *Splat.* Hair. *Splat.* Square jaw. *Splat.*

My breathing becomes labored. It feels like someone has doused me in scalding-hot water. Intense feelings of betrayal course through my veins. My layers of composure slough away. I turn back to Mira, her pint glass now placed back on the table and her eyes giving me a sad, pleading look as she nervously wipes at her lips.

She knew. *She knew.*

And she didn't tell me.

Never mentioned it.

The utter shock of it all lances through me. Hot and painful and nauseating. I need to leave. I need to compose myself before I say or do something I'll regret.

Hank's head quirks, the emerald eyes that match mine

so full of questions. "You all right, son? You look like you've seen a ghost."

Son. The word fills my mind and blankets my vision. After all this time, he's been sitting right under my nose. And the woman I thought I might be falling in love with fucking *knew.*

I've experienced betrayal in my life, more than most people have. But this is different. Only people who had already let me down in some way have ever betrayed me.

Mira bowled me over by being perfect for me, and I didn't even have the sense to see it coming.

"I'm fine." My voice is brittle. "Enjoy your dinner." I spin on a heel and march toward the heavy front door of the dingy pub.

I need fresh air. I need distance. I need time to process. I can't do that with Mira's doe eyes pleading with me.

And I sure as fuck can't do that while I stare into eyes that are a perfect mirror image of my own.

Pushing into the cool night air, I keep my strides even and controlled until I get to my SUV. I round the front of it toward the grass ditch and heave. It's been hours since I've eaten, so nothing comes. Just silent nausea and the choked sounds that accompany it.

When the episode passes, I'm still bent over, hands on my knees, trying to catch my breath—trying to cool my head.

"Stefan?"

Her voice is quiet, pained. Uncertain.

"I don't want to talk right now." And I don't. At this current juncture, I have nothing to say to Dr. Mira Thorne.

Her steps don't falter as she approaches. "Let me explain." Her voice cracks.

I turn on her, eyes blazing. Heart throbbing. "Explain what, Mira? How, after everything I've divulged to you, you can't so much as mention this to me?"

"I—"

I cut her off, words coming out hard as I stand up tall. "I trusted you. I told you things I've never told *anyone*."

"I had a plan. I was going to tell you."

"How long?"

She blanches, her face going deathly white under the light of the moon, almost blue beneath the dark sky.

"How long did you know?"

"Listen." She holds her hands up in a gesture that tells me she wants me to slow down. But I can't do that right now. My head is spinning. I've spent years languishing over this secret, and she's had the power to put me out of my misery for...how long?

"Did you know before we got involved?"

"Define *involved.*"

That's my answer. Rage churns in my gut, and I quirk an eyebrow at her, scoffing as I do.

"Everything between us has happened so fast. Just let me explain before you cut me off again."

"So now this is my fault? No, Mira. This was a simple conversation you could have had with me. It doesn't matter now."

Her face stays stoic while silent tears trickle down her cheeks. "What does that mean?"

"It means…I…fuck!" I shout as I run both my hands through my hair. This is not how this was supposed to go between us. "I'm not sure I can be with someone this dishonest. In fact, I'm almost positive I can't."

A hollow gasp erupts from her lips as she slams a hand over her mouth. "Stefan, just—"

I wave a hand to stop her. "Nah. No, thanks. I've already got one woman I loved who lied to me up on a pedestal. I don't have room for another. It's no wonder you wanted to keep us a secret." I shake my head and walk around to my driver's-side door. "I mean, really, Mira? Do you ever do anything that doesn't benefit *you* in some way?" The noise she makes in response is deep and guttural. "Tell Nadia I had to go."

I don't let my eyes anywhere near her as I get in and pull away. I can't. Because as angry as I am with her, I know one look at her face will kill my resolve to protect myself.

I watch the outline of her body shrink into the dark as I drive away and realize protecting myself is something I've already failed to do, considering I just admitted I'm in love with her.

CHAPTER 28

Mira

I FEEL LIKE I'M ON AUTOPILOT. FLOATING, BUT NOT IN A good way. I walk back into the bar on wooden legs. I barely feel in control of my body, like a marionette on a string and the universe is having a good laugh as it walks me around. Hank and Nadia must be able to tell because she's taken my place at our table, and they're both looking at me with confusion written all over their faces.

I'm accustomed to tragedy, but I'm at a loss for what to say right now. I can't think of a way to cover this up. I don't know what to do.

"Everything okay, Mira?" Hank asks, concern lacing his voice.

Nadia looks at me sadly, her brows knitting together in concern.

"No. Not really." I wipe at my eyes, realizing that I walked in here with tears pooling on my cheeks.

"Here." Hank stands and pulls another chair up to our table, lining it up behind me and giving my back a quick rub as he does. "Take a seat. You look like you're going to topple over."

I sit rigidly, twisting my hands in my lap. Usually when I deliver bad news, I take solace in knowing I've done everything in my power to avoid this outcome.

Tonight, I can't say the same.

I could have handled this differently. But I'm not sure that would have been preferable. I don't know. I don't know anything other than I'm drowning in guilt. My chest aches with such raw pain, it radiates up my throat and steals my words.

I've been so unfair to Stefan. He's done everything he can to protect me, and I repaid him by withholding something he's been killing himself trying to figure out. I thought I was protecting him too.

A wave of shame hits me, soaking me, chilling me to the bone.

"I've made a huge mistake."

"Well"—Hank shifts in his seat, eyes darting to Nadia— "let's see what we can do about solving that." He pushes my beer toward me, but I can't handle the thought of consuming anything right now.

"I… Hank, I can't. I still don't feel like it's my place to say anything. I had hoped to talk with you tonight. I had some certainty, but this…god. This really blew up in my face."

"Talk to me about what?"

I glance over at Nadia, white teeth nibbling at

heart-shaped pink lips. I have no clue if she's aware of this whole thing. *How did I make such a big mess? How did I blow this so badly?*

I opt for a very general line of questioning, just in case.

"Did you know someone by the name of Nora when you worked here?"

Hank clears his throat and shuffles his broad shoulders around in his chair. "I did."

I nod, looking down at my hands again, rolling my lips together. I feel like I could hurl. My voice drops an octave and comes out as almost a whisper. "How well did you know her?"

A shadow passes over Hank's face, a memory maybe. I watch his proud chest rise and fall under the plaid shirt he's wearing. His head tilts, and a sad smile touches his lips. "Well enough that I still think about her often."

My heart cracks and tears spring up in my eyes again. *Fuck my life.* This whole thing is just painful.

I blink rapidly and grab Hank's knee right as Nadia pipes up, confusion lacing her tone. "Are you talking about my mom?"

My hand pulses over Hank's jeans as his eyes snap down to mine. Shock weaves its way between the different shades of green as the realization sinks in.

"You need to talk to Stefan. That's all I can tell you." I stand and wrap my arms around the shocked man's neck, squeezing him in a bone-crushing hug. I whisper so only Hank can hear me, "He really needs you."

The stinging in my nose overwhelms me, and without

saying anything further, I turn to pay. "Come on, Nadia. I'll drive you home."

She says nothing but pushes to stand, clearly trying to piece things together. And when I get to the front door, I check over my shoulder to see Hank spinning his pint of beer, staring at the golden liquid. But he's not really there.

He's lost in a memory.

CHAPTER 29

Stefan

I woke on a pillow that smelled like Mira's honey-scented shampoo. I stripped the bed and threw everything in the wash—hot water and an extra pod—as though washing my sheets would help scrub her from my mind.

Now I'm sitting at my kitchen counter staring at the steam rising off my black coffee. The coffee that has done nothing to wake me up after a long, restless night. I've been fixating on the fact I've probably finally found my father. I don't know where to go now, and I don't know what to say. I don't even know *if* I should say anything or if it's best to let sleeping dogs lie.

I don't know if the man has a family. I have no clue what I'd be interrupting. *I don't know a fucking thing.*

But Mira did. She knew everyone's situation perfectly and opted to keep me in the dark. She let me spill my guts to her. She let me expose all my inner misery, and she did nothing to ease that.

She made me care for her. She wiggled her way into my life. She made me want things I wasn't sure I'd ever want. And then she turned around and ruined it all with her dishonesty.

Letting her go should be simple. A clear-cut choice. An obvious answer. But I feel like I'm sitting here sawing off a perfectly good limb.

It *hurts*. More than I thought it would. More than I knew it could.

Quiet footsteps pull me from my moping as Nadia pads across the kitchen straight toward the coffee maker.

With her back to me, I say, "Sorry I left you last night."

"It's okay. Mira drove me back."

I sigh and scrub at my face. "I'm sorry I have such a terrible habit of leaving you behind."

My sister turns, her golden curls a wild mess in a bun on top of her head. "I wish you'd forgive yourself. Do you have any idea how much happier you'd be if you stopped blaming yourself for all the bad things that happened to us in our lives? They aren't worth it. Not even a little bit. Don't let them keep the power. I want you to be happy. I hold nothing against you. Yes, I was stuck with them for longer before I left, but you're still stuck there in that house even though you're standing here before me."

I swallow. I am. I live in that house every damn day. I relive it. I'm trapped there, and I've made it my life's mission to undo everything he did—but at what cost? Who am I really punishing? Constantin is dead in the ground on the other side of the world.

My mom is in the lake.

And Nadia is sitting here. Giving me advice that is wise beyond her years.

"I know we don't have the same dad."

"Pardon?"

"Look at us, Stefan. I'm a dead ringer for Mom. You look like you belong to the milkman. Or as it's currently looking, the barn manager down the road."

"Jesus. You have no filter, do you?"

She smiles, wide and cheesy, not looking the least bit upset about this conversation. "Unapologetic honesty. You should try it some time."

I groan, scrubbing at my face even harder. "Fuck."

"Oh, wow." She lifts the steaming mug up to her lips and bats her lashes. "Things must be bad if Mr. Proper is swearing."

"I'm sorry."

"For what?"

"For…" God, where do I even start? "The course your life has taken."

She scrunches her face and shakes her head like I've said the most ridiculous thing in the world. "I'm not. Not everything happens for a reason. Some things happen because we make the conscious decision to stop letting shit happen to us. And no matter what, you're my brother. We're family. DNA doesn't change a damn thing."

I swallow. My little sister is usually nonchalant. Carefree. A pain in my ass. But today she feels more like a big sister, hitting me with all the things I need to hear.

"Don't blow it with Mira."

Except that. I don't want to hear that.

"I'm not sure what you're talking about."

Her brow arches. "You spew an awful lot of bullshit for someone who goes on about valuing honesty."

"I—"

One hand shoots up to stop me. "Stefan, stop. I know you guys are together. She told us."

My stomach bottoms out. "What?"

"Yeah. Girls' night. Billie said something bitchy about you, and Mira wasn't having it. Told us all that you guys were a thing. Or whatever. I stopped listening because it was gross—you're still my brother." She shudders.

She told them. I was certain she planned on keeping us a secret. She's so hard to get a read on. She keeps her cards so close. Why wouldn't she have told me this? That was the night I showed up at her apartment because she missed me.

"At any rate," my sister continues, "don't let her get away. She's the best thing that has ever happened to you. And you have a bad habit of not letting good things happen to yourself."

The doorbell rings, effectively cutting off our conversation. Which works for me because I'm still irrationally angry with Mira. I'm still not ready to forgive her.

I don't know if I can.

But all thoughts of Mira flee my mind when I swing the front door open and stare back into eyes that are exactly like mine. I've never taken a very close look at Hank. The dark-golden hair swooped back off his face, the deep lines on his tan skin from years spent in the sun, his broad shoulders and trim waist. He's fit for his age—whatever that is. Strong in a way only a lifetime of manual labor can achieve.

"I have a feeling that you and I should chat."

He smiles, but it's a nervous smile. Not the typical happy-go-lucky grin that I've seen him sporting. The man couldn't be less like Constantin if he tried. Looks-wise, personality-wise, life-wise. It's something I instantly love about him.

I give him a nervous smile of my own. "Come on in." I hold the door open wide and gesture with my arm for him to enter. "Coffee?" I ask, walking away toward the kitchen, trying to catch my breath and looking for something to fix the dry throat situation I have going.

"Got anything harder?" Hank chuckles.

I've never heard a better idea in my life. Instead of reaching for the coffee, I reach into the cupboard above the sink and pull out a bottle of bourbon and two whiskey glasses.

"It's five o'clock somewhere." I hold them up and face the man who is most likely my father.

He chuckles again. It's warm and comforting and genuinely happy. I ache for that sound. The sound I missed growing up. And when he winks at me, my mind flashes with moments in my life when I missed that exact look. My graduation. Swim meets. I could have had *that*.

I clear my throat and will the emotion clouding my eyes away. "Living room is that way."

Once we're both seated on the plush leather couches with a healthy two-finger pour of whiskey in hand, Hank leans back, arm over the back of the couch, and lets his eyes soak me in. I can feel him analyzing me, cataloguing our similarities with a small sad smile on his lips. I wonder how this must feel for him.

I'm about to ask when he says, "So, Stefan, tell me about your life."

And I do. I start at the very beginning, and I leave absolutely nothing out.

★★★

I'm drunk. It's 11 a.m. on a Wednesday, and I'm drunk.

With my dad.

Talk about things I never thought would happen. We're both pretty sure he's my dad. The timing works out. We'll get a DNA test done to confirm. It all makes sense. Except my mom's decisions. Those will never make sense to me. Hank says he begged her to stay. He says he loved her.

That part was hard to hear.

Just like me, having to tell him what became of her life was hard for him to hear. I'm not above admitting that we both shed a few tears over the course of our two-hour conversation. We have that in common too, I guess.

And now, we're walking down the driveway toward the farm, both a bit tipsy, because Hank wants to see Loki.

"See that lake?" I point to the small body of water at the base of the valley. "Or pond? Slough? I call it a lake, but maybe it's too small."

"It can be whatever you want it to be." Hank laughs, hands in his pockets, strolling down the driveway with a tipsy grin on his face.

His smile melts off the minute I drunkenly blurt out, "That's where I spread her ashes."

His Adam's apple bobs in his throat as his eyes gaze out over the sparkling water reflecting the clouds on its still surface. "I think she'd have loved it here." His voice is thick with emotion, and I instantly regret saying anything. I immediately start beating myself up about it, staring at the ground, wondering why I would blurt that out. I'm so accustomed to walking on eggshells around people that I'm taken by surprise when a warm hand lands on my shoulder.

"Thank you for telling me." He smiles a real smile. "It's nice to know where she is."

I feel like a little kid. A sad little kid with daddy issues basking in the glow of someone with kind hands and a friendly face. I've spent so many years dreaming of this day, and somehow it still doesn't seem real. I feel like I'm hovering above, looking down at myself.

And it's not just the whiskey.

We walk side by side in a companionable silence until we reach the stable parking lot and come face-to-face with Mira's big Gold Rush Veterinary Services truck parked in front of the large sliding doors.

I go rigid and stop in my tracks. I'm not prepared to see her. I have too many feelings to process first. I said things last night I wish I hadn't said. Things I'm not ready to apologize for yet. To be honest, I'm still not sure they warrant an apology.

I still can't believe she kept this to herself.

I catch sight of her in Farrah and Loki's paddock, doing

her daily check, stooped down over her workbox full of needles and bottles.

"You should talk to her," Hank says.

"I…" I get lost soaking up the expression of concentration on her face. The way her intelligent eyes dart around, her teeth worrying at her bottom lip while she looks for something. My first instinct is to rush over and help her.

I wonder if that need will ever wane.

"I'm not sure I'm ready."

"I'm not telling you what you need to say to her. Only that you need to talk to her. You both need closure. *If* that's what you want. She's a tough cookie. She's not an open book, but she has a good heart. She came to your defense on more than one occasion. That woman cares about you. Don't doubt that for a moment. Because we all only have so many moments left to live." He looks over at the lake thoughtfully before adding, "I'm going to go have a chat with your mom."

And with one final squeeze of my shoulder, he's gone, strolling away like giving fatherly advice is something he's been doing for me my entire life.

His movement catches Mira's attention, and she stands abruptly to stare at him before her eyes search the driveway for me. And when her eyes meet mine, emotion moves between us. There's always been a palpable tension between Mira and me—something that hasn't lessened just because I broke it off last night.

It might even be stronger. It feels like there's an elastic between us and I've pulled it taut by yanking myself away. I wonder if the more I pull away, the harder we'll collide.

I wonder if we'll survive the collision.

"Hi," she says tentatively as I move toward her.

"Hey." My voice is slightly slurred, and I stop a few meters away.

I don't trust myself to get any closer, and at least this proximity has eased the throbbing in my chest. As long as I don't get lost in her eyes. Her wide onyx eyes, the ones that give everything away lately. Every thought and feeling. Every insecurity.

Today they look sad. Devastated even.

We stare at each other stupidly. Awkwardly. Two intelligent adults who've shared one another's deepest, darkest secrets and still can't think of a damn thing to say.

"I need you to listen to me. I don't need you to respond. I don't even need you to understand. I just want the opportunity to present my reasoning for what I did. Then I'll leave. I promise."

All I can offer her is a terse nod.

With a deep sigh, she starts in, her hand gently scratching at Farrah's ear. "I didn't know Hank being your father was even a possibility until the night we drove back from my parents' place. When you told me what your mom said. The only connection I had to go on was that he'd been a bartender in town. I knew Hank had bartended before he started working here. But, Stefan"—she pauses, looking at me imploringly—"there has been a lot more than one bartender in town over the years."

I know she's right, but I just keep staring.

"I had no idea if there were more bars or restaurants in

town back then. It didn't *have* to be Neighbor's. I suspected, but what was I supposed to do? Get your hopes up when it could be nothing? Tell Hank, who is almost like family to me, that maybe I was on to something?"

"Yes, Mira. Either of those options would have been preferable."

Her hands land on her hips, and her eyes swim with sadness. "And who should I have told first? Who is entitled to my completely unproven hypothesis? I asked you about your mom for more information. Even just her name. And then last night, my plan was to ask Hank if he knew her."

"Wow, you really had this all planned out." My voice is cutting. I hate feeling like she was plotting something behind my back.

She ignores the dig, but I don't miss the tears that spring to her eyes.

"This was *so* not any of my business. I was trying to make responsible decisions with big information. It's not in me to run around spouting a theory without any good evidence. My brain doesn't work like that. I didn't know how quickly things between us would"—she sighs and looks up at the puffy clouds overhead—"evolve. I didn't see you coming, Stefan. Not like this. And I couldn't tell Hank because that would break your confidence in me. And I couldn't tell you because I didn't want to be the one to hurt you if I was wrong." Her voice cracks on the last few words, and she looks away, foot tapping against the ground anxiously. "Believe me when I say that I was trying to protect you."

"You hurt me anyway."

Any happy buzz I had before has leached into the ground at my feet. Now, I feel monumentally depressed. I'd have to be an idiot to not see her point. But it doesn't change the result. She lied to me, kept a secret, and I can't get over that hurdle. But pain traces her every feature. I want to wrap her in my arms and kiss away every hurt, but my pride won't let me. The sad little boy inside me won't allow it.

I lean into that childish side of myself when I respond in a wooden tone, "I…I need some time to wrap my head around everything." Her lashes flutter in a failed attempt to stop the tears from spilling down her cheeks. "Thank you for explaining your line of thinking."

She sucks in air like she can't breathe. There's so much pain there, and I hate thinking I caused it for her. I never wanted to hurt Mira, but I'm feeling too fragile to save us both. I want to be able to let it go, but my mother's betrayal is a wound that's been freshly ripped open. The truth of the matter is, I'm not in the right headspace to make big decisions. And Mira might be the most important decision I've ever had to make.

"Thank you for hearing me out." Her broken voice is a searing lance to my heart, but I knock it away. I can't afford a killing blow right now. "I don't think Loki will require regular checkups anymore, so you won't have to worry about seeing me."

"Perfect" is my quick response.

And I instantly want to take it back. I meant perfect that he's better, not that I won't have to see her. That part stings in a way I didn't expect.

297

A few minutes ago, she asked me to hear her out, and hope welled in her eyes.

Now, thanks to me, it's spilling down her cheeks.

CHAPTER 30

Mira

IT'S BEEN THE LONGEST WEEK OF MY LIFE. I'M A SHELL OF myself, and I'm not even succeeding at hiding it. My heartbreak is on my sleeve for everyone to see. I thought foaling season sucked, but getting over what happened between Stefan and me is worse. It's truly a torment I've never known.

I haven't heard a single thing from Stefan all week. He hasn't called or texted. And I haven't either. Giving him space seems like the most grown-up approach at this time.

I wish I could make him see things the way I do, but I'm not one to force things on another person. If I were more like Billie, I'd march over there and browbeat him until he relented. I'm more live and let live though. If that's what he thinks of this, of me, then that's fine. I'll get over it.

Eventually.

But not soon enough. Because this hurts. I feel like we've spent months building a complicated puzzle together, and now he's taken one piece and hidden it on me. It's annoying to look at, no matter which way I spin it, what perspective I move to—the puzzle is incomplete.

I'm incomplete.

How it happened is beyond me. All those quiet nights on the barn floor, I guess. All the inappropriate jokes. All the times he asked me on a date. All the times I turned him down.

All the time I wasted when we could have been together.

If I'd said yes, I might have had more time with him before this happened. Maybe it wouldn't have happened at all. Maybe it all would have come out more organically if I hadn't been so fucking stubborn.

Instead, I'm here in the office replaying our interactions and nights together, feeling his hands sliding over my skin, hearing the filthy words spilling from his lips.

I'm missing him like crazy and trying to pretend I don't. Nadia eyes me speculatively now and then. We both know talking about my relationship with her brother would be weird. And he's *her* brother, so I fully expect she takes his side in this nightmare. If there are sides to be had at all. Plus, I know he loves her more than anything in the world, so it feels wrong to lament anything about him to her, even if she's become a friend.

If you ask me, it's just one big sorry situation. She asks me how I'm doing with a weird intonation that tells me she doesn't believe me when I say I'm good.

I am not good. I'm fucking sick.

"What are you staring at?" Billie says from behind me where I'm staring out the enormous windows at the front of the clinic.

I spin, startled by her presence. She must have come in through the back door closest to the barn.

"An eagle," I lie.

"Huh." She peers at the sky in an exaggerated fashion. "I must have missed it."

We both know she didn't miss shit.

"Must have."

"You holding up, Mimi?"

"Jesus Christ. Can you not?" I cross my arms and shake my head.

Her hand falls across her chest in mock alarm. "Not what?"

"Your nicknames. I've escaped them for this long. I thought I was doing okay, and now all of a sudden I'm *Mimi*?"

She snorts. "It doesn't suit you at all."

"Yes. Exactly. Thank you."

"But that's why I like it."

I groan and drop my chin to my chest. "Sometimes I wonder why I love you so much."

"Because I'm honest."

Ugh. I really don't want to hear about honesty. According to Stefan, I'm dishonest. And that hurts too. I don't think I'm a dishonest person. Not at all. I got tangled up these last couple months, but I'm not a liar. And I don't like being called one.

"Uh-huh…" I peek at Billie out of the corner of my eye, wondering what's coming next.

"I'm here to tell you to pull yourself up by the bootstraps. He's just a boy. And you are a fucking rock star."

301

This conversation is the epitome of what I don't want to talk about. "Thanks," I reply tersely.

She snorts. "Maybe Dalca the Dick really is a dick after all, huh?"

I know she's trying to make me laugh, but this doesn't feel funny right now. It feels like she's diminishing what happened between us. And the more time I spend away from Stefan, the more I realize what happened between us is love. Or at least something a lot like it.

"Funny." I don't laugh.

Her amber eyes dart over to mine. "I wasn't trying to be funny, Mira. I was right. The guy *is* a dick, and you deserve better."

What are the stages of grief again? Because I'm pretty sure my best friend just catapulted me into the anger phase.

"You know what, Billie? Fuck you. This isn't the moment where I need you to be right. I need you to be wrong."

Heat lashes at my gut, and I spin on my heel to walk away. I need to get out of here. But I come face-to-face with a wide-eyed Nadia. "Can you lock up, Nadia? I'll see you tomorrow."

It's only been one week since Stefan asked me if I only do things when they benefit me, and I'm still not over it. Still not over him.

And I'm not sure I ever will be.

★★★

"You're really out?" My nana is not buying my story about how I came to see her for more samosas. "Because you don't *look* like you've been eating."

I haven't been.

"Yup. Can we make some?"

Folding samosas with my grandmother is therapeutic. It's soothing. And right now, I need to be soothed. Even her lilting accent soothes me—until it reminds me of Stefan's and the way it's more pronounced when he's turned on. A shiver races down my spine.

She hobbles back into my parents' house, shaking her head. "Your parents are out right now."

She moved in here a couple of years ago after my grandfather passed. She tells me it's because I'm her favorite grandchild, but I'm pretty sure it's because my parents have a separate suite she can live in.

I follow her to the kitchen and try to pull stuff out, but I'm moping, and I keep getting in her way. I feel like Eeyore dragging his sad ass around just being generally brutal.

"You"—she points at me and then points at the table—"go sit down."

"Okay." I tuck my tail and drop into a chair, relieved to be resting and away from prying eyes, disapproving stares, and awkward conversations with Hank. *God*, are they ever awkward. He's trying so hard to be chipper around me while also not talking about the elephant in the room.

It's brutal, and I'm ashamed to say I've taken to avoiding him.

"Where is the blond boy?" Nana has her upper body shoved into the fridge, where she's pulling ingredients.

"Probably working."

"Did he break your heart?"

My throat constricts. But I don't respond.

"Yes?" She shakes her head as she bends down to pull a bowl out of the lower cupboard, her cotton sari draping with her every movement. "I knew he would."

"I thought you said he wasn't my type?"

She looks at me now, her eyes fierce, her index finger pointing straight at me once again. "Exactly. Your type wasn't working for you, so I knew he would. All smart and sexy and established, why wouldn't he?"

Did my grandmother just call Stefan Dalca sexy?

I clear my throat and pick at a dent on the dated wooden table.

"So?"

"So what?"

"Did he break your heart?"

I feel my bottom lip wobble. "Yeah."

"And what are you going to do about it?" she asks as she continues organizing ingredients and cooking utensils.

"I mean…nothing. I don't think he can forgive me. I'm not one to grovel. I'm still not even sure I did anything wrong. It's…complicated."

"Mira, Mira, Mira." Her head shakes, and she makes a tutting noise. "You work so hard for everything else that you want in life. School, career, your independence—you haven't cared about what anyone thought about all that. What makes this any different? What makes you think you won't have to work for this?"

"I…" I trail off.

I don't have a good answer. The only thing that runs through my head is Stefan asking if I ever do something that

304

doesn't benefit me. Going after him with reckless abandon would serve me, but would it just upset him? I feel like I'm living each day with that one sentence haunting me. Do I really do that? I became a veterinarian to help animals, to be a voice for those who don't have one, and I know I've helped countless people along the way. As a general rule, people love their animals and appreciate my work.

But I'm paralyzed by the sentiment that I do nothing unless it helps me in some way. Do I only save animals because it makes me feel good? And if I do…is that even a bad thing?

"Do you want him?"

That's a question I barely need to think about. "Yes."

"Then take him. I saw the way that fool looked at you when you were here. You might have thought you were tricking us by bringing a fake date to fend off the questions, but not me. And nothing about that day was fake for him."

I think she's trying to reassure me, but it's not working. The cracking pain in my chest is sharp enough to take my breath away.

"Okay." My breathing hitches as my brain whirs.

What have I done? How have I so easily dismissed our connection as something fleeting? Why did I give up on him when I've never given up on anything that matters to me in my life? Maybe it's not so bad that I do things that benefit me.

Maybe my mistake is failing to make Stefan one of those things.

"Well?" She props her tiny fists on her full hips and gives me a suffering look. "Why are you still here pretending that you're out of samosas?"

Why does she know absolutely everything?

"Get out of here. Go get him. Nobody walks away from my favorite granddaughter unless she lets them."

I was so concerned about what everyone else would think that I failed to notice the way a great man worshipped me. The way he was *good for me*. And now I've hurt him. And it doesn't even matter who's right or wrong. There's no fault. My intention doesn't matter. None of that matters because I hurt a man who has done nothing but care for me in a way no one ever has.

I don't even respond. There's no point in denying that my freezer is practically overflowing with samosas. My plan was to pawn these new ones off on Billie and Vi. I nod, swiping my keys off the counter and striding out the front door.

My heart knows how I feel about him. But my head—well, my head is a complicated place to be sometimes. I exist in a world of absolutes and science. But there is nothing absolute about falling in love.

No, that's a matter for the soul.

The minute I hop in my truck, all fired up and feeling determined, my phone rings through the Bluetooth system. Nadia is calling. I press the button, expecting her to have some question about closing the clinic for the night.

What I don't expect is her panicked voice. "Mira! The barn at Cascade Acres is on fire!"

★★★

I've never driven so dangerously in my life. I know the back roads around these small towns like the back of my hand, so I cut every corner I can and break every speed limit. Nadia

306

didn't have much information other than she'd gotten a call from the barn manager and was heading over there.

I got a hold of Vaughn to close the clinic for us, and I've made it back to Ruby Creek in record time. I can see the smoke billowing ahead of me like an omen. My stomach sinks at the sight of the dark clouds over Stefan's picturesque farm.

Inhaling deep breaths into my lungs, I try to force myself into the right headspace for what I might walk into. Barn fires aren't exactly unheard of. Unfortunately, hay and wood make for excellent kindling. But the outcome never gets easier. Burns, smoke inhalation—it's almost always ugly and heartbreaking.

Especially with the size of the smoke cloud overhead. This isn't some small spark.

I confirm my suspicions when I turn into the driveway. The scenic barn is covered in smoke, flames licking up the back side of the building. Lights flash in the darkening night, and I hear the firefighters shouting as I park and jump out of my truck—heading straight for the fire.

I see the barn manager, Leo, staring at the scene before him, mouth agape, standing with the glow of flames lighting his face.

"Are the horses out?" I ask him.

"I—no. Not all of them. We'd just put them all away for the night when it happened."

My heart lurches. *Loki. Farrah.* Rage courses through me. "And why are you just standing here?"

"What am I supposed to do?"

Absolute idiot. "Were you here when it started?"

He nods solemnly. The coward was here when it started and didn't do shit except stand here catching flies.

"Where is Stefan?"

"On his way."

"Where is Nadia?"

"She went in."

A chill starts from the ground, seeping up through my bones. "Excuse me?"

He points at the barn. "Just a couple minutes ago."

"Fuck, Leo. Has anyone ever mentioned that you're a pussy?" I storm toward the barn and stop near a fully out-fitted firefighter. "There's someone in there, did you know that?"

"We just got here, ma'am. We're assessing the situation."

Not good enough. Nadia is in there. Stefan can't lose her. It will kill him.

Moments later, Nadia stands at the wide-open doors, eyes wild and searching. My relief is short-lived.

"I need gloves," she shouts. "I can't get the stalls open! The metal latches are too hot."

Then she turns and races back into the building. A fire-fighter runs to the door, trying to grab her before she disappears back into the smoke.

My stomach sinks as I stare at the barn. Her words haunt me as I watch the flames building on each other. Everything Stefan has worked so hard for. The redemption he's thrown himself into. His horses who he loves so quietly. Sweet souls who have no hope of helping themselves in this situation.

His sister.

The thought barely crosses my mind before I'm moving. I grab a pair of gloves sitting on the bumper of the fire truck and sprint for the barn before anyone can stop me. No chance I'll stand here watching a barn full of horses and a friend of mine burn to death while they formulate a plan. It's simply not an option.

I hear shouts behind me as I shove my hands into the big gloves and charge through the door. It crosses my mind what I'm doing is monumentally stupid, but I don't linger on that thought. Even if I can save a few horses and get out, I'll be happy.

Thick smoke fills the dark barn. The whinnies are loud over the crackling of the fire. I can almost *taste* the fear. And then I see Nadia, trying to grab a latch but jerking away when it sizzles against her skin.

Her eyes find mine, her voice imploring as she points down the barn alleyway to where the smoke is thickest. "Mira! Loki is down there! They're *all* in here."

She looks down at her hands, and it doesn't take a medical degree to see that she's burned them in her failed attempts to open the stalls.

"Nadia. Out. You need medical attention. I've got this."

"Let me help you!" She's in shock, tears streaming down her face.

"No."

"Mira. You don't understand. If he loses Loki, I don't think he'll ever forgive himself. That foal is proof that not everything he touches turns to shit. I have to get him out."

"And if he loses you, Nadia? Then what?" I grab her, sheltering her underneath my arm and walking her toward the open doors. "Go. I'll get Loki out."

The look she gives me is full of pleading as the emergency crews descend on her, but I'm back in the barn before they can grab me.

Moving quickly, I pull my coat over my nose and grab the metal latch of the first stall. I step in, slap the horse on its haunches, and watch it run for the door. Horses are flight animals. I just hope someone out there has the good sense to corral them off somewhere. Even if they don't, running free is better than burning.

I work my way swiftly down the barn, thankful that many of Stefan's horses live at the track and this is not a full stable.

The smoke thickens the farther I get down the alleyway. The heat is intense, but I push on. Luckily, the fire seems to be worse on the outside of the building than on the inside. I feel like I've gotten almost all the horses out, but not the ones I desperately want.

I mutter into my jacket, "Fuck my life," as I trudge to the end of the barn where Loki and Farrah have been living.

I specifically picked the back because it's less drafty. A choice I now regret. Farrah is pacing nervously when I get to them. Loki huddles by her side, all signs of his spunky personality replaced with pure terror.

"Hey, guys. I got you." I swing the door open.

Farrah doesn't need any prompting. She bolts for the

safety of the front door with Loki at her haunch, galloping to keep up.

I spin to follow them when a wave of dizziness hits me.

I need to get out of here.

That's my last thought before everything goes black.

CHAPTER 31

Stefan

I HAVE NO IDEA WHAT I'M WALKING INTO, BUT I KNOW IT'S
not good. I could see the glow of my property from down the
road as I sped back from a court date in Vancouver where I
was really looking forward to burying that slimeball Patrick
Cassel.

When I drive through the tall iron gates, with my heart
firmly in my throat, I'm met with chaos. Lights flash and
horses are loose around the property. I sigh when I see Farrah
and Loki closed off in the paddock closest to the house.
Thank god.

I'm relieved to see Mira's truck is here. I suspect we're
going to need her help, and I'm willing to endure the pain of
being around her if it means saving my horses' lives.

Nauseating butterflies erupt in my stomach as Nadia
runs toward my car, waving bandaged hands, tears clinging
to her mascara, leaving black smudges down her cheeks. For

a girl who looks constantly put together, she is downright frantic.

I sit frozen, not sure I'm ready to face what I'm about to walk into. I'm watching my goal go up in flames. Literally. I've spent the past several years chasing a vendetta. And here I am, watching it all turn to ash. I don't even know how to feel.

Nadia yanks my driver's-side door open. She's shouting frantically, but I can't quite wrap my head around what she's saying. I'm too lost in the flames, what they represent.

It's almost hypnotic.

Her hand lands hard and fast across my cheek, forcing my attention to her. "Wake the fuck up! Mira is in there! She hasn't come out!" She's screaming now. Distraught.

And in a blast, I absorb all her anxiety. Her horror. I'm in motion before I have a single second to think about it. I leave my door open as I jog toward the barn, the devastation of the fire dawning on me.

"Stefan! They said they can't go in. But *she's in there*! She sent me out and went in instead, promising to get Loki and Farrah! They both came out. They were in the last stall. But she hasn't followed!" The pain is palpable as it rolls off my sister in waves.

Everyone is just standing back, watching.

"Where is she? Where is Mira?" I hear Billie from just behind me, her golden eyes desperately searching the crowd while Hank stands at her side, his green eyes alight with pure agony as he wraps an arm around Billie's midsection to hold her back.

Word travels fast in a small town, and I'm certain they

could see the fire from their property. They must have arrived mere moments after me, and I'm sure they overheard Nadia's shouting.

The lack of action enrages me. *I* enrage me. I told Mira she only ever does anything to benefit herself. Now she's in *my* burning barn. Saving *my* horses. Saving *my* sister.

And I said *that* to her. What I should have said to her is that I love her. That I needed some time to lick my wounds. That we would be fine. That I was going to come back. That I'd never felt this way about another person before.

That I never wanted to again.

The need to tell her overwhelms me. And instinct overtakes all sense. All I know is I *need* her.

I need to tell her I love her.

I take one look into my newfound father's eyes, and something passes between us. An understanding. An agreement. I only just found him, and now I might lose him. But if I don't at least try to get her out of there, I will lose myself. He nods at me, and with his blessing, I push through the line of firefighters.

"Sir!"

"Sir, stop! The structure isn't stable!"

A hand reaches out to grip me, but I'm stronger. My strength is coming from somewhere else right now. *Adrenaline.*

I shake the person off and hold an arm up over my mouth to stifle the smoke. Once I cross the threshold, I realize they localized the flames on the outside of the building but the smoke inside is suffocating. It's captured in here like steam from a shower in a closed bathroom. Deep down, I know I'm making a stupid decision walking into a burning building.

But even deeper down than that, I know it's the *right* decision. It's the *only* decision.

Every stall door is open as I rush down the hall, checking for where she might be located. Panic rises in me every time I check a stall and don't find her. It chokes me. The smoke I can handle. Losing her when I've only just found her is what I won't survive. It's what's closing my throat and making my eyes sting.

Flames, spurred on by the hay stall at the back, cut through the smoke. The heat is borderline overwhelming, and the thought that I might have to turn back flits across my mind before I shake it away.

And then I see it, a dark lump on the floor. *Mira.*

I rush forward, shucking my jacket off and covering her head with it. The long tips of her hair are singed from the close flames. I pat them out over the top of my jacket before scooping up her limp form.

"Stefan…" I can barely hear her. "I got them out for you."

Her words cut me off at the knees. *I did this.* I told her something so cruel that she walked into a burning building to show me otherwise.

"Mira. I love you." But she doesn't hear me. Her body goes heavy in my arms.

Sagging. Lifeless.

She doesn't respond. But I chant my confession as I turn and run for the door.

"I love you. I love you. I love you."

All those months ago, in almost this exact spot, I carried a limp, lifeless foal out of this barn. And she sat in the rain with me digging a hole for that foal, even though she didn't need to help. I don't know why she did it. I don't know how she knew I needed her steady, quiet company that morning. But I fully intend to spend the rest of my life repaying her for it. For sticking it out. For not shunning me or hating me or thinking the worst of me when everyone else did.

For *protecting* me.

And now it's my turn to protect her.

I rush out of the barn, staying low and holding her as tightly as possible. Her limbs swing as I hug her to my chest and pray to whatever power is listening to please not let this be it for us. I tell her over and over again, hoping she can hear me through it all.

"I love you. I love you. I love you."

I stumble out into the fresh air, gasping to get it into my lungs. "Help!" I cough, moving as far away from the burning building as possible. "She needs help!"

Bodies surge in around us as I drop to my knees and place her on the gravel road as carefully as I can. "Mira." I smooth her burnt hair away from her beautiful face, smudges of ash trailing in the wake of my fingers. "Mira." I shake her gently and am met with the heavy feel of a body that offers no resistance. The firefighters descend around us, but I can't take my eyes off of her. "I love you."

What if the last thing I ever said to her was harsh? What if the last thing I ever did was make her cry?

316

"Sir, we need you to move." Hands grip at me, pulling me away from her when all I want is to cover her body with mine. To give her anything she needs. Lungs. Skin. Life. She can have it all.

I love you. I love you. I love you.

"Stefan, they need space." Hank's soothing voice filters in through the chaos as his hand squeezes at the back of my neck to urge me away from her. "Move back so they can do their jobs."

What if I never see her again? I don't think I'll ever forgive myself.

Nausea surges in me, and for the second time in a week, I get up and run toward the lake, where I can empty my stomach in peace. Paramedics surge past me in the opposite direction carrying duffel bags and oxygen. The surrounding noises are loud, but all I can hear is the whoosh of blood in my ears, the quickened thump of my heart beating through my body as I lean up against a tree and give myself over to the sickness.

What if she dies saving everything that she thinks is dear to me without knowing she is everything to me?

I love you. I love you. I love you.

The guilt eats at me, tearing at my flesh. I feel like I'm being ripped apart piece by piece. I gasp for air and stare out over the lake, wishing my mom were here when a warm hand slides over my shoulder.

Hank says nothing, but I know it's him. We have a connection and barely know each other. Deep down, I know he's my dad. Sure, a DNA test will prove it, but I already know it. I know it in my bones.

His firm grip on my shoulder soothes me as I try to recapture control of my breathing.

"She's breathing. She's got this."

I peek over my shoulder. Relief and regret pummel me with equal strength. "I can't lose her."

He gives me a solemn nod. "I know."

"I just can't."

"I know."

"I love her."

He sighs. "I know, son. I know."

I stare back out over the lake, silently begging my mother for some of her strength. Her strength to endure years of what she did to keep us safe. I need that strength to keep Mira safe.

"She'd be proud of you."

My breathing goes raspy.

"I know I am."

My eyes sting, and I wish I were man enough to properly respond to that. It's all I've wanted to hear for years. But my brain fixates on Mira.

I squeeze his hand back. "Thank you."

"Go be with her. She needs you."

I don't like the way he says that. It sounds far too final. It makes me feel like a shmuck for wasting precious time retching when I should have been with her. Even though what she needs is medical attention.

I rush across the grass, watching them load her unconscious body onto a stretcher with an oxygen mask affixed firmly over her delicate face. Billie and Nadia stand huddled close to each other, tears twinkling on their cheeks. The back doors of the ambulance open, and Billie moves to get in with Mira.

"No," I say. "I'm going."

She glares at me, her eyes bright like the flames as they rake over my face, assessing me and looking like they find me entirely lacking. "I'm not sure what she sees in you. I'm not sure what drives her to defend you, to choose you when she could have anyone she wants—to walk through fire for *you*." Her finger presses into the center of my chest. "But this is your chance to prove yourself to everyone. And if you ever make her cry again, I have a lot of land at my disposal to bury your body."

I've always thought Billie was a bit of a loose cannon, but her love is absolute. I love that Mira has friends like this in her corner. I've never had anyone like this in my corner. And her challenge is one I'm happy to accept. I nod, never dropping her eye contact.

"Who's with her?" one paramedic calls out of the back of the ambulance.

And I don't miss a beat. "I am!" I grab a handle and pull myself onto the small bench beside Mira's still form.

Moments later, I take one last look at the wide eyes looking on. Her friend. My sister. My dad.

And then the doors close, and it's just us.

I grip her hand and drop my head to my chest.

I need it to be us *forever*.

The hospital is a blur. I spend the night drifting off in an uncomfortable chair, too anxious to sleep but too exhausted to keep my eyes open. People I know or recognize flit in and out. And when Mira's parents rush in through the door, I stand.

Her mom envelops me in a full hug before she breaks down in my arms, her tears soaking through my thin dress shirt. "Thank you."

If she knew the things I had said to her daughter, she wouldn't be thanking me.

"You saved her. Th-thank you."

She holds on to me like I'm a lifeline. The hug more than just an embrace. Deeper than that. I feel her gratitude wrap around me as she clings to my body, vibrating under my arms. Her dad and grandmother stand behind her looking stoic.

When Sylvia pulls away, her father shakes my hand, tearing up, unable to say anything. Which works just fine for me.

Her nana, though, steps up close, gripping my chin tightly in her bony hand. And then she smiles. "How are you feeling?"

"Guilty," I reply honestly because there's no lying to this woman.

Her head quirks, eyes twinkling. "Why?"

My palm rasps across my face. "I can't help but feel responsible for her being here. Injured. God knows wha—" My voice cracks, and I look away.

She pats my chest and shakes her head. "Poor sweet fool. That girl was coming back for you. Don't you know her well enough to know she doesn't quit? She walked into that barn because that's the type of person she is. A little prickly, but as loyal as they come once you get her. And don't worry, you've got her. I rather think you're stuck with her."

Claws rake down the back of my throat. I know she's trying to make me feel better, but the guilt is still there. Magnified by the longing I feel. I just want to be with Mira.

I want to hold her.

When she wakes up, I'm never walking away from her again. I'm going to bask in being stuck with her.

No matter what it takes.

And I'm going to tell her I love her. Over and over and over again.

CHAPTER 32

Mira

NOTHING MAKES SENSE.

A steady beeping sound filters through my consciousness. My eyelids are heavy like lead, and my body aches. I roll my tongue through my mouth, chasing away the dryness as best I can, but my throat feels like sandpaper, raspy and sore enough to make me whimper.

I feel a squeeze on my forearm and a firm hold on the opposite hand.

My eyelids flinch as I force them open. It feels like there's dirt inside them. I'm in a mostly dark room. Dim lights give it a sort of warm-yellow glow. It strikes me that it's probably nighttime.

"Hey." I glance over at my best friend, into eyes lined with anxiety.

"Hi. God." Her voice quavers. "It's really fucking good to see you."

I try to smile, finding comfort in the crass way Billie talks. It feels so normal. "Am I…?" Jesus, my throat feels terrible.

"You're in the hospital." Her hands stroke my forearm, and she nods to my opposite side. I slowly turn my head, realizing I can feel someone holding my hand, but it's not my friend. When I look down and to my left, I'm met with a slumped figure in a chair pulled close, a mop of beautiful dark-gold hair resting on the bed beside me.

He's here.

I sigh, my lungs burning and chest aching.

He's clutching my hand like I'm his lifeline while he sits in an uncomfortable hospital chair, face resting on the bed by my thigh. He looks exhausted, but I soak in his face like I haven't seen the sun in years. His sharp cheekbones, covered in more stubble than I'm used to seeing. His full lips slightly parted. The dark smudges beneath his eyes.

I feel confused about everything that is going on around me.

Except him.

I've never been so sure of anything in my life.

"He hasn't left your side," Billie whispers. "Nadia had to bring him fresh clothes because he reeked of smoke but refused to leave you."

Tears spring up in my eyes as I watch the beautiful man sleeping beside me. All I want is for him to hold me and tell me everything is going to be okay.

"He went into the burning barn—when everyone told him not to—and carried you out. If it wasn't for him, I'm not sure we'd be sitting here today. I mean, he literally walked through fire for you."

Tears roll down my cheeks.

Billie reaches up to wipe them away, drawing my attention away from Stefan. "The guy is a total nightmare." Her voice cracks, but she blinks quickly and forges ahead. "But not in the way I thought. Never mind his barn, I think he's been ready to burn this whole fucking hospital down to get you the best care available and what I'm pretty sure is like a twentieth opinion." Her laugh is tearful, and I smile back at her.

"Listen, Mimi." I groan and shake my head. Billie is insane in the best possible way. "I was wrong. And I'm sorry. Any man who loves you as much as he does is a winner in my book."

"Thank you," I rasp. I know I don't need my friend's permission, but knowing she accepts him—accepts us—well, that makes my heart happy. "Did he tell you much?"

She snorts and rolls her eyes. "That Hank is his daddy? Or that he named my horse?"

I scrunch my face up and nod, whispering, "Yeah. Kinda big news. I know Hank is like a dad to you and has been for a long time." Then I point at her. "And you know that name is a good one."

"Yeah. I have to confess, it is." She chuckles tearfully. "And man, Hank is so happy. It's downright infectious. I can't *not* be happy for them. The world works in mysterious ways, Mimi." She winks saucily, clearly getting hold of her emotions. "I mean, I need another dumb brother like I need a fucking hole in the head. But here I am with one anyway." She gestures across at Stefan's sleeping form.

He stirs, like his ears are burning. I give his hand a quick squeeze, and his head snaps up. Dopey eyes latch onto mine instantly.

"I'm gonna go," Billie says with a gentle squeeze of my arm and a kiss to my hair.

I don't even look at her. "Okay, bye." I can't tear my gaze away from Stefan, his entrancing green eyes, his slightly crooked nose. I drink him in, trying not to think about how I almost let him get away.

"Hi." I smile, unable to discern the expression on his face as the door clicks shut. Like he's almost angry.

"How do you feel?" His fingers push between mine.

"Sore." Why lie? Every part of me feels sore.

"You suffered smoke inhalation and a concussion from when you passed out. You've been out for about a day."

"Oh. Okay."

He's all business right now. "The doctor said your trachea and lungs should heal completely. But I've got a second and third opinion on the way." Rigid tension lines his body as his eyes rake over mine. "I'm not taking any chances they missed something."

"Okay." I'm sure I'll be fine. I'm capable of understanding any diagnosis I might have, but if micromanaging this makes him feel better, I won't interfere. "How are *you*?"

I brush my thumb across the underside of his hand, reveling in the feel of his skin on mine. In the way energy crackles up my arm with the simplest touch. This man sets me on fire. Maybe that's why I ran in there with no regard for my safety. I'd already endured the most intense heat I could imagine. That barn was no comparison for our chemistry.

"Mira, you shouldn't have gone into that barn." His jaw ticks with annoyance.

"Neither should you," I scold him right back.

"I couldn't leave you in there." His voice breaks as his eyes land where our hands are joined.

I reach up and run my hand through his hair, savoring the feel of the strands running between my fingers. Something I never thought I'd feel again. "You love so fiercely. Just like I told you. Just like me. I didn't think twice about walking into that barn."

His sad eyes meet mine. They more than meet. His gaze plunges into mine. The way he looks at me is borderline invasive, like he's staring straight into my soul. "Love?"

My hand slides down his cheek, the feel of his stubble against my palm sending goose bumps up my arm. "Yeah. You love me."

He looks so intense, which emboldens me. A man who was done with me wouldn't be regarding me like this.

"Who told you that?" His eyes dart to the opposite side of the bed where Billie sat earlier, but I tip his chin back down toward me.

"You did."

"Did you hear me in the barn?" His voice is raspy, his accent shining through a little more than usual as his free hand lands on my knee and strokes me there.

I quirk my head, knowing I've struck a chord. "No…

but have you walked through fire for any other girls lately, Stefan?"

I smile, but his facade cracks right before my eyes. His face falls and a sob wracks his body as he gives up all pretense of control and crawls onto the small hospital bed beside me, turning my body in toward him with the utmost care. With heartbreaking gentleness. I bury my face in his chest. Rejoicing in the feel of his hard arms around me and his warm skin against mine.

His breath shudders, and his hand shoots into my hair, lovingly cupping my head. "I can't ever lose you. I'm so sorry I walked away." His words rumble across my scalp as he burrows into me. "I love you too fucking much."

"I know," I reply, stroking his hair. "I love you too, Stefan."

"Nothing else mattered when I thought you might die. *Nothing.* There is nothing you could do to make me leave you behind. And I'll never forgive myself for doing it once."

I nod into the warmth of his chest, feeling my eyes leak again.

"I don't know if I'll be able to keep you safe. But I want to spend forever trying if you'll let me."

"Oh, Stefan. You already do." My voice is thick as I stroke my hand over the length of his broad back. "You saved me last night. You believe me. You listen to me. You protect me. You stood up to my family for me, Stefan. And Patrick? You took him out for me." I laugh through the tears. "I mean, shit. You lied to the cops for me when I egged the principal's car with Nadia."

"That guy fucking deserved it."

I laugh again, but it's cut short when he pulls away and tips my chin up. "I love you, Mira." His confession is quiet and deep. Private and just for us. Even though he's already said it, this time it really sinks in. "You make me a better man. A happier man. I said it once before, and I meant it: you are mine, and I am yours. I will drink whatever ungodly coffee concoctions you bring me. I will worship your body." His eyes drop to my lips, and even in a hospital bed feeling more roughed up than I ever have, when *he* looks at *me* like *that*, I feel more beautiful than I ever have. "I would walk through fire for you any day. Over and over again."

And then his lips descend on mine. Soft and searching. Perfect and panty melting. His hands cup me like I'm the most precious thing he's ever held.

And I melt. I melt into him. Into us.

I whimper, overcome with emotion. Soaking in the feel of him and how he surrounds me, feeling infinitely safe in his arms.

"Does it hurt?" He draws back, concern etching his handsome face.

I fist the neckline of his T-shirt, gathering it between my fingers as our legs tangle together on the small hospital bed.

"No," I murmur. "Please." I sigh. "Don't ever stop," I implore.

He drops his forehead to mine. "I love it when you beg, Dr. Thorne."

His lips press against one cheek, in the sweetest kiss. "I love you." Before moving over to the other, butterflies erupt in my stomach. "I love you." Our lips meet in a soul-searing kiss, the perfect fit, and he says it a third time. "I love you."

And nothing in my life has ever felt more real.

I love him. I love him. I love him.

EPILOGUE

Stefan

THREE MONTHS LATER...

I feel Mira's fingers dig into my thigh from where she sits at the dinner table beside me. Hank sits across from us, and we've just finished a beautiful dinner I cooked for two of the most important people in my life. Seared duck breast, complete with a special blueberry sauce Mira concocted. Just to remind me of our very first "fake" date.

I've just placed an envelope in the middle of the table. It holds the results of our DNA test. It's what I've been waiting for, except now that it's here, I'm not sure I want to open it. Hank and I have been spending time together as though he is my father. Making up for lost time. And I've been soaking it up. No matter how much time I spend with the man, it's just never quite enough. I always feel like I want more. I have so much to share with him in whatever time we might have left. My perception of making the most of the time we have has drastically changed since the fire. Some might say it was a wake-up call to stop living in the past.

"Is that what I think it is?" Hank asks, eyes glued to the yellow envelope.

Who knew something so life-altering could come in such a generic-looking package?

"It is."

He swallows, and I watch him, feeling Mira's steady presence beside me. The tips of her dainty fingers press into my inner thigh, making me think about things I shouldn't be at a moment like this. But then she's always had that effect on me.

"It's funny"—Hank's voice is all gravel as he smiles and looks up at us—"because I've been looking forward to this, and now that it's staring me in the face…well, I think I'd be happy to go on pretending that it's exactly as we think it is."

A silence descends over the table before Hank continues, "You know, Stefan, even if this envelope doesn't hold what we're both hoping it does, I'd…well, I'd like to keep doing what we've been doing. Everything I felt about your mom is still true, and I like to think she'd be happy to see us spending time together regardless of DNA."

I lick my lips and wish away the stinging sensation across the bridge of my nose. "I would like that."

"Do you guys want me to read it first?" Mira asks quietly, her thumb rubbing soothing circles against my jeans. Her head volleys between us, her shiny black hair brushing the tops of her shoulders. After the fire, she cut the burnt ends and went for a straight blunt bob, and it suits her to a tee. She is striking, and there's still plenty for me to wrap between my fingers when I take her from behind.

Hank and I make brief eye contact before both nodding. Her hand darts out, and I see the anticipation shining in her eyes. Feelings about this have been a bit of a roller coaster for me, but Mira is *so* certain. She's the only thing keeping me grounded.

In a flash, she tears the top of the envelope and pulls out crisp white papers. Intelligent eyes scan the first page, her practiced impassive face giving nothing away. She flips the papers onto the place mat before her, rolling her lips together as her almond-shaped eyes find mine. Like always, I could get lost in those eyes. I often do, but right now I'm staring at them looking for some sign, some tell. She's giving me nothing.

"Stefan…"

This is torture.

I can't even tell if she's taking forever to say it or if time is standing still. Her full soft lips tip into a smile. "I'd like you to officially meet your father."

Hank barks out a loud laugh, leaning back in his chair with an exaggerated clap. But I just reach for Mira and yank her to me, gathering her in my arms. Her hair smells like honey, and her T-shirt smells like fresh laundry soap.

I realize that without her, without the universe placing her in my path, without a sick horse, without a dead mom… without all of that, I may never have found Hank. Without Mira, I may never have met my dad.

"Thank you." I nuzzle into her neck, momentarily distracted by all the ways I plan to thank her later tonight.

"Always" is all she says before holding me back and smiling at me, eyes twinkling with unshed tears. "Now go hug your dad."

So I do. I round the table and walk right into Hank's wide-open arms. My *dad's* wide-open arms.

God. That feels good.

"Nice to officially meet you, son."

I hear the emotion in his voice, and to be frank, I don't really trust myself to respond. So I just squeeze him tighter. It feels like I've spent a lifetime looking for him. And now I've found him.

We spend the next thirty minutes talking, laughing, and just feeling immensely relieved. When the night winds down, he hugs Mira, and I don't miss the way he whispers, "Thank you for bringing me my boy."

I also don't miss the way she wipes at her eyes and nods.

I don't know how I'll ever repay her. Repay the universe for giving me her.

Actually, I do. I know exactly how I'm going to do it. Which is why after Hank leaves, I suggest a walk down to where the barn used to stand. They have cleared away the rubble, and now it's just a big flat space. Ready to be rebuilt.

Next to the lake, Loki and Farrah graze happily in their field. Loki whinnies when he sees me.

"Your heart horse is saying hello, my love," Mira says.

I wrap my arm around her and pull her closer, feeling endlessly grateful.

After the fire, Billie approached me with a deal. Half-ownership of the little colt for everything I'd done to help with saving him. The woman I thought hated me is now calling me her "brother from another mother" and giving me half of one of her most prized horses. The world works in truly mysterious ways.

We walk into the middle of the cleared space. Hand in hand. After the hospital, Mira moved straight in with me. I wouldn't take no for an answer. Life was too fragile to spend another moment not together. This much I have learned. Plus, since finishing her courses, Nadia has decided to attend a college in the city to become a veterinary technician. That's how much she loves working with Mira. She'll be moving to Vancouver to pursue that soon, leaving the house to just the two of us.

A companionable silence stretches between Mira and me. Today is already one of the happiest days of my life. And I'm about to make it a whole lot happier.

There's this part of me that thinks standing here in the aftermath of a fire that took so much should make me sad.

But I feel relieved.

This is where I almost lost Mira. This is where I roped her into my arrangement. This is where I spent quiet nights learning Mira. This is where I laid my life on the line to save her.

I believe my mom is overlooking this exact spot from where I sprinkled her ashes.

This spot is my whole world. This spot is fate. This spot is my future.

This is where I'm going to rebuild.

Mira and I? We're like a phoenix, born from the ashes. And I wouldn't have it any other way.

She's looking up at the sky, all pink and orange as the sun crosses the horizon of the mountains, when I drop to one knee.

Her head snaps down to me immediately. "What are you doing?" One hand lands across her chest.

I grin. "What does it look like I'm doing?"

"It—"

"Do you think I'm down here trying to fix your shoe again?" Her eyes widen as she looks down at her simple slip-on sneakers. "Don't worry, Kitten. I can"—I wink at her—"fix your shoe later. First, I have something I want to ask you."

"Oh my god." Her hand slides up around her neck, and I can see her pulse jumping in her throat as I pull a small velvet box out of my pocket.

"I've never considered myself a particularly good man. I never thought I was a bad man either. I was just a man with a sad past and no one to love. And then I saw you. It only took one look, and I swear some part of me knew."

Her free hand cups my cheek lovingly.

"I knew my life would never be the same. You didn't treat me like I was a bad man. You didn't always treat me like a good one either. But you made me want to be a *better* one. You make me want to deserve you. And I have every intention of spending the rest of my life trying."

"Oh, Stefan." A tear trails down her cheek as I flip the

box open to display the thin yellow-gold band with a sparkling teardrop-shaped emerald affixed to it. All she can talk about these days is how green is her favorite color because it reminds her of me.

"This fire almost stole you from me. I almost lost you. And that's a mistake I never intend to make again. I intend to cherish you like the treasure you are. This fire burned everything else away. My anger, my vendettas. The only things that mattered to me I pulled out of it. And so I'm taking this as a fresh start. Everything else is ash—dust in the wind. And now I realize that the only thing that matters is what made it out. You and me." I pause here, watching my love reflected at me in her eyes. "Mira Thorne, would you do me the incredible honor of being my wife?"

She falls to her knees before me in one swift motion, hands cupping my face. "Yes. Yes, yes, yes. Nothing would make me or my aunt happier."

The smile on my face is huge as I slide the vintage ring onto her delicate finger. And when I gaze back up into her eyes, all I can see is our future.

I love you. I love you. I love you.

"Green is my favorite color, Stefan." She looks down at her hand with a tearful smile. I laugh and brush the tears off the apples of her cheeks before I erase the space between us and press my lips to hers. The lips I plan to kiss for the rest of my life. *Mine.*

A better man would have let her out of our arrangement.

I am not a better man.

And I've never felt less sorry about anything in my life.

BONUS EPILOGUE

Stefan

TWO YEARS LATER...

"I'm nervous," I blurt.

Mira smirks. It's slow and full of amusement. "I know. But he's here for experience. The win doesn't matter."

We're standing right at the finish line at Bell Point Park, where the little horse who brought us together will run past the post for the very first time. His first race. His maiden voyage.

"How do you know?" I jangle my keys in the pocket of my bespoke brown suit. I had it made to match Loki for today. And I don't care if that's lame.

Her lips roll together. "I can tell."

I scoff. "How?"

She lifts our joined hands up. "Well, for starters because your hand is so clammy that I can feel mine starting to shrivel." My brow furrows, so she clarifies, "You know, like when you spend too long in the bathtub?"

My eyes roll, and I release her hand. She's not wrong about the clammy part, but when I flip her hand over and trace the lines of her palm with my thumb, the only thing I notice is gooseflesh creeping up her arm. "Kitten. Your hand is not shriveled...but I can see the goose bumps when I do this."

"Do what?" Her voice has dropped an octave. It doesn't matter that strangers are starting to press in around us. When Mira and I touch, the world falls away, and in two years that hasn't changed a single bit. I can get just as lost in her eyes today as I could sitting on that dirty stall floor.

So I trace her palm gently again, and this time I watch a shiver race down her spine as she looks away from me. Like she's annoyed with herself for reacting to me so unmistakably.

Now it's my turn to smirk. I lean down toward her, letting the tip of my nose graze the shell of her ear. "You love my hands on you."

A low groan erupts from her lips. "Only you could go from being stressed out to horny at the drop of a hat like this."

I laugh because if nothing else, this conversation has distracted me from how nervous I really am. "You love me for it though." I wink at her and bask in the glow of the full smile she returns.

"I do. Very much."

The loudspeaker crackles to life right as I murmur that she can sit on my face later and I'll show her how much I love her back.

Her cheeks flare, but our attention is drawn away to the dirt track where the horses are spilling through the gate. It's a weeknight, and this is in no way, shape, or form an important race.

Except for me.

This is the most important race in the world because the sick little colt that Mira and I saved—the one that had no business making it through what he did—is out there.

My eyes find him immediately, and I feel my wife's hand pulse in my own. He looks like a brand-new copper penny. He shines so brightly, he's not just brown; he's metallic.

He looks flashy as all get-out with his high white stockings and wide white blaze. He also looks like a hormone-filled teenaged boy at his first high school party.

That is to say, he is leaping everywhere like an absolute fool. Violet is stuck on his back like a little fly with a long blond braid down her back, and I can see her grinning from here—not the least bit put off by his antics.

No, the surly-looking frown is reserved for her husband Cole, who is riding the pony horse, GD, that's walking beside Loki. His job is to keep the racehorse calm, and GD does it well. If a horse could roll his eyes, I'm fairly certain that's what he'd be doing to Loki right now.

Cole gets them loaded up into the gate and then trots away. He gives us a quick salute as he rides past where we stand, and I can't help but notice the amused look on his face as he takes me in.

Everyone has been making fun of the suit. Mercilessly. And clearly he heard about it too. But I don't care. This suit looks killer on me. Mira even agreed. Of course, she then asked if Loki and I were exchanging friendship bracelets as well.

The announcer is talking, but I register little of what he says. My eyes are glued to the gate. I don't even hear the countdown. Suddenly the bell rings and the gates fly open, horses surging out like a tidal wave.

I lean forward eagerly, watching them thunder down the stretch. Violet and Billie's plan for this race is to keep him in the middle of the pack. Where he's possibly packed a little too tightly to goof off the way he likes, where he won't fall too far behind or tire too quickly to make a move.

Basically, this race is one big experiment.

As they move into the turn, I can see that they're exactly where they wanted to be. In the middle, but there's still this part of me that wants to see him right up at the front.

Billie is all about giving him a positive experience, which I love. But…deep down I'm still really, really invested in him winning. In proving to the world that he's the real deal, like his dad, DD.

The main group of horses turn the corner, heading toward the final straightaway. Some have fallen away toward the back now, and a few have pulled ahead.

Loki is still running even and comfortable in the middle of the pack, and as I take a deep breath, I resign myself to the fact that his first race might not be the one he wins. After all, he's just getting started. He's a playful young stallion whose focus leaves something to be desired. Champions aren't made overnight.

But that's the moment Violet opens one rein to move

him over, just enough that he's now looking down a perfect open lane up the middle of the pack.

And I swear he goes from looking around at the other horses to the eye of the tiger, tunnel vision straight down that path. Like there's some instinctual part of him that just *knows* what to do with all that space.

Violet goes low on him and shoves her hands at his neck forcefully, urging him to take the bit and run.

And he doesn't hesitate.

He shoots up the middle like he's been rocketed out of a slingshot. To be honest, I wasn't aware he had a streak quite like this in him.

He's a spitting fucking image of his dad right now. That inherent competitor in him—the winner in him—just leaping out to play. It's truly incredible to see.

And based on the flash of teeth coming from Violet's petite face, it must be a pretty incredible feeling too.

They thunder ahead; the ground vibrates beneath me. Passing the third-place horse, then the second, and with only moments to spare, they really stretch out. Covering the ground with an incredible final few strides, they push out to the front. A full length in front of the next closest horse.

And with a flash of the finish-line camera, Loki is officially a winning racehorse.

"Ahhh!" Mira screams, and her hands shoot up into the air above her head like she's just won an Olympic medal or something. Then she launches herself at me. Nuzzling into my neck while her arms squeeze tightly. "He did it! He fucking did it!"

My eyes water, and I bark out a loud laugh. "I thought he was here for the experience and the win didn't matter?"

She's vibrating with laughter now, and when she draws away, I realize there are tears sparkling in her beautiful dark eyes too. "I lied. I wanted him to win so badly I could barely stand it. I was trying to play it cool for you."

We laugh and hug again, and my chest feels so full of happiness that I think I could burst.

"Let's go revel in the winner's circle!" She grabs my hand and tugs me in that direction. Where I know all of our friends will be waiting with equally big smiles. Friends I never thought I'd have. Family I chose. I only wish Nadia was back from school to soak it up too.

We round the corner, and sure enough, there they are. Waiting for us. Billie waving at me wildly as she calls out, "He did it, Stef!" Vaughn grins playfully as he adds, "It was the lucky suit!"

I can see Cole leading Violet and Loki down the path toward the circle, and I soak it up. There's nothing in the world that could make me look away from them in that moment.

"Daddy!"

Except that. That is one of my new favorite sounds. My son's voice and my dad's deep chuckle to accompany it.

Hank and Trixie walk up, grinning broadly. My dad holding my son, Silas, who is reaching his chubby little arms out in my direction while my wife clutches my arm.

And all I can think is…

How did I get so damn lucky?

Read on for a sneak peek of the
final book in the series **A FALSE START**

CHAPTER 1

Nadia

TOMMY KOSS IS A TERRIBLE KISSER.

He's mashing his lips into mine with zero finesse, and I
wonder if a girl has ever taken the opportunity to tell him
how utterly awful he is at this.

"You're so fucking hot," he murmurs between messy,
slobbery kisses.

"So are you," I whisper back, arms slung loosely over
his shoulders, rolling my eyes and wishing I could shut this
running monologue off and just enjoy myself. His tongue
tastes like cheap beer, and he's pawing at my breasts like a
bear mauling a tree. The taste of alcohol in my mouth is an
instant turnoff. A relentless reminder.

I had it in my head that making out with Tommy might
make me feel something. It might be the cherry on top of
an unusually wonderful day. Turns out, I only feel repulsed.

Maybe I'm outgrowing these antics?

His hands glide up under my tight tank top as he steps between my legs where I sit on the vanity in the men's bathroom. It smells like urinal pucks and whatever cheap body spray Tommy is wearing. I'm not so sure the scents are very different.

He yanks one of the slim straps of my tank top down and moves his lips to my chest. My head tips back, resting against the splattered mirror, and I stare up at the ceiling. The water stains on the foam panels are so old they've turned a rusty-brown color. Tommy's elbow bumps the hand dryer, and a loud blowing noise fills the small room.

My lips tip up in amusement, and I stifle a laugh. If this weren't so sad, it would be hilarious. At nineteen years old, making out with boys in the bathroom of shitty bars is supposed to be fun. Nineteen is when you're allowed to hit the bars in British Columbia. Going out is supposed to feel like living. But legal ages have never stopped me. It used to make me feel rebellious and excited. Now I just feel numb and bored. This idea that I'm missing something and hoping I might find it near some guy's tonsils is getting old.

Chalk it up to daddy issues, I guess.

My brother thinks I'm a wild card—reckless. Possibly even promiscuous. And I am, but what he doesn't understand is that I'm looking for something.

I'm just not sure what yet.

Tommy is about to pull my breast out over the top of my neckline. He's fumbling with it when the bathroom door swings open. I glance over at who walked in, but all I catch is a flash of dark eyes beneath the brim of a cap and a bearded jawline before the guy turns his back and makes use of the urinal like we're not even here.

Talk about big dick energy.

My lips part in a mixture of shock and glee, and Tommy gives me this sweet, boyish expression before shrugging and grabbing the nape of my neck, pulling me in for more unskilled face sucking. I should tell him to stop, but my body isn't attuned to him. For a few moments, I keep my eyes open, but I'm not looking at Tommy. Every ounce of my awareness is on the man taking a piss. The confidence. The sheer gall.

I'm honestly impressed.

I let my lashes flutter shut and pretend I'm kissing someone else.

The sound of a zipper closing draws me away from the wet smacking noises Tommy is making. And then the deep gravel of the stranger's voice makes me pause entirely. "Move."

The boy with his lips on mine pulls away and looks into the eyes of the man beside him. "My dude, just use the other sink. There are two."

The man's features are shadowed beneath the low-slung brim of his worn cap. Dense brows and deep-set eyes top off a strong nose. But mostly, he's too obscured beneath the brim of the cap for me to really make him out. Like he's hiding in plain sight.

The white mesh covering neatly trimmed brown hair has a faded brown panel at the front and the outline of a cowboy on a bucking horse. I lean in closer, inextricably drawn to the man, trying to make out the writing just beneath it.

Someone only wears a hat into that state if it's special to them. And I want to know more about what's special to a man like this. One who can take up all the space in a room without even trying.

"Go!" he barks, and I startle.

Raised voices always do that to me. I freeze, fire licking up my throat. I *hate* when anyone takes that kind of tone with me. All it does is make me combative.

Tommy just scoffs, totally oblivious to the steel in the man's voice, behaving like a boy who has seen nothing bad in his life and has no concept of the consequences. "Whatever, man. Let's go, Nadia," he says, moving toward the door without a backward glance. He doesn't stop and wait for me. He doesn't hold the door open for me. He just assumes I'll follow him back out into the bar where all our mutual acquaintances are waiting, where the other girls who I barely know will glare at me with envy in their eyes like Tommy is some great catch.

If they'd ever kissed him, they'd know the glares aren't necessary.

I don't follow. I sigh and lean back against the mirror, facing off with the mysterious stranger. The one glaring at me. I've always promised myself I won't respond when a man uses that voice on me, when they try to intimidate me, and today is no exception.

You're going to bark at me? I'll bite you back.

I give the man my best resting bitch face before peering down at my nails with disinterest. "I'm not well trained like that, so you really are going to have to use the other sink."

A FALSE START

I gesture across the vanity, and he glares at me, irritation rolling off him in waves. The only part of him that moves is his broad chest as he breathes heavily and stares me down.

"And if you're going to talk to me like that again, I suggest you cup your boys to soften the blow."

He shakes his head and steps over to the other sink, flicking the tap, agitation lining every movement. A breath rattles past my lips, and the tension in the room begins to dissipate.

"I know. This is the men's room. I shouldn't be in here. Yadda, yadda, yadda. But you just pulled your dick out and took a leak without a second thought, so it's kind of hard to believe you're averse to washing your hands in front of me."

He says nothing. Just pumps a few gelatinous blobs of pink soap into his wide calloused palm. He looks older. He must be. The confidence, the thin lines highlighting the tense set of his eyes, the whole brooding act.

"You know," I continue, completely unprompted, just prattling on now, "I should thank you. That guy is the worst kisser. All teeth and saliva." I shudder dramatically as a small giggle escapes me, and I trace a finger over my puffy, ravaged lips while staring for too long into one of the pot lights above me. "Like, really bad."

Bright spots dance across my vision, and the quiet stranger just grunts, white T-shirt stretching across his thick chest, and then says, "Why?"

"Why what?" I ask, leaning in again, trying to get a view of his face. To make heads or tails of what this guy actually looks like. His light-wash jeans hug his ass, and his thighs fill them out just right, not too thick. His waist is trim, and a sea of intricate black tattoos that I could spend hours deciphering cover his arms.

His eyes flit to mine as he rinses his hands methodically. He swallows, and his Adam's apple bobs heavily in his throat. "Do that with him."

"Kiss him?" My head quirks, and he nods, stepping closer as his long arms reach across my lap to use the hand dryer. The loud whooshing sound fills the bathroom again, substantially less funny this time around.

I watch the way his hands fold over each other under the warm air, the odd droplet of water landing on my bare thigh just beneath the hemline of my jean skirt. When the dryer stops, he turns to me, and the weight of his gaze winds me. I suck air in through my nose, my shoulders coming up high as I do.

"I wanted to celebrate tonight. Found out I got into school today. I'm finally doing something for myself. I guess I just wanted to feel good for a bit."

He stares wordlessly, so I fill the space with words instead.

"Today I found out they accepted me into the program I applied for months ago. I'm going to be a veterinary technician. It's the first thing I can say I've ever really wanted to do entirely for myself. I was so nervous about applying that I haven't even told anyone I did—let alone that I got in. Not even my boss, who should probably know because she's going to need to hire a new receptionist by the time September rolls around."

The man hits the dryer again, as though to drown out my rambling. The warm air envelops my thighs, and I can almost imagine him palming them instead. To distract myself, I keep talking, hands gesturing animatedly.

"So I'm supposed to be celebrating my accomplishment tonight. Having *fun*. And if nothing else, Tommy has always been fun. Easy. A nice enough guy—if a terrible kisser. Best of all, he doesn't want any sort of commitment. Which is perfect because I don't have any commitment to give."

The dryer stops, and lights glint off the deep-brown irises that trace my face now, his nose wrinkling as he turns my words over in his head. This nameless man is studying me like I'm nuts.

A nervous laugh spills out over my lips before I lick them. *He is so intense.* "I don't know why I just told you all that."

His face is impassive, but he lifts one hand, hooking a finger through the strap of my tank top that is still pushed off my shoulder, making me feel just as disheveled as I must appear. But rather than pulling it down farther, like I hoped he might, he slides it up and places it back over my shoulder, the first knuckle of his pointer finger dragging across my collarbone.

My breath catches at the contact, goose bumps racing out in its wake, the man's dark-mahogany eyes fixed on where he touched me.

"Kiss me." I blurt the words out before I even think about them. His gaze snaps up, searing into mine. "A congratulatory kiss. A real kiss."

Here it is. My reckless side is out to play.

I swear I can see him thinking, weighing his options. Anyone could walk in at any instant.

"Why?" Suspicion taints his gaze.

I shrug. "Why not? Two perfect strangers who will never see each other again. What have you got to lose?"

He continues to stare at me for a beat, and I watch some of that wariness melt away. Within moments, his hand comes up underneath my jaw, his thumb pressing gently into the cleft of my chin as he pulls me to him, and like a moth to a flame, I go.

Up close, I get a glimpse of how ruggedly handsome he is. He turns his head to allow for the brim of his hat, giving me the perfect view of his stern face. This is a man who knows what he's doing. Knows exactly how to tilt his head, how to angle mine.

His face descends, and when his lips land against my own, I swear the world stands still. He smells like laundry soap and freshly fallen pine needles. His lips move with precision, with a longing I've never felt. And his mouth tastes like cinnamon.

I lean closer and sigh into the kiss, letting my palms press against his chiseled chest where the thumping of his racing heart beats against them. I find myself wishing he'd hold something more than just my chin. Wanting his calloused hands on me the way Tommy's smooth ones were minutes ago. I already know it would be better. This is the universe's cruel version of a side-by-side taste test.

And I already know who the winner is.

His mouth is firm, and I open for him, softening and surrendering as his tongue dances against the seam of my lips. His teeth don't clash against mine. His beard prickles at my skin, a sensation that sizzles over every nerve ending. I push closer to him. The unyielding pressure of denim sliding up my thighs makes me ache as he comes to stand between them. And when his hips press into the cradle of mine, I shiver.

I melt.

This kiss is like a dance with a man who knows how to lead rather than one who keeps stepping on my feet. It's effortless, and I want it to go all night.

But it doesn't.

He pulls away slowly, eyes raking over me, an almost confused expression on his face. My breathing is labored as I gaze up into his eyes, trying to figure out what's going on in here—in a dirty bar bathroom with a perfect stranger.

I want him to do it again.

Instead, he lifts his thumb and rubs it down over my slack bottom lip, sending a zing of arousal right between my legs. There's something possessive about the act. It's a filthy secret in a grungy restroom. It makes me want to follow him out of here and spend the night unraveling the mystery.

But his hands fall limp at his side, and he steps away, leaving me cold without his body heat. "Congratulations, Wildflower." His voice is so deep and so low that I almost don't hear it as he turns toward the door.

My eyes bounce back and forth between the blades of his shoulders, the ones straining against the fabric of his simple T-shirt. The expanse between them held taut.

"Again." I sound breathless, bordering on desperate. This can't be it for the dark stranger and me. Not when he just scorched the small bit of earth I'm standing on. Not when I feel like I might have just found *something*.

He doesn't turn around as he wraps one big hand around the door handle. He doesn't need to look at me to embarrass me, to make me feel small the way that most men in my life have. He only needs a few quiet, well-placed words.

"Once is an accident. Twice is a mistake."

CHAPTER 2

Nadia

I'M PMS-ING, I'M HUNGRY, AND I'M TIRED. IT'S A DEADLY combination, and I'm taking that deep-rooted anger out on the keyboard as I put together invoices for the month.

As it stands, I'm working part-time at the vet clinic and also taking my last few remaining high school courses by correspondence. So I sit at this front desk, alternately doing schoolwork or odd jobs that get handed off to me— something my boss, Dr. Mira Thorne, is totally fine with. In fact, it was her idea.

I answer the phone and greet people when they walk in the door. For those parts of my job, I'm supposed to be chipper and polite.

Both of which I'm not today.

I want to go home, curl up with a filthy book and a bottle of Midol, and play out that kiss with the hot-as-fuck stranger from the bar bathroom on the back of my eyelids.

Apparently, orgasms are good for cramps. At least that's what my personal research has proven.

Which is why, when I hear the front door open, I stifle a groan and glance at the clock. One hour left. So close and yet so far away. Right now, I do not want to talk to a single person, and that's the only consideration in my mind as I swivel my chair around to face the entryway with a big fake, cheesy smile plastered on my face.

A look that freezes in place for a moment before transforming into one of utter shock, mouth hanging open like I'm about to say something. But then I just…don't. I literally can't because I especially don't want to talk to *this* person.

The dirty bathroom guy—that's what I'm calling him now—is here. At my place of work. Holding a brown paper bag and wearing a scowl that would scare most people. But not me.

Because I'm giving him an equally unimpressed look right back. I lean back in my chair, fingernails digging into the armrests as I force a grin onto my face. I don't want to be embarrassed around this jerk. There is nothing to be ashamed of because I am a modern, single woman. I can kiss ten guys a night if I want to.

But none of them would stick with me like this prick. And that's what really chaps my ass about him. I never let guys get to me the way he has.

"Hi. Can I help you with something? Do you have an appointment?" I take a mental note to scour the schedule and find out who he is so that I can google the hell outta him later.

But he doesn't respond. He just holds up the paper bag. Like that explains a single thing.

"Yes. It's a lovely bag. Do you have an appointment?" I grit my teeth. Pretty sure my forced smile is making me appear downright deranged.

His dark eyes narrow from beneath the brim of that same hat, and this time, he holds the bag up, shaking it at me. *Oh, hell no.*

"Dude. I don't know what that means. How about you use your big boy words?" Oh, yeah, my patience is absolutely shot.

I swear he growls at me in response, which just annoys me more. He talked enough to tell me I was a mistake or an accident or whatever the other night, but now he won't talk to me at all? Rich. Really fucking rich.

"Listen." I use the most condescending tone I can drum up. "I can't read whatever kind of sign language these dirty looks are using. You're going to have to *talk* to me. Or write it down or something." I hold up a finger and pretend to check under my desk. "Wait, let me grab my *crystal ball.*"

It's at that moment Mira pushes through the swinging door and waltzes into the reception area with an accommodating smile on her face.

"Griff! Good to see ya. You got those samples we talked about?"

Dirty bathroom guy nods at her, but he doesn't take his eyes off me. It's honestly a little unnerving. I lick my lips and hold his gaze, refusing to drop his gaze. He drops the paper bag on the front desk countertop and then swaggers back out the front door.

"Piece of work," I spit out, rolling my eyes.

Mira stays suspiciously silent. When I glance at her, she's a million miles away, staring just past me.

"Do I have something on my face?" I rub at my mouth and wave a hand in front of her.

She blinks and shakes her head. "No. No. Sorry. Just tired. I zoned out."

"What the hell is wrong with that guy? He walked in here like he's some sort of celebrity, like I should know him. Wouldn't say a goddamn word. Manners leave something to be desired." I shake my shoulders out and scoff just thinking about it.

"Griff? He used to live around here."

I turn back to the computer screen and mutter, "Still a dick."

Again, Mira barely notes what I'm saying. "I need to go check on the foal," she blurts out, changing the subject entirely. "I, uh, won't be back. Can you lock up?"

She's acting totally weird. "Of course."

"Thanks." She grabs her coat and takes off, leaving me thoroughly confused, in a terrible mood, and stuck at work for another fifty-seven minutes.

Just great.

Acknowledgments

All throughout junior high and high school, my parents would pull me out of school for one day every month so that I could go volunteer with my horse's veterinarian.

One day we were called out to a barn fire. Luckily, the worst of it was smoke inhalation, on the one young horse that was stuck inside the longest. Her breathing was worsening by the minute, so we rushed her back to the clinic. But by the time we got there, she could barely breathe at all. So this veterinarian pulled out a textbook, read for a few minutes, and then proceeded to perform an emergency tracheostomy on the spot—a procedure she had never done before. She saved that horse by winging an unfamiliar procedure, and I just remember thinking that she was a stone-cold badass.

She was beautiful, smart, funny, and kind, and completely took me under her wing. Major girl crush over here!

My days with her are some of the most memorable from that time in my life.

My mom always said that not all learning takes place in the classroom—and boy was she right. I learned *a lot* on those days. That castration scene? It really happened… except the next time she actually did let me do it on my own.

For years I swore I was going to become an equine veterinarian when I grew up, but I think Dr. Mira Thorne is as close to that as I'm really going to get. Something I'm okay with because her character is so full of personal pieces of me and I just love her so much.

I hope you all did too.

This is my third book! One that really fell to the page for me. I'm very proud of it. On top of that, I'm eternally grateful to all the people who helped make it possible.

To my husband, who encourages me to lock myself in a room and hang out with fictional men, you are my rock. *My person.*

To my son, who has taken to telling people, "My mom is on a deadline," you are a procrastinator too; I'm pretty sure you got it from me. Sorry about that. But I love you to the moon and back anyway.

To my editor, Paula, I feel so blessed that I get to work with you. Your feedback is not only helpful, but it brings me comfort. I trust you so much with my words and my worries, and I still think you should charge me extra for being my therapist sometimes.

Krista Callaghan, I'm so glad we crossed paths! I can't even explain to you what a huge help you've been. You're a superstar!

Anna P., who gave this manuscript a very thoughtful sensitivity read for me. THANK YOU. Thank you for helping me do Mira and her family justice. I also promise to never call it naan *bread* again.

To Mary, I think our covers just keep getting better. I adore working with you and can't wait to make more beautiful covers with you.

Brandi, Shannon, and Laetitia, hats off to you for your exceptional eye for detail and time spent poring over my words. I so appreciate your help.

My beta readers, Lena, Amy, Amber, and Christy, thank you for reading my manuscript even when it still feels all jumbled. Each of you helps me see things more clearly.

My ARC and street team members, I am absolutely overwhelmed by all of your support! It makes me a little misty-eyed to think about how much you have all done for me. I'm really not sure how I'll ever thank you all. I send hugs to each and every one of you.

Melanie Harlow, who gives so much of herself and her knowledge to helping new authors, thank you for your thoughtful responses every time I harass you about something.

Sarah and Jenn from Social Butterfly, thank you for sharing your wisdom and offering me so much direction and encouragement. I absolutely love working with you both.

Finally, thank you to The Golden Girls. My partners in crime. My friends. I love you both, meaty balls and all.

About the Author

Elsie Silver is a Canadian author of sassy, sexy, small-town romance who loves good book boyfriends and the strong heroines who bring them to their knees. She lives just outside Vancouver, British Columbia, with her husband, son, and three dogs and has been voraciously reading romance books since before she was probably supposed to.

She loves cooking and trying new foods, traveling, and spending time with her boys—especially outdoors. Elsie has also become a big fan of her quiet 5:00 a.m. mornings, which is when most of her writing happens. It's during this time that she can sip a cup of hot coffee and dream up a fictional world full of romantic stories to share with her readers.

Website: elsiesilver.com
Facebook: authorelsiesilver
Instagram: @authorelsiesilver
TikTok: @authorelsiesilver